THE UNCERTAIN MIDNIGHT

When is a machine not a machine?
When it is an android . . .

Machines — creations of plastic and metal — are made in the exact outward likeness of man, fulfilling man's functions, but always with perfect efficiency. They start with programmed emotions, factual data, logical reactions and reasoned thinking. They can 'create' in themselves something more than the original input — original thought, other emotions. Furthermore, they can, and do, reproduce themselves.

These benevolent daleks are more intelligent, more amusing, more likable, more human than the effete descendants of their original creators.

These androids, this new race of near-men, are a better strain than mankind. Why does one primitive Twentieth Century man have the right to destroy these creatures who lack the spark of original sin?

Because he has the right to survive — if he can.

D1158866

The Uncertain Midnight

(Formerly Deadly Image)

Edmund Cooper

CORONET BOOKS
Hodder Paperbacks Ltd., London

First published 1958 by Ballantine Books, Inc.,
New York

Coronet edition 1971
Second impression 1974

———————————

The quotation on pages 129–31 is from
'The Golden Journey to Samarkand', from
Collected Poems of James Elroy Flecker,
published by permission of The Richards Press, Ltd.

Printed in Great Britain for Coronet Books, Hodder Paperbacks
Limited, St. Paul's House, Warwick Lane, London EC4P 4AH,
by Cox & Wyman Ltd., London, Reading and Fakenham

ISBN 0 340 15132 3

FOREWORD

The Uncertain Midnight is my first novel; and for this reason alone I have a special affection for it. I suppose most writers have similar feelings about their first-born. When the novel first appeared, it was received very favourably; and its success was not confined to the United Kingdom. Over the years it has been translated into French, German, Dutch, Italian, Japanese. It is in its second printing in the U.S.A., its second printing in Italy and its third printing in West Germany. In 1969 it was adapted as a ten-part television serial in the French language and has also been shown in Switzerland and Belgium. The serial was chosen to represent Swiss Television at the 1969 Prix Futura in Berlin.

The book has been out of print in this country for several years; and I am particularly pleased that it is now possible to bring out a new edition. An earlier paperback edition was published as *Deadly Image,* after the title of the American paperback edition. At the time, my New York publishers thought it a more appropriate title; but now, as then, I prefer the original.

From my remarks so far, it will be apparent that the novel was written a long time ago. When I consider the science fiction that has since been translated into science fact, I realise that it was a very long time ago. It was before the Space Age, before the development of lasers, before it was possible to give a man a new human heart. It was written when the population of the world was about eight hundred million less than it is now. In short, *The Uncertain Midnight* was completed in the autumn of 1957.

It is a regrettable fact that war is a great stimulus to science. Radar, rockets and the peaceful use of atomic energy are among the many products of war stimulus. In *The Uncertain Midnight,* I wrote briefly of an atomic war in the late nineteen-sixties. It was not my intention to predict such a war. As we know, it never happened; and I hope fervently that atomic weapons (once belonging only to the realm of science fiction) will never be used again. The bombs that were dropped on Hiroshima and Nagasaki are peanuts compared to what is available now.

But, for the purposes of the story, the war stimulus was used to generate the rapid evolutionary progression of computers-robots-androids. However, a war is not really needed to bring about the existence of androids. All that is needed, I believe, is time and the tireless ingenuity of mankind.

But, though machines may become very complex, will it ever be possible to regard them as living beings? That was the question that began to fascinate me in the spring of 1957. Ironically, as scientific research intensifies, as the secrets of D.N.A. are unravelled and the prospect of laboratory-created life looms before us, the question is reversed. Shall we come to regard living beings as machines?

And, in the end, will the history of man be reduced to the dynamic competition of machines against machines?

Less than one human generation ago, ENIAC, the first large electronic computer — a monster conglomeration of 18,000 vacuum tubes — was built at the University of Pennsylvania. It became obsolete, comparatively senile, at twelve years old. During one human generation, computers have passed through several evolutionary phases. ENIAC is now regarded as a dinosaur among computers. How many generations of computers will have developed in one more human generation? And what will the end of this rapid evolutionary process be?

I certainly don't know. I am just a compulsive guesser, an addict of possibilities. And, I hope, an entertainer.

EDMUND COOPER

Autumn: 1970

For man, as for other animals, the limitations of environment are an emotional and intellectual challenge. But, to meet his own peculiar challenge, man has created weapons and tools and language. Therefore it has become his destiny to continually create new worlds, new problems.

This, then, is the story of a *possible* world and its problems. A world in which machines have taken from man the ancient burdens of work and responsibility. A world, dominated by leisure, in which permanent love and happiness seem irreconcilable; and in which . . .

CHAPTER ONE

FIRST, there was pain; and after the awareness of pain, a flock of dark shadows fluttering like silent birds against a backcloth of darkness. Then cloudy images, and in their wake a vague feeling of identity. Then dreams, drifting by without meaning until suddenly the symbols dropped into focus and the meaning took on greater reality than the dreams.

In a remote twilight of consciousness, memories burned like minute candles. He watched them, fascinated, shaken by the stupendous sense of being alive.

A girl's face surged toward him out of the mist, recognisable. It was Katy's face — Katy as he had first known her. She came near and smiled. She was wearing a candy-striped blouse and carrying an armful of documents. That was when they had first met, when he was installing the heat-exchange unit in the block of offices where she worked.

'Hello,' said Katy. 'Would you like some coffee?'

'You bet I would.' But it was not his voice speaking. It was the voice of a ghost.

Katy turned away and disappeared. Presently she returned with two steaming mugs of coffee. The ghost said thank you and told her that his name was John Markham, that he was twenty-two years old, that he had lived in London for only a few months, that his home was in Yorkshire, that he like Beethoven and Gershwin, and chess and musical comedies. And he told her that one day he would ship out to the moon.

The ghost talked so much because he was a lonely ghost. Since he was fresh from the provinces, London had swallowed him at a single gulp, and he was afraid of dissolving away entirely in the city's cavernous stomach.

Katy laughed. She tossed back her golden hair and laughed. She thought the moon idea was just the modern equivalent of running away to sea, and she was surprised at — almost resentful of — the possibilities of deep space travel. Of course there were the satellites, the space platforms and all the other crazy machines that men kept putting in the sky. But somehow they didn't *belong* any more. Not to ordinary people. They were just — and literally — out of this world . . . No, she didn't like Beethoven, but Gershwin was still all right. And had he seen *The Commissar and the Deb*?

The ghost had not seen it, nor even heard of it. He had been too busy poring over fuel statistics, free flight trajectories and accelerating G forces in his room in the suburbs. But here was a chance to get to know Katy, to destroy his consuming loneliness. He offered to get tickets for the show . . .

He didn't watch *The Commissar and the Deb* nor hear much of the many hit songs. Instead he watched Katy, and heard her occasional excited whispers magnified to a quiet thunderous murmur in some strange hollow dimension. He had known then that he would marry her and that he would never ship out to the moon.

Now his body lay on a trolley in a room whose temperature had climbed infinitely slowly over a period of days. There was still a heavy hoar-frost on his hair, eyebrows and stubbly chin. But the frozen clothes, caked with ice crystals, had been carefully cut away. And in his stillness, his gaunt nakedness, the possibility of life was utterly fantastic but real. He was a corpse with a beam of steady white light playing on his chest directly above the heart. But he was a corpse whose heart was beginning to stir feebly; a corpse who had begun to dream. A corpse that was being resurrected, drawn mercilessly down long corridors of pain . . .

Katy . . . the honeymoon . . . A cheap furnished cottage on the East Anglian coast, where they could have the luxury of a home of their own for two full weeks before they returned to a bed-sitting-room in the city.

The seashore. Bathing. Katy changing her wet costume under the eroding cliffs. Her body was thin and brown and hard, yet her breasts flowed out from it with starling softness, somehow emphasising the duality of woman.

Katy was proud of her body. In the evenings before she came to bed she would stand in front of the long mirror admiring it, turning slowly to watch the play of light and shadow on her arms, her shoulders and the tiny roundness of her belly.

He, the ghost, was proud of it, too. Watching her, his longing became more than longing, grew into a spearhead of necessity that was rarely demolished even when they had exhausted all the gambits of love.

Eventually there was a baby — Johnny-Boy. Fat-faced, loud, implacable. The legacy of that carefree honeymoon — Johnny-Boy climbing over tables, chairs, Katy, blueprints, everything. Johnny-Boy, whose expensive upkeep accounted for most of their spare money and turned the possibility of a car into a fast receding mirage.

The ghost had enjoyed being a father. It was something positive, something purposeful. More important than spaceflight, because Johnny-Boy belonged to Katy and Katy belonged to him . . .

Another wave of darkness in the body under the beam of light. Succeeding waves of oblivion and pain. And still the temperature climbing, the hoar-frost receding hour by hour. Figures bending over the inert body, unfelt injections. Unfelt pain . . .

Childhood! The ghost discovered that he had once been a child himself . . . Rain and sunlight in the Yorkshire dales. Trout in the summer streams. Toboggan rides on the bleak December hills. A schoolroom.

'Markham!'

'Sir?'

'What is fifty per cent of point five of a half?'

'One-eighth, sir.'

'Expressed as a decimal?'

'Point one two five, sir.'

'Expressed as a percentage?'

'Twelve and a half per cent, sir.'

'You'd better get that scholarship, Markham.'

'Yes, sir.'

And with the scholarship came a world that was wider than that of childhood.

'I say, Markham, what are you going to do when you leave this dump?'

'Haven't thought about it yet, Stringer. What about you?'

'My Dad says he can fix me up in International Refrigeration. Like me to ask him if he can get you in, too?'

'I don't know.'

'Come on, don't be a drip. We'll stick together.'

The body on the trolley moved. It was the first movement; a nostril twitching. White-coated figures observed the movement. More injections. No pain now — only a divine sense of non-attachment. And the images came brighter, faster, more confused.

Johnny-Boy at the zoo. Elephants. A small hand clutching a coin. 'I want to go on the big one, Daddy. With the man with the black face.'

And Katy: 'He can't go alone, John.'

The ghost laughing. 'Then you take him, darling.'

The zoo faded ... Katy undressing, big with child again. The ghost watching her, still finding her beautiful after six years. How could a ghost know that it was six years, even in a dream? How does a ghost know anything?

'We should have waited, Katy — about the baby, I mean.'

Katy smiled. ' "Nobody asked you, sir," she said.'

'We'll never have enough money to buy the house.'

'We will.' Katy always knew better than the ghost. 'And anyway, if we have our family while we're young, darling, we'll have so much more time for each other.'

The ghost said, 'I'm greedy. I want it now.'

'Take back your baby, then!'

'I'll get a better job. That's the answer, more money.'

International Refrigeration, Limited. Cheesebody's office. Cigar smoke. Why wouldn't anyone called Cheesebody change his name? It only costs a fiver. Deed poll.

'It's a big thing, Mr. Markham. A big thing!'

Cheesebody nodding over his cigar like an owl wishing to created the illusion of humanity. Bald head, pot belly, no soul. Pawed all his secretaries until they left him.

'I'm aware of that, sir.' The ghost was looking keen, resourceful. This was his big moment.

'A lot of responsibility for a young man, Mr. Markham. Can't fool about with government contracts, you know. They say December 1967, they mean December 1967.'

'I can handle it, sir.'

'You'd better ... Know something, Markham? We're doing fifty of these underground units all over the country. Know why they want 'em so deep?'

'Bomb-proof,' suggested the ghost.

'Radiation-proof,' corrected Cheesebody. Armageddon, Mr. Markham. It's got to come sooner or later, what? Then open the deep-freeze units and bring out the uncontaminated food.'

'Yes, sir.'

'No point in winning the war if we have to dine on radioactive sausages, what?' A great balloon of laughter shaking in Cheesebody's stomach.

'No, sir.' The ghost smiled dutifully.

'Big responsibility, Markham. The nation's future, you know.'

'Yes, sir.'

'Well, you'd better get down to Epping Forest and familiarise yourself with the project. Get to know your opposite number on the construction side. Maybe have to butter him ... I understand the first chamber will be ready for installation at the end of the month.'

'Very good, sir.'

Epping Forest. Fifteen miles north of the City. Epping in autumn, with the leaves red and gold; and the rustle of crisp, multi-colored waves blown tumbling along the concrete highways. The sudden stillness of trees, and then a wind-whipped turbulence bringing them to life, scattering the leaves in a dance of death.

Autumn and falling leaves — and bulldozers, excavators, tractors, trucks. Men sweating in the late sunlight. Burrowing into the earth like moles; creating tunnels, chambers. More tunnels, more chambers. Churning angrily and noisily into the patient skin of the earth.

'B Chamber ready, Mr. Markham.'

'Right. Check the powered exchange.'

'Yes, sir.'

'C Chamber ready, Mr. Markham.'

'The hell it is! Tear out the roof insulation and start again.'

'D Chamber's O.K. now, Mr. Markham.'

'Give it a week of self-drive. Get me a graph of the fall.'

'E Chamber completed, sir.'

13

'Put it on automatic exchange. Storing begins next week. Here's the lay-out tables.'

Ice caves hollowed from the warm and living soil. Convoys of trucks bringing the food that would save the Cheesebodys of England from a diet of contaminated sausages. Wheat, dried milk, beef, fat, sugar, dehydrated fruit. A hundred tons, a thousand tons, a hundred thousand tons. This was the big pile-up.

The ghost was happy then. It wasn't a pointless preparation for a suicidal war that nobody believed in. It was just a job. A good job, a big job, an important job. One that bought a house in Hampstead for Katy and Johnny-Boy and Little Sara. One that bought a car and a holiday and tailor-made clothes.

There was the leisurely drive back to Hampstead in the evenings, with sunlight turning the road into a ribbon of fire, and the leaves scurrying in the wake of the car . . .

The body shivered under the beam of light. Muscles contracted. Eyelids flickered. The hoar-frost had faded into dew, and the corpse was no longer a corpse but a man bathed in ice-cold sweat. A man with no pain, but too many memories. A man who had no right to be alive.

The dreams fell into a kaleidoscope: the memories rotated, producing colorful patterns.

'Have you seen *The Commissar and the Deb*?'

'Tear out the insulation,' said the ghost.

'What is fifty per cent of point five of a half?'

The ghost laughed. 'A radioactive sausage.'

'I want to go on the big one, Daddy. With the man with the black face.'

'You can't fool about with government contracts,' explained the ghost.

'*Stop!*'

The body on the trolley had spoken. The white figures huddled over it like giant seagulls inspecting the harvest of the tide. For a moment the man opened his eyes and stared at them vaguely, seeing only what was not in the room. The beam of light that was directed on his chest became more intense. He closed his eyes again, knowing that this was just another dream.

'Will there be a war, John?'

'Of course there won't. Not unless the top men go completely off their rockers. We can't afford it. Nobody can.'

'They're spending an awful lot of money on your ice-boxes.'

'We should worry,' said the ghost with a cynical smile. 'We're getting some of it.'

Katy began to darn a pair of socks. 'Sometimes,' she said, 'I lie awake at night, thinking about the kind of world Johnny-Boy and Sara will grow up in.'

The ghost sat on the arm of her chair and laid his hand on her shoulder. 'You think too much. You aren't equipped for it. They'll be all right, Katy. Every generation has its problems.'

'They're talking about rearmament again.'

'It's the season for it,' said the ghost. 'It comes round regularly, like football and cricket.'

'You're sure there won't be a war, darling?'

'I'm damn sure,' said the ghost. 'We may be nuts, but we aren't *that* nutty. Let's go to bed.'

Katy smiles. 'If that's the way you're feeling . . .' She put away the sewing basket, stood up and stretched. The ghost took her in his arms.

'*No,*' said the man on the trolley, '*there can't be a war!*' But in the quiet room the statement was somehow translated into a question issuing urgently from the lips of one who knew he was no longer dead. Carefully the white-robed figures toweled the icy dew from his naked body. Then they switched off the beam of light, laid a sheet over him and then a blanket. The crisis was past. Now he could begin to get warm quickly. One of them gently raised his head, gave him a drink. He did not open his eyes; but the liquid became an elixir, filling his throat and stomach with the fire of life.

Epping . . . white and still. No drifting leaves now; only the hanging whiteness of snow on laden trees. But still the endless caravan of food trucks crawling like fat, heavy beetles down to the deep-freeze chambers.

'G Chamber full and sealed, Mr. Markham.'

'Good. How many loads over?'

'Nine, sir.'

'Divert to K.'

'H Chamber sealed, Mr. Markham.'

'Any left?'

'Three.'

'Divert to K.'

'I Chamber complete and closed, sir.'

'Divert the residue to K.'

Epping — still as a Christmas card, lovely as a dream country, except for the groaning convoys of trucks. Only one more chamber left to fill, then the job would be over and the trucks would depart; and only the ghost and a maintenance team would stay behind. The forest would forgive all the indignity of digging and boring and churning. The forest would forgive and forget. The dispossessed would return and reclaim their lost territory. First the birds; then the rabbits, squirrels, foxes, rats, stoats, moles, badgers. The silent community of the wild.

Epping and Christmas. The world of evening. A tiny tree with blown glass bubbles and colored lights in the sitting-room. Firelight dancing intimately over walls and furniture. The vague roar of London shut completely out of a private universe.

Johnny-Boy and his electric train. Sara with a teddy-bear twice her size. Katy opening the parcel that contained her first fur coat.

Johnny-Boy goggling. 'I want to make it pull ten full trucks, Daddy. You be the guard.'

Sara squealing. 'Teddy-bear-Daddy-bear, Teddy-bear, Daddy-bear.'

Katy posing. 'Pardon me, Duchess, but that happens to be *my* fur coat!'

A massed choir:

> *Oh bring all ye faithful*
> *Food to Epping Forest.*
> *Freeze it and store it for evermore.*
> *Come and dehydrate*
> *Milk and meat and raisins!*
> *Then pack it all in boxes*

In half a million boxes
In deeply frozen chambers —
All sealed up!

Merry Christmas Katy, Johnny-Boy, Sara. Merry Christmas London, Moscow, Washington. Peace on earth, goodwill to men. The world's gone sane . . .

The man on the trolley began to sing: '*Oh bring all ye faithful . . .*' He stopped, opened his eyes, stared at the white figures around him and screamed. Then he shut his eyes tight, rolled onto his side and slowly, painfully, brought his knees up to his chin. The last dream was the worst. The last dream was the last reality. Everything else was an illusion, the product of a mind that was trying to escape and couldn't.

January, Epping. Rain, sleet, snow. More rain. The sky creeping low over the trees like a falling shroud.

'It's K Chamber, Mr. Markham. A fault in the automatic. The servo-change has packed up.'

'Hell,' said the ghost. 'Get somebody down there. Get Martin.'

'Mr. Martin has gone home, sir. Influenza.'

'I'll go myself, then.'

Into the tunnel. Footsteps echoing like an army, the footsteps of a ghost. Down, down into the earth, a ghost wrapped up like an Eskimo. Through the first manhole. Down the metal ladder, fifteen rungs. Open the second manhole. Down again. Crawl through the inspection panel and into K Chamber.

Frost. Frost everywhere. Hans Andersen — the Snow Queen's Palace. Cases of food stacked in neat, frosty phalanxes, rising to the roof. Nothing but a frozen silence, and the floor a thick sheet of blue ice. Who the hell said the servo-change had packed up? It's operating perfectly. Somebody's hammed the instrumentation in the control room. K Chamber will stay frozen for a thousand years. Frozen by its own heat. The great freeze-up maintained by engines driven by heat extraction. Perpetual motion. Until the temperature of a billion cubic yards of soil equalises — which will be never. Ain't science wonderful!

The ghost walked up and down the alleyways of K

Chamber, listening to the frozen silence, staring at the white-rimmed cases, the neat mountains of food.

Then suddenly the floor shuddered. Ice groaned, cracked and splintered. Food cases danced crazily out of their stacks, tumbling and slithering along the heaving floor. The ghost was lifted bodily, rolled the length of an alleyway like a knocked-down skittle. An angry roar filled K Chamber, bursting from the walls, the roof, the flaking slabs of ice; swelling into a vibration that took command of everything — even thought itself.

The sound grew until it seemed as if the earth would split in two from the colossal discharge of energy. Then suddenly there was silence. The crazy jumble of food cases became still. And the aftermath, the silence and the stillness were even more intolerable than the upheaval itself.

Earthquake! As he slithered over crates and debris, the ghost tried desperately to believe in an earthquake. Any old earthquake would do. But, please God, not the other thing!

The inspection panel was hidden deep under a pile of cases, maybe a hundred tons. He stared at the untidy mountain, stupefied. Then he remembered the emergency telephone, and crawled toward it over a sea of frozen food. It took a long time to clear the debris away from the little recess. Too long. The intense cold was already creeping through his clothes, insinuating itself in his body. He took off his gloves, blew on the numbered fingers, stared dully at the tiny ice crystals. Then he wrenched open the door of the insulated cupboard, picked up the telephone and began to shout. Dead line!

He shook the phone, kicked it, hammered it. Still dead. He roared at it, willing it to operate. And finally he smashed it and began to sob.

Don't panic! Think of Katy and the children. He crawled back to the mountain of cases that blocked the inspection panel. He began to fight his way through them, knowing that there was not enough time. His arms began to flail awkwardly. Fingers refused to grip. His legs buckled. Think of Katy and Johnny-Boy and Sara! He picked himself up again, lurched toward another broken food case, fell down and stayed down.

Too cold to think now. Too cold for regret or hope. Too

cold for anything but a profound sense of peace. This was the Snow Queen's Palace. The end of the journey . . .

'Will there be a war, John?' Dear, distant Katy!

'It's the season for it,' said the ghost. 'It comes round regularly, like football and cricket.'

He began to pray. And the cold crept steadily inward, faster, faster, until in mid-prayer he closed his eyes and went luxuriously to sleep. No dreams, or none that mattered. Only a last tableau of Katy, wearing a candy-striped blouse and carrying an armful of documents.

'Have you seen *The Commissar and . . .*'

Nothing! Nothing at all.

The man on the trolley woke up, stared round the room, knew he was no longer in K Chamber. They had pulled him out after all. He wanted to go home.

A white-coated woman, standing by the trolley, was watching him. He sat up.

'How long have I been here?'

'Several days, sir. Do not worry. You will be all right now.'

'Good God! Does my wife know?'

'Please lie down, sir. Exertion is not good at the moment.' Her accent was flat, peculiar. Like a tape recording.

'I'm all right. I want to go home.'

'Sir, you must rest. You are not yet ready to move. I would suggest a sedative.'

'To blazes with sedatives, I want to — what is this place?' He looked round him curiously. The room was entirely bare, but he noticed that the walls were lined with panels of insulating material.

'This is a cold-room, sir. You are in the North London Sanatorium.' Her voice was monotonously even, her face almost expressionless.

He was fascinated by the face. Although she could not be more than twenty-five, it was somehow ageless — masklike. Its immobility began to disturb him in a way he could not quite define. He looked at the woman closely. She was tall, dark and shapely — but strangely unfeminine. Statuesque — that was the word. In spite of the white coat, she looked as if she had just stepped down from a pedestal.

He tried to get a grip on things. 'Why the devil did you

stick me in a cold-room?' he asked irritably. 'I've just been hauled out of one.'

'That was some time ago, sir. You were discovered in suspended animation. We had to raise the temperature slowly.'

Markham gave her a dazed look, trying to comprehend, willing the information to sink in — and at the same time rejecting it.

'Suspended animation! What damn nonsense! ... I'm sorry, I didn't mean to say that.' He heard his own voice, squeaky and unnatural, the voice of a stranger. He rubbed his forehead with clammy fingers, and noticed that they were trembling. He made an effort to pull himself together. 'By suspended animation,' he said carefully, 'I presume you mean I was unconscious and half-frozen ... Lucky to be pulled out in time, I suppose.'

'Sir,' said the woman in white, using that fixed, monotonous tone, 'you were not unconscious, you were for all practical purposes dead. Fortunately we have developed techniques for restoring animation after sub-zero suspension. It is only by the merest chance that your cellular structure was not damaged in the original freezing. We were afraid that —'

'Who are you?' snapped Markham. In some indefinable way her voice was wrecking his nerves. It was as if she were there and yet not there — as if, somehow, she were a kind of telephone and someone else were doing the talking: someone very far away ... He knew he must check the wave of hysteria that was rising inside him. 'Who are you?' he heard himself shouting.

She did not lose her temper or show any sign of emotion. 'Sir, I will call a human being. It would be better, I think.'

There was a moment's silence. His muscles tightened uncontrollably. Then he began to laugh. 'A human being, by God! What the devil are you?' He met her gaze, and suddenly his laughter died.

'I am an android, sir. A humanoid robot.'

But Markham had already fainted. He slumped back onto the trolley silently and heavily. This time the dreams were horribly grotesque ...

Presently there was another voice — a man's voice, still sounding very far away. Yet even before he opened his eyes Markham knew that it was human. He gave no sign of returning consciousness for a few seconds but lay there trying to think. He didn't know what to think because all thought was fantastic, and all conclusions utterly absurd. Finally, in desperation, he opened his eyes. He remembered.

The man was definitely a man, whereas the woman had not been quite a woman.

He was tall, round-faced, and wore a short, pointed beard. His clothes were peculiar, like something out of a pantomime or a satirical period piece. A long-cut jacket of what looked like green velvet; a semi-transparent waistcoat of some kind of plastic; and a white shirt with an extraordinarily long collar. The trousers were hidden from view, since he was standing close to the trolley.

'They were supposed to tell me the moment you were recalled,' said the man. 'These damned androids seem to think they can handle any situation themselves. Can't appreciate the human touch, of course ... My name is Bressing, by the way.'

'Androids!' said Markham hoarsely. 'Androids!' The hysteria began to build up. 'God damn it! What kind of—'

'Take it easy,' cut in Bressing. 'You're in for a few shocks. Shall I unload now, or would you like it in measured doses? And what about a needleful of tranquility first?'

There was a question exploding in Markham's numbed brain. 'How long?' he murmured with an edge of fear in his voice. 'How long was I — was I out?'

'Before they found you?'

'Yes. For God's sake, how long?'

Bressing smiled. 'Hold on tight,' he said. 'It's going to shake you ... About a hundred and fifty years — plus or minus. Do you remember the year you were trapped?'

It took all the strength he had to answer without screaming: 'Nineteen sixty-seven.'

'Then you've been in S.A. for a hundred and forty-six years; this is twenty-one thirteen A.D.'

There was silence, an appalling silence. Markham heard his own heartbeats swell into accelerating throbs of thunder — a hundred and forty-six years!

He tried to imagine the decades of frozen stillness, the tomb-like immobility, the remote and relentless passage of time while he lay stiff and lifeless yet not quite dead in K Chamber. A hundred and forty-six years!

It wasn't true. It couldn't be true. This was some kind of delirium. Maybe they were even now digging him out. Maybe he would shortly wake up to find Katy by his bedside ... A hundred and forty-six years!

He looked at Bressing and tried to will him away. But Bressing, secure in his three-dimensional reality, just stayed and smiled. Markham shut his eyes, making himself believe that when he opened them again the scene would have changed — to Hampstead, to an *ordinary* hospital, to K Chamber even! To anything but a world where nurses were non-human and doctors wore fancy dress ... A hundred and forty-six years!

True or not, it was real; real or not, it was true. Unless he was in a madhouse; and he, Bressing and the android woman were all patients together ... A hundred and forty-six years!

He thought of Katy. Katy, Johnny-Boy and Sara. Christmas Eve. The day before yesterday. One and a half centuries. Katy, warm and unattainable. Lost in a pit of time. The tears streamed down his face. It was damn silly to cry. It was weak and childish and futile. But Katy and the children — dear, lovely Katy ... Christ Almighty! *A hundred and forty-six years!*

Bressing coughed. 'Steady, old man. Weep if you want to, but don't let it iron out the old circuits. You're taking a hell of a bounce, but it was coming to you anyway. And if you were going to crumple, you'd have curled up in your shell by now. What about a shot of tranquility, eh? Have you laughing it off in ten seconds.'

He wanted to smash this odd, insensate character of the twenty-second century into little pieces. He wanted to rise up and tear away the stage scenery, expose the whole elaborate joke. Sweep the curtain to one side and find his own sane world again.

But he couldn't. He could only lie on the trolley and stare up at the stupid smiling face, and let a crossfire of thoughts riddle his brain with anger and longing and futility.

'What happened?' he whispered, thinking of Katy. 'London ... what happened to London?'

The man was cheery, reassuring and damnable. 'London? Oh, I see what you mean ... Immortal, dear fellow. London survived. At least, the City did. Well, most of it. Haven't got much taste for history, you know. Wait a minute — what year did you say? Ah, nineteen sixty-seven! That was the lot, old chappie. But positively. The last days of the Empire system. The North American continent and what they use to call the British Commonwealth versus a whacking great stack of Asiatics. Damn me, what a blow-up! In the history-tapes they call it the Nine Days Tranquiliser. Everybody ironed everybody else out flat. Must have been quite joyful. But it was the last one, you know. When the Estates began to develop, atomic war became unfashionable. Do I make myself clear?'

Markham gave a harsh laugh. Clear, by heaven! I'm para-lysed with clarity!' The laughter trailed away. 'Sorry about that. Tell me one more thing — how was I discovered, Dr. Bressing?'

The man's face suddenly whitened. 'For your information, I am *not* a doctor,' he said stiffly. 'I'm a gentleman and an artist. The androids who looked after you are doctors. You needn't apologise. It's quite understandable.'

Bressing had reacted as if to a deadly insult. And in some peculiar way this shocked Markham more than anything else. But he persisted with his question. 'I'd like to know how I came to be — resurrected.'

Bressing recovered himself. 'Some android archaeologist was poking about with a troop of robo-diggers,' he ex-plained. 'They picked up the noise of your freeze unit and started excavating. Had to cut you out of the ice, I be-lieve.'

Markham was silent for a moment or two. Then he said wistfully, 'I suppose there will be records of — of the old days. You see, I had a wife and family. I'd like to know—'

The man of the twenty-second century cut him short. 'The androids will take care of that. They take care of every-thing practical. Incidentally, your P.A. should be along any moment. She'll fix you up with all you need. The main thing, old man, is to relax. I expect you'll need to stay in the sana-torium for a while, but your P.A. will settle the release date when she's seen you.'

'P.A.?' inquired Markham.

'Personal android,' said Bressing impatiently. 'We all have them. What would life be without a P.A.? Well, I must trot, now, dear fellow. My release is fixed for tomorrow.'

'You're a patient, then?'

'Guest is the word we use,' said Bressing. 'I'm a psychiatric guest — most artists are, sooner or later. Now you just lie down and let it roll over you. I'll send your P.A. in — if they've allocated you one. The odds were you were going to die, so maybe they didn't bother.'

Bressing gave him a broad smile, turned and went out of the room before Markham could digest or comment upon this latest information. He had not been alone for more than half a minute, however, when a woman came into the room.

She had a mass of golden hair, a compact oval face. She wore clothes that were almost twentieth century in style. And she looked . . . She looked . . .

Markham gazed at her. 'Katy!'

But simultaneously, he knew it wasn't Katy. The eyes were blue but there was no sparkle. The lips were full and red but they were also stiff and somehow inert. No, this couldn't be Katy! It was only her soulless twin — a macabre twenty-second century joke. An android!

Markham felt anger rise in him. Reasonable anger. Righteous anger. Why in hell were they doing this to him? Why, in the name of sanity, did—

'I am sorry not to have been here for your recall, sir. But it was not known whether you would survive. My modification has only just been completed. I am Marion-A, your personal android.' Her voice had a greater variation in tone than the other one. Not so remote.

Markham lacked the strength to sustain his anger. He began to tremble, and was ashamed of his weakness. 'You — you look like my — my wife,' he said, painfully aware that he was speaking to a non-human being.

'I was remodeled on the style of the photograph found in your wallet,' said Marion-A. 'It was decided that you would appreciate the resemblance . . . Now, sir, if you wish, I will take you to your apartment.'

CHAPTER TWO

JOHN MARKHAM stayed as a 'guest' in the North London Sanatorium for a further six days. It was the normal period of recovery from what the android doctors called S.A.R. — Suspended Animation Recall.

Although he was a freak survivor from another age, he was not — as he later learned — the only case of suspended animation in the sanatorium. In fact, most of the other guests were either recovering from S.A.R. or preparing to go into deep freeze for periods of a week to a year.

In the twenty-second century suspended animation was rapidly becoming the standard treatment for deep-level neuroses. The strange thing was that it worked.

Toward the end of his stay, when he had become sufficiently oriented to speak to an android normally, Markham asked one of the doctors to explain, the theory behind the treatment. He discovered that it differed very little in principle from the twentieth-century electroplexy and insulin techniques: the patient was allowed to endure a subthreshold trauma, the experience of which would erase the signs of neurosis. Usually the period of suspension did not matter a great deal, for the value of the treatment lay in the processes of withdrawal and recall. Variations in the length of suspension were useful only if the time factor had any bearing on the individual's problem.

Before Markham left the santorium, he asked to see one of the suspension units. For a while the androids were evasive without actually refusing, but at last they pointed out that it was not customary for guests to know more of the routine than was absolutely necessary. To which Markham replied that as an engineer he was interested in the technical aspect. Eventually Marion-A took him down to an insulated vault that was oddly reminiscent of K Chamber.

But instead of being filled with cases of food the vault was lined with row upon row of what looked like large filing cabinets. He wanted to open one of the drawers, but Marion-A was firm in her refusal — although the refusal was presented first as a suggestion, then as a piece of advice, and finally as an urgent recommendation.

Each drawer, she explained, contained a human being in suspension. It was a rule of the sanatorium that none should be disturbed until recall. Markham saw that each of the drawers had a plastic label which carried the name of the person in suspension, the date of withdrawal and the date of recall. He shuddered involuntarily, although the heated clothing he wore was remarkably efficient.

But what puzzled him most about the sanatorium was the apparent lack of personal contact among the guests. His single experience of twentieth-century hospital life, occasioned by an appendectomy, had led him to believe that patients were naturally gregarious. But not, evidently, in the North London Sanatorium.

During the whole of his stay he saw less than a dozen guests and spoke only to three of them. The first was Bressing; the second was a portly middle-aged man who was short-sighted enough to mistake him for an android; and the third was a girl of about twenty whom Markham discovered in a corridor weeping. He had asked her if there was anything that he could do to help. She stared at him; then with an emphatic 'No! No! No!' she turned and fled. He had the impression that he had made her even more unhappy.

He was not sure whether his lack of human contact was accidental or intended. The apartment the androids had given him was a penthouse on the flat roof of the sanatorium. There were similar apartments nearby, but none of them was occupied.

In many ways he was grateful for the isolation, since it gave him time to get used to the idea of having 'jumped' from the twentieth to the twenty-second century. It gave him time to sort out his own thoughts, to try to come to terms with his private sorrows, to consider his future even . . .

Perhaps, then, the androids had intentionally selected this apartment for him. Perhaps they realised that for a while he would need an ivory tower, a private citadel where he could grapple with his problems in peace.

It was a comfortable retreat, consisting of a bedroom, a bathroom and a lounge. Three walls of each room were painted in light colors, but the fourth was simply a sheet of double-thickness glass. The furniture in the bedroom was simple, functional: a low-built swivel bed on slender spider-legs of polished hiduminium, a black and white plastic dressing-table, a wall-wardrobe unit and a couple of chairs. But the floor was covered with deeply piled carpet, and at night the indirect lighting contrived to give the austere furnishings an intimate glow.

By contrast the lounge was a study in luxury, if not decadence. Its whole style was just a shade too voluptuous for its

26

twentieth-century occupant. The walls were pink, the ceiling crimson, and the floor was covered with a black-based carpet whose repeat motif was a dancing nude. There was a rustic brick fireplace complete with imitation coal-fire; and on each side of it a ceiling-high bookcase, one of which contained real books while the other proved to be a disguised cocktail cabinet.

Against the wall opposite the fireplace was a long settee, upholstered in a silky fabric whose color matched the ceiling. There was also an easy chair covered in the same material, a pair of small tables whose surfaces were decorated with the same enlarged motif as the carpet, and a plain whitewood stool.

During the few days that he occupied the apartment Markham had to adjust himself to a new concept of solitude — for Marion-A, as his personal android, was constantly with him. His first introduction to the functions of a personal android came when she had wheeled him on the trolley out of the cold-room, down a corridor, into an elevator, and finally into the penthouse lounge.

There she had helped him onto the settee and had taken the trolley away, returning a few minutes later with a selection of twenty-second-century clothes. Markham chose the least garish; and was about to ask the android to help him into the bedroom so that he could try them on, when Marion-A promptly and efficiently began to dress him. He was too surprised to object, too shaken to make any comment until she had finished.

Her hands were warm, he noted. Her touch was impersonal but gentle. The texture and feel of her 'skin' was curious but not distasteful. She put the clothes on him as though it was a routine to which she was well accustomed.

'So you are my personal android,' he said thoughtfully, when he had inspected the result with the aid of a hand mirror. He put the mirror down and looked at Marion-A once more. It was only then that he realised that he had avoided looking at her directly ever since they had left the cold-room.

He had got over the shock of her resemblance to Katy. It was, in fact, a poor resemblance and had probably had such an effect upon him because he had been subconsciously hoping that Katy would miraculously appear.

Marion-A was taller than Katy. Her features were more symmetrical, her shoulders broader, her limbs longer and her waist more slender. Too perfect. Too perfect to live.

She wore a plain red jersey and a black divided skirt. Pinned to her jersey, under her throat, was a silver brooch. Looking at it closely, Markham saw that it was just an ornamental letter A. A for android. In case, he thought cynically, anyone was doubtful.

'Yes, sir,' said Marion-A. 'It is customary for every adult human being to have a personal android.' She stood still, enduring his inspection without betraying any reaction at all.

'Do you know anything about me?' asked Markham abruptly.

'I only know, sir, that you belong to the twentieth century but have been accidentally preserved in S.A. The archaeologist who discovered you estimated that your suspension began between the fifth and eight decades.'

Markham gave a bitter smile. 'Good enough — the actual date was nineteen sixty-seven.'

'Yes, sir.' Marion-A relapsed into silence, standing quite still, rewarding his continued stare with total indifference.

Now that he was past the initial shock Markham was in the mood for information — and vengeance.

'Give me,' he said coldly, 'a definition of an android.'

'An android, sir, is a robot modeled in the style of a human being.'

'Just a machine, in fact?'

'Yes, sir, essentially a machine.'

'What is the function of androids, then?' His stare became quizzical, if not insolent. He was behaving like a child, and reveled in it. Although he was relaxing on the settee, he had left her standing. Idly he wondered if she would stand there until he told her to sit down.

'The function of androids,' said Marion-A, 'is to further the interests of human beings.'

'In fact you are a mechanical hybrid of nursemaid and servant?'

'Yes, sir,' she agreed blandly. 'I am also programed to be companionable.' She hesitated. 'There are two main types of android — the personal and the executive. The first functions for the benefit of the individual and the second for the benefit of society.'

28

Markham settled back comfortably and gave her a thin smile. 'Tell me about them. I've got a lot to learn about the twenty-second century. I might as well make a start on the interesting subject of androids.' The sight of her standing in front of him, without any sign of fatigue or resentment, became unnerving. 'I'm sorry,' he said awkwardly, feeling a burning sensation in his cheeks. 'Do sit down.'

'Thank you, sir.' Marion-A drew up the whitewood stool. Then in the impersonal voice of a lecturer she began to trace the development of robotics.

During and after the atomic war — the Nine Days Tranquiliser — that had been responsible for Markham's predicament, the populations of most of the industrialised countries throughout the world had been reduced to fractional percentages of their former numbers. But those who died as a direct result of atomic warfare were overshadowed numerically by the incredibly high mortalities from disease, pestilence and famine during the next ten years.

Britain, being one of the most densely populated countries, was naturally one of the worst hit. In 1967, it had boasted a population of sixty-five million. The Nine Days Tranquiliser and the succeeding ten years of disaster reduced that number to a little over sixty thousand.

These sixty thousand survivors were clearly not enough to keep the country going as an economic unit. And since the monarchy itself was destroyed by the war, there was no longer even a symbol of unity in the country. Government was ineffective and ludicrous simply because policy could not be implemented and legislation could not be enforced.

It was not long, therefore, before the concept of national unity was completely abandoned and the country split into three autonomous regional groups: Scotland, the Midlands and the South. Meanwhile, the critical shortage of manpower had forced the surviving scientists and engineers to concentrate on the development of servo-mechanisms, automation and ultimately robots.

Robots and electronic computers had started on their serious phase of development in the early nineteen-forties. But since manpower at that time was relatively abundant, they had been designed to fulfill only functions that were either beyond human ability in terms of time and energy, or simply too dangerous.

29

The first computers had been cumbersome machines the size of a large house. In fifty years, new techniques had reduced them to the size of a suitcase. The first robots had been heavy, monstrous, tanklike creatures. They, too, underwent a proportional reduction in size — and shape.

Previously they had been designed to carry out abnormal or hazardous tasks. Now they became substitutes for ordinary factory workers, farm laborers and clerks. And in order that the existing machines, which they were destined to use, need not be modified, the robots had to be reduced to roughly the size and shape of a man.

Their vision mechanism needed to have the same sensitivity and be about the same height from ground level as human eyes. Their arms and fingers needed a parallel range of dexterity, as did their legs. For they were destined to drive tractors and trucks, operate lathes, lay bricks, dig ditches and use typewriters and calculators.

But for several decades robot-designers had to concentrate on increasing the efficiency of their machines without paying much attention to the appearance of the robots. Though, for example, it was necessary for robotic vision to be as near as possible to human vision, it was not necessary to provide the robot with a neck and a head separated from its trunk. The whole 'body' was merely a joined metal case with 'eyes', 'ears' and 'voice' in the top section and all co-ordinating, executive and interpretive circuits down below. The arms were similarly jointed tubes with solenoid 'muscles', and the hands were based more upon the mechanical grab than on the human pattern. Also, by human standards, the legs were slender, though the feet were exceptionally large and heavy to give stability.

Eventually, however, the numbers of robots increased along with their industrial adaptability, and they were able to take charge of virtually all heavy industry and agriculture — with just a few human supervisors to deal with problems that were beyond the scope of electronic microbrains.

There came a time when it was evident that the sheer struggle for industrial survival was over. The robots – who already outnumbered their masters— had won a battle that human beings could only have lost.

So far it had required men to build robots. But the point

had been reached where a robot was built that was capable of designing and building another robot. Soon the first completely independent production unit was set up, where super-specialised robots designed and fabricated others of their own kind. The robots were at last controlling their own evolutionary processes.

Meanwhile the industrial demand for robots having been met, there now remained the domestic demand. The robots had solved the problem of industrial manpower. There followed, inevitably, the problem of domestic womanpower.

At first the ugly, heavy-footed monsters were confined to the kitchen and garden. But as their ability to perform household chores was developed, there developed also the need for a type of robot that looked less like an animated washing machine and more like a human being — in short, a robot able to operate in the living-room and the nursery as well as in the kitchen. A robot that could wait at table, look after the children, make the beds and dust the lounge ... A robot that could mix cocktails, tell fairy stories, play chess or bridge or whist ... A robot that would remember birthdays and appoinments ... A robot that would provide conversation for the lonely and assistance for the aged ...

It was the beginning of the androids.

The first models resembled lightly armored medieval knights. Then the humanising process began in earnest. New techniques enabled the weight problem to be overcome; consequently feet became smaller and human in shape. The developement of the micropile — a miniature atomic power station — allowed the energy course to be contained in a lead capsule hardly larger than the human heart. Mechanical hands were remodeled on the human style. The head was humanised and separated from the trunk by a neck. And finally a synthetic skin was added to fleshlike contours; natural hair was set in a plastic scalp; a face was created with artificial eyes, ears, nose and mouth. And lips capable of smiling ...

The ultimate product bore no resemblance at all to its one and a half ton ancestors. It was in every respect a humanised robot. An android.

Because of their human appearance, they produced an even greater change in society than the conventional robots. People quickly grew used to the idea of having androids in their homes, and soon it was unfashionable to be without one.

It became a sign of breeding and good taste to allow an android to perform all those tasks which were not innately interesting. The activities of the androids expanded. They took over the entire housekeeping; they became chauffeurs and escorts. It became acceptable for a single or neglected woman to be taken out to dine or dance, or be escorted to the theatre by a 'male' android. It was natural for a lonely bachelor, or a man whose wife was on holiday or otherwise occupied, to use a 'female' android as a temporary companion.

Eventually the idea grew that each adult human being should have a personal android capable of being valet, maid, chauffeur, nurse, adviser and housekeeper as and when required. In the end human beings began to depend upon androids in many spheres of activity for which they were not originally designed. After all, the androids were simply convenient machines. And almost infallible ones!

Toward the end of the twenty-first century the androids had reached such a pitch of efficiency that they were able to enter what had been regarded as necessarily human professions. They became doctors, dentists, policemen — even psychiatrists. And so the burden of work was finally lifted from the shoulders of mankind.

It was no longer necessary for a man to do anything productive since, whatever his task, it could be safely left to an appropriately programed android. Thus, in the world of the twenty-second century leisure did not belong only to a privileged class but was the natural birthright of all human beings. A man was free to make what he wished of his life — he was even free to work if he really wanted to. But few men did, since work had become unfashionable.

Markham heard Marion-A's account of the development of the androids with increasing distaste. To his twentieth-century mind, the way in which machines had superseded human beings was not only incredible, it was also sinister.

'Bang goes initiative and intelligence,' he said grimly. 'In my world, work was regarded as a challenge. Now the challenge no longer exists. What is there to take its place?'

'Leisure is also a challenge,' said Marion-A. 'Human beings are so constituted that they need a purpose in life. If work is no longer a necessity, people are free to explore other fields of activitity — the arts, for example, social accomplishments and all forms of psychosomatic discipline from sport to religion.'

'You seem to know a devil of a lot about what human beings need.'

'Yes, sir. It was a major part of my programing.'

Markham was silent for a while. Then he said, 'Tell me, how old are you?'

Marion-A gave one of her rare stiff smiles. 'I was created a year ago, sir. I was then given a basic programing and stored until I could be used. After your discovery, and when it seemed possible that you might be recalled, I was activated and given a special programing based upon extrapolations of your probable requirements.'

'I see. I forgot for a moment that you were not — ' He floundered.

'Of biological origin?' suggested Marion-A.

Markham laughed. 'That's right,' he said. 'Not of biological origin. A magnificent description. I'll remember it.'

'I think, sir,' said Marion-A, 'that it would be good for you to rest now. It is important that one should not exert oneself greatly for a few days after recall.'

Markham yawned. Besides being tired, he felt utterly depressed and nervy. 'I think you're right. A good dose of natural sleep would improve me considerably. There's plenty of time to get my bearings. I presume the world of the twenty-second century will still be real when I wake again?' His question was only half joking.

'Yes, sir,' said Marion-A. 'It is unlikely that you will sleep more than fifteen hours.'

He grinned. 'I don't know about that. The last time I closed my eyes it was for one and a half centuries.'

Then Marion-A gave another of her stiff smiles and really surprised him. 'Perhaps, sir, you should have used an alarm clock.'

'My God!' he exploded, jerking upright. 'A sense of humor! Thank the Lord for small mercies. How on earth did you get it?'

'It is a synthetic sense of humor,' explained Marion-A gravely. 'I was programed with it. True humor depends primarily upon a sense of shock, which can be fully developed

33

only in biological systems. But I am able to appreciate the bisociative process of thought, and can therefore interpret some humorous ideas and also create some.'

He sank back exhausted and yawned again. 'You really surprise me — a sense of humor. That's something, anyway.'

Marion-A stood up. 'With permission, I will take you into the bedroom, sir.'

As she helped him to his feet he managed a weak, tired smile. 'In the twentieth century that might have made for an interesting situation. No androids, only men and women. What a wonderful bloody world!'

He leaned on Marion-A heavily, but she supported his weight easily and led him into the bedroom. In a minute or two his day clothes were exchanged for a light sleeping suit and he was wriggling luxuriously between clean, warm sheets.

Marion-A put the clothes away and said, 'Good night, sir. I hope you sleep well. If there is anything you need, it is necessary only to call me.'

'Thank you. ... Androids don't need to sleep, I suppose?'

'When a personal android's master or mistress does not require attention the android goes into low alert — which correlates approximately with human relaxation. We maintain high alert only when on continuous duty.'

Markham gave her a look that was neither bitter nor mocking. 'I hope you have a nice low alert,' he said seriously. Then he closed his eyes.

Marion-A turned out the light and returned to the lounge. There she sat on the whitewood stool, closed her eyes and remained quite motionless for the next thirteen hours until Markham awoke.

CHAPTER THREE

THE face in the bathroom mirror, did not look a hundred and seventy-seven years old. It merely looked like the face of a man who was thirty-one. Staring critically at it as he

34

shaved, John Markham saw that the skin on the lined fore-head was still fresh-looking, even youthful. Above it, the untidy mass of dark hair gave no sign of receding or thinning. In fact, if anything, it was too long, for he had badly needed a haircut a hundred and forty-six years ago and had meant to get one on the way home from Epping.

He tried hard not to think about the past, for the past meant Katy. Katy as he had seen her a couple of days ago — a couple of days that had grown into the meaningless inter-val of one and a half centuries. He fought back the sudden wave of nostalgia, the hopeless longing . . .

Breakfast was waiting for him in the lounge, breakfast and Marion-A.

'Good morning, sir. You look much more relaxed after your sleep. Perhaps when you have breakfasted you would care to spend a little time in the sunshine. It is a very fine day.'

He glanced at the sunlight pouring through the wall-window. Sunlight and a blue sky — the rich, enduring things. He felt a subtle release of vitality deep inside him. So much had been lost, but he was still alive.

Then he caught sight of a little pile on the breakfast trol-ley. His wallet and key-ring, a cigarette lighter and a tiny white elephant from the last Christmas cracker that he and Katy had pulled.

Suddenly his legs gave way, and the next thing he knew, Marion-A was helping him onto the settee.

'Damn!' he said angrily. 'I'm as weak as a kitten. How did — how did those things get here?'

'I thought you might want them, sir, for reasons of sen-timent. I am sorry if you prefer not to — '

'No, that's all right.' He looked at the android and smiled. 'Just that I wasn't expecting . . . Will you pass me the wallet?'

He looked to see if the photograph of Katy was still there. It was. Crinkled, but not faded. He looked at it for a minute or two, then he handed it to Marion-A. 'Now go and look in the mirror.'

She took the photograph, glanced at it, then examined her own features. 'The resemblance is not good,' she said. 'Your wife was beautiful.'

35

'How do you know what beauty is?' he asked harshly. 'No, don't tell me — you were programed with an esthetic sense.' He gave a bitter laugh.

'Perhaps,' said Marion-A, 'you find my appearance distressing. It can be remodeled if you wish.'

'Not necessary. I've got to learn to take the world as I find it. Got to learn to cut out the self-pity, too.' He put the photograph away. 'Now what's for breakfast? Ham and eggs, by heaven! The world is still civilised.'

He knew that his voice was a little too hearty, that he was only trying to prove to himself — and failing — that he could take whatever came. But he didn't care. What, he asked himself silently, was the point in being inhibited for the benefit of an android?

While he ate, Marion-A sat motionless on her whitewood stool. He tried to ignore her presence, but the odd thing was that she did have a presence. Maybe she was only a complex machine, but the humanised exterior gave her the illusion of personality. He would not have felt disconcerted eating in front of a tape-recorder, or a camera, or an electronic computer. But he was disconcerted by Marion-A. She was the sum of all those things, but she was also something more. The whole was greater than the parts ... not quite a machine and not quite human. He wondered idly if he would feel the same about a conventional robot.

After a time he felt the need to make conversation. 'That'll be the day,' he said thoughtfully, 'when androids are able to eat.'

Marion-A smiled. 'We already can, sir — if necessary. Most of the androids produced during the last decade have artificial stomachs. Since, among human beings, eating is a social function as well as a necessary one, it seemed desirable to create androids capable of taking their place at table if required. . . . Do you wish me to join you, sir?'

Markham shook his head violently. 'What do you do with it?' he asked.

'With what, sir?'

'The food.'

'It is received in a small plastic sack which can be removed when convenient.'

'My God!' he exclaimed. 'I suppose procreation will be next on the list.'

'I do not think so, sir. For non-biological material, factory reproduction is more feasible and more efficient.'

He began to laugh. 'You have quite a subtle sense of humor.'

She smiled again. 'Actually, sir, I was not joking.'

After breakfast Marion-A took him out onto the roof and placed a light canvas chair in a wind-trap facing the sun. He had expected to find the North London Sanatorium on the outskirts of the city. But all around, as far as the eye could see, there was nothing but rolling wooded country and farmland.

'Where are we?' he asked. 'I thought this place was somewhere near the city.'

'London is about fifty miles away,' said Marion-A. 'The nearest town is Colchester.'

'Why call it the North London Sanatorium, then?'

'Because it is in the Republic of London, sir.'

'Yes, you said something about that yesterday. . . . I want to get out of this place. I want to see what's happened to the world. . . . Do you know, I haven't any idea what time of year it is? The weather's so magnificent it could be spring or early autumn.'

'This is the third day of September, sir.'

Markham took a deep breath. 'The best month of the year. I remember —' He stopped suddenly. 'To hell with that . . .' He looked at Marion-A and smiled. 'I want you to do something for me. Stop calling me "sir". It makes me feel like a company director.'

'Yes, Mr. Markham.'

'That's worse — better make it John.'

Marion-A hesitated. 'It is not customary for a personal android to be so familiar.'

'It is also not customary for men to be resurrected after one and a half centuries in an icebox . . . I'd like you to call me John.'

'It would be advisable, then, to restrict it to private conversation. There is a strong convention of formality between human beings and androids.'

He yawned. 'Maybe it isn't a necessary convention. . . . I wish I didn't feel so tired. Dammit, I've just had a really good sleep.'

'Suspended animation usually brings fatigue and lassitude.

That is why it is important for you to spend a few days recovering your stamina.'

'Marion?'

'Yes, sir?'

'No — not "yes sir." '

She smiled. 'Yes — John.'

'The illusion of your personality and intelligence is fascinating . . . How long will you be my personal android?'

'Until you require a different model, sir.'

'Good. Then I can have a go at educating you. It should be interesting.'

'I have already been given a basic programing in science and social studies.'

'That's not the kind of education I was thinking about.'

She remained silent, and Markham said irritably, 'If you were human you would have asked me for a definition.'

'Would you like me to?'

'Yes.'

'Then please define the type of education you have in mind, John.'

'That's better.' He yawned again, and gazed drowsily at the horizon. 'Intellectual independence and curiosity. Without them you're just a box of electronic tricks. With them you can become a self-conscious being.'

'Self-consciousness,' said Marion-A, 'is a metaphysical abstraction that I can apprehend but not appreciate.'

'Self-consciousness,' he retorted, 'is the gift of God — also a metaphysical abstraction, but valid nevertheless. God gave it to men. The question is: can men give it to machines?'

Marion-A placed a pillow behind his head and a light rug over his knees. 'I think that is a question that only human beings can hope to answer.'

Markham looked up at her and grinned. 'Until androids begin to ask themselves the same thing . . . You're a ready-made Galatea, and I'm an out-of-date Pygmalion. I wonder what the result will be?'

'I'm afraid I do not know the terms of reference.'

He laughed. 'Neither did Pygmalion.' A moment later, his eyes were closed and he was sleeping soundly.

Sleeping and eating, talking and walking — that was the pattern of his life for the next few days. The fatigue induced by suspended animation went deeper than physical fatigue. Its aftermath was a short but profound lethargy of spirit.

But slowly his vitality returned to normal, and by the fifth day he was seething with impatience. He wanted to break out of the cocoon of the sanatorium and explore the world of the twenty-second century.

It was on the fifth day that Marion-A took him to see the suspension units. By that time, during the course of several medical examinations, he had made the acquaintance of two android doctors who seemed to be subtly different from the other androids he had encountered, including Marion-A. He learned later that they were psychiatrists, and deduced that their conversations with him — which always seemed to strike an oddly personal note — were part of some kind of psychiatric assessment.

Also, on the evening of the fifth day, he had his first actual encounter with the outside world. It was really only a one-sided affair, since he was interviewed by an android tri-di television announcer; but it gave him a few more pointers on the kind of world he could expect.

The interview took place in his apartment shortly after he had finished a late and substantial dinner.

The android was tall and with features that were surprisingly flexible. When he smiled it looked like a real smile, and he could register a whole series of convincing expressions — doubtless for the benefit of television audiences.

The tri-di camera was a small egg-shaped canister with a cluster of tiny lenses on the larger end. It was set upon a tripod facing the settee on which Markham was sitting. As far as he could judge, its focus and direction were remotely controlled by the interviewer, who carried a gadget something like a watch strapped to the underside of his wrist.

Marion-A remained out of camera range, but Markham was amused to find himself looking at her now and again for reassurance. He had come to depend on her a great deal during the last few days. He had come to depend on her, in fact, far more than he cared to realise.

The interviewer signaled to Markham, touched his control gadget, then faced the camera.

'Hello, dear people. As always, Persona-Parade brings you the most interesting personality of the week. Tonight we have with us Mr. John Markham, who has been accidentally preserved in S.A. for a hundred and forty-six years. It couldn't happen, but it did. Here is living history, friends. Here is *the* dramatic situation — a man of the twentieth century flung forward a hundred and fifty years in time. Remember, dear friends, to him we are dreams of the future; to us, he is a ghost from the past. And what does he think about it all? Let's ask him, shall we?'

The camera swung slightly to Markham, and he felt the sweat on his forehead. This, he thought grimly, was a fitting end to convalescence.

'Now, Mr. Markham,' continued the android, 'what do you miss most from the old days?'

'My wife and children,' came the prompt answer.

The interviewer laughed. 'A natural sentiment! In the twentieth century you were still conditioned to primitive family life, weren't you?'

Markham betrayed surprise. 'We didn't exactly regard it as primitive, but I'm quite prepared to believe it's old-fashioned now. I expect you grow children in bottles these days.'

'Hardly, dear sir. But humanity no longer submits to the unhealthy parent-child relationship. It has achieved psychosomatic freedom in the pursuit of creative art. Incidentally, what was your own favorite art form?'

'I didn't have much time for it,' said Markham drily. 'I was too busy earning a living.'

The android gazed archly at the camera. 'Dear people,' he murmured, 'don't think the Survivor is just out to shock us. Disgusting though it seems, men really did waste most of their time actually *working*.'

'And quite a number of us,' added Markham, 'were so depraved as actually to enjoy it. . . . Am I right in thinking that work has become a trifle obscene since then?'

'Humanity has been liberated,' said the interviewer impressively. 'Work is the business of robots and androids, and mankind is free to seek the Full Life — which brings us to my next question, sir. Is it true that after marriage in your day a man slept only with his wife, and vice versa?'

The camera turned to Markham, who was registering a slightly dazed expression. 'We regarded it as the ideal arrangement,' he said carefully. 'Most of us believed that a happy marriage depended on being faithful to one's partner.'

'But there were exceptions?'

'Yes.'

'Were you one of them?'

'No.'

The android gave what seemed a slightly malicious laugh. 'So you actually believe in possessive love, Mr. Markham. How utterly quaint!'

'It might be,' conceded Markham dangerously, 'in a world of prostitutes and gigolos.'

The android turned to the camera with a delighted smile. 'My friends,' he said in a stage whisper, 'would you believe it? Our Survivor is a genuine sexual barbarian.'

Markham was suddenly angry. 'I also use a stone club and beat my chest in the mating season. . . . Now is there anything else you'd like to know?'

'Certainly,' said the android calmly. 'What do you propose to do now that you are ready to leave the sanatorium?'

'I'd like to see what kind of a world I've waked up into, but I suppose I'll have to do something to earn my keep first.'

'No, sir. Your name will be added to the Male Index and you will be awarded the Republic's basic pension of five thousand pounds a year, which will not be reduced unless you inadvertently fertilise more than one female within any five-year period.'

'Good God!' The feeling of shock quickly gave way to a mild hysteria. 'What happens if I fertilise half a dozen?'

The camera focused on the android. His face was grave. 'Such behaviour,' he said slowly, 'is regarded as psychotic. The usual treatment is prolonged suspended animation. The creation of new life, Mr. Markham, is not undertaken lightly. In your own day, doubtless, it was of little consequence. Perhaps that is one of the reasons why your culture was destroyed by the Nine Days Tranquiliser.'

'I think,' said Markham cautiously, 'that I have a great deal to learn about the twenty-second century.'

'Yes, indeed!' The interviewer's frown gave way to a genial grin. 'And now, as we have about a minute left, perhaps you would like to conclude our interesting discussion with a few words to all the dear people.'

Though the camera hadn't moved, Markham had the conviction that it was re-focusing for a close-up. He glanced quickly at Marion-A, then faced the camera squarely and cleared his throat.

'To me,' he said hesitantly, 'the twentieth century is as real as if it were only a few days ago. You must remember that I belong to an age when the population of this island was counted in millions rather than thousands — an age when men worked, when marriage was binding, and when the desire for children was not psychotic. Bearing that in mind, you'll understand my difficulties in adjusting to a new world where, as it seems, many of the old ways are no longer acceptable. But I shall do my best to adapt to the twenty-second century, and if I'm guilty of any social blunders perhaps you'll make allowances for me. . . . Thank you, and good evening.'

The android immediately took over. 'That was Mr. John Markham, the Survivor — and Persona-Parade's personality of the week. Now we take you to the Scottish Estate, where one of my colleagues is about to ask the Laird for his impression of the recent campaign in the Highlands. . . . So, dear people, over to New Glasgow.'

The interviewer touched his wrist-control. 'We're off the screen now, sir. Therefore may I apologise for any familiarity rendered necessary by the interview. I hope you'll understand that — '

'Don't worry,' said Markham with irony. 'No bones broken. Anything to keep the dear people amused.'

'Exactly,' said the android, his face impassive once more. 'Thank you for your co-operation, sir.' He dismantled the tripod and placed the camera in a case.

Until he had gone Markham maintained an air of stolid indifference. But as soon as the apartment door was closed he began to walk nervously up and down the room. Marion-A watched him but remained silent. Presently he put his hand in his pocket, took out his cigarette lighter and stared at it.

'Damn, no cigarettes! I haven't had one since — since nineteen sixty-seven. Does nobody smoke in this idiotic brave new world?'

'Very few people, sir,' said Marion-A. 'And those chiefly of the older generation. The habit began to die several decades ago. But I took the liberty of having some cigarettes

42

made in case you required them.' She took a small box from the cocktail cabinet that was disguised as a book case.

'Thanks. Genuine tobacco?'

'Yes, sir. London grown.'

He examined one of the cigarettes, sniffed at it cautiously, then finally lighted it. 'Not bad. We used to import tobacco from America, you know.'

'Yes, sir. But international trade declined considerably after the Nine Days Tranquiliser; and there is now virtually no need for it.'

'For the love of Mike stop saying "sir"!'

'Very well, John.'

He inhaled deeply for a few moments, savoring the luxury. 'I might as well be a real devil and have a drink. I could use it. What kind of fire-water is there in the poison cupboard!'

'Brandy, whisky, gin, red and white wines, and cordials.'

'Pour me a double whisky, then ... please. And give yourself a drink, too. It helps the illusion of humanity.'

He took the glass and waited until Marion-A had poured another. 'In my day we used to say "Cheers!" or "Down the hatch!" or something like that. What's the password nowadays?'

Marion-A smiled. 'If I were a human being, I might say "Take the lid off your id." Then you would respond with "Here we go, libido." '

Markham laughed. 'Might as well begin my reorientation. O.K., Marion — take the lid off your id.'

She lifted her glass and said gravely, 'Here we go, libido.'

He drank the whisky, and was glad to feel it burning his throat. Then he watched Marion-A sip hers, knowing that it meant nothing to her.

'What kind of an ass did I make of myself in that interview?'

'You behaved very well. I think you will have made a good impression. People will understand that you cannot be expected to be familiar with current social attitudes.'

Markham grimaced. 'Something tells me that your current social attitudes are going to make me yearn for suspended animation.'

'I think you will adjust in time, John.'

'My God! I hope not. ... And another thing. What the devil am I going to do when I leave here? I've been living in a daze for the last few days. I suppose I was subconsciously expecting everything to be planned out for me.'

'Tomorrow,' said Marion-A, 'it would be advisable to go to the City and register on the Male Index. Then you will receive a checkbook and your basic credit rating.'

'Five thousand pounds,' said Markham, 'providing I don't absent-mindedly fertilise a few females.'

Marion-A gave another of her stiff smiles. 'I would suggest a good night's sleep, John. You are still tired and there is much to be done tomorrow. It will be necessary to decide where you wish to live and to arrange for accommodation.'

Markham looked at her, then went to the cocktail cabinet and poured himself another double whisky. 'I have news for you, Marion. I'm going to get slightly drunk. It appears to be indicated. ... So here's to my favorite nursemaid.'

CHAPTER FOUR

THE helicar was a two-seater; a light plastiglass and hiduminium bubble with three road wheels and two compact air vanes, the smaller vane being under its chassis. Altogether, the machine looked too fragile to operate either as a helicopter or a car. But when he examined it carefully Markham saw that he had greatly underestimated the quality of its design.

Marion-A slid along the comfortable bench seat and took the wheel. He got in beside her and shut the door. There was a faint whine as the atomic motor came to life, then the helicar rose slowly from the roof of the sanatorium and headed southwest toward the City at a leisurely seventy miles an hour.

It was a fine warm morning and the mellow sunlight, with a golden quality peculiar to early autumn, played evenly over the rolling countryside. Eight or nine miles away, the town of Colchester was just visible — a sharply defined island of glass and concrete in the rippling sea of green.

Now that he was leaving the sanatorium, Markham felt irrationally that a door was closing on the past. Intellectually he knew that it had closed long ago — the moment he felt the first shock wave in K Chamber. But while he had enjoyed the solitude of his penthouse apartment there had always been the sneaking conviction that somehow it was all an elaborate dream, that presently he would open his eyes, roll over and tell Katy all about it. And because he had needed to sleep so much during the last five days the dreamlike quality had been reinforced so that he had almost begun to believe in a real and final awakening.

But this was the real awakening — helicar journey to London with a companion who was capable, considerate — and soulless. This was the true moment of rebirth: the entry into a world that had already given frightening hints of its own inescapable reality.

Before he left the sanatorium four letters had been delivered to his apartment. They were the result of his appearance on Persona-Parade. The first was from a man who wanted to paint his portrait in a crimson monochrome on glass, two were from women politely offering to initiate him in the sexual customs of the twenty-second century, and the fourth was an ornately printed dinner-party invitation from the President of London.

As the helicar continued on its journey and Colchester disappeared in the undulating countryside, Markham took the President's card from his pocket and looked at it again.

It read:

BUCKINGHAM PALACE　　　7-9-13
From Clement Bertrand
PRESIDENT OF THE REPUBLIC OF LONDON
John Markham Esquire
GREETINGS
You are cordially invited to present
yourself at 2100 on 15-9-13
Dinner & Diversions
(Androids optional　　　R.S.V.P.)

Dinner and diversions! Markham smiled cynically to himself as he imagined the kind of diversions that might be provided by the President of London. He began to wonder what

45

kind of a man Clement Bertrand would be, and was about to ask Marion-A. But he changed his mind and put the card back into his pocket. How could an android adequately describe a human being?

Meanwhile the helicar was passing over thickly wooded country. But less than a mile ahead the trees thinned out, suddenly exposing a wide area of rock and barren earth. It was roughly circular in shape, and nearly half a mile in diameter. Hardly anything was growing in the whole area except a few stunted bushes and thin uneven patches of grass. From the low altitude at which the helicar was flying Markham could make out the disintegrating surface of three disused roads that converged on the barren area.

With a shock of recognition he realized that he was passing over Epping Forest, and that in a few seconds he would be almost directly above K Chamber where he had lain like a slab of frozen meat for all those appalling years. The barren patch was evidently caused by the atomic bomb or missile that had sealed him up with the force of its blast.

He stared at the forest, fascinated, turning to gaze at it until it was out of sight. When he looked ahead once more, he saw the outskirts of the City, still bearing the broad unhealed scars of the Nine Days Tranquiliser; but alive and enduring — looking as if it would yet survive the race that built it.

Presently he saw something that brought a watery film to his eyes, that set up a sharp, searing pain inside him — a pain that was somehow not physical but yet too deep to be borne for long. He tried to dismiss it by a sheer act of will, but it stayed — heavy as lead, colder than all the ice of K Chamber.

Down below was Hampstead Heath — incredibly unchanged.

'Circle,' he said to Marion-A in a voice that was hoarse and indistinct. 'Circle slowly, and take it low . . . Hampstead. I — I used to . . . I want to have a look.'

'Yes sir.'

He knew that Marion-A was not surprised or curious. Androids are never surprised or curious — unless it's necessary. He didn't even bother to make her say, 'Yes, John.'

The Heath was cleaner, fresher than it had ever been. Where were the lovers who had walked there arm in arm?

46

Where were the children who had romped and flown kites and scattered the wrappings of innumerable sweets over the worn grass? Where were all the ghosts of a thousand yesterdays? And, above all, where were the ghosts of the three he had loved?

Such warm and living ghosts. All that a man should want. And all that he could no longer have . . .

But the Heath was deserted — except for trees and grass and flowers and sunlight. And all the whispers that were ever swallowed by the wind.

'Find somewhere and put down,' he told Marion-A. 'I want to stay here a while. I want to stay and think.'

Without answering, Marion-A selected a smooth patch of turf and set the helicar gently down. For a minute or so he didn't get out. He just sat there, watching. Watching and thinking. And remembering.

'Would you like a cigarette, John?'

He looked at Marion-A in surprise, and suddenly grinned. 'You're learning.'

He smoked the cigarette silently for a while, then opened the helicar door. After a moment's hesitation he got out and stretched.

'Think I'll take a walk . . . There's no particular hurry to get me registered, is there?'

'No, the bureau is open all the time. Would you like me to come with you?'

'Yes.'

Marion-A came out of the helicar and stood waiting, while he glanced round at a landscape that was still curiously the same — but somehow a little wilder because it was no longer punished by thousands of weekend strolls. Presently he took Marion-A by the hand and began to walk briskly toward a hillock three or four hundred yards away.

'Fantasies and illusions are important,' he said quietly. 'When human beings lose them, they begin to die . . . Androids don't die, do they?'

'No, John.'

'Why not?'

'Because they do not live,' said Marion-A. 'Their motivation is synthetic, their aim functional.'

'Well, you can stop being functional for a while, Marion. You can become part of my fantasy. You can become an honorary member of the doomed society of the living. In short, you can pretend to be human. You can pretend to enjoy the wind and the sun and the feel of grass under your feet.'

After four or five minutes they reached the hillock and Markham found a suitable spot to sit down. He was sweating and breathing heavily — not with the sun's warmth, but with the exertion of having walked a quarter of a mile. He lay back for a time, closing his eyes, feeling the secure hardness of the earth beneath him and the gentle interplay of wind and sunlight on his body.

He let himself sink into a haze of daydreams and memories, until Marion-A's voice jerked him back to the present.

'Someone is approaching, John. Perhaps he wishes to speak to you.'

Markham sat up with a jerk and saw a plump, oldish man coming toward them. The stranger wore a dark red tunic — much the same as Markham himself was wearing— and a pair of loose, bell-bottom trousers: the normal dress for a man of the twenty-second century. He did not have a hat; and as he got nearer, Markham saw that his white hair was as long as a woman's and was held back close to his scalp by a couple of silver clips. The face was brown and pouchy with lines of discontent, but a pair of wide-set eyes somehow redeemed these features with their suggestion of secret amusement.

'Lo,' said the stranger. 'Fine weather for the uninhibited, don't you think? I never came across a sexual barbarian before — excepting lions and swans, of course. They have a kind of misguided faithfulness, too. But then *they* don't want to work, they just want to live . . . Mind if I sit down?'

Markham was bewildered. 'No valid objection, it's a free country.'

'So they say,' grunted the stranger, easing his bulk gently down onto the grass. 'And who are we to disbelieve 'em? Nice android they gave you. Almost looks intelligent.' Then he suddenly snapped at Marion-A: 'Classification, mark and function — quick!'

'A-three-alpha,' said Marion-A. 'By what right, sir — '

'Forget it. I'm just absent-minded.' He turned to Markham. 'A nice bright one. They may be fast, but sometimes we can still be faster. You can always get them to admit their operation level if you pick your moment. Now tell her to go and look for four-leaf clover for twenty minutes.'

Markham became angry. 'What the devil do you think you're doing?'

'Fixing to have a quiet chat with you,' said the stranger imperturbably. 'Little androids have big ears, my friend — and long memories. A fact that you cannot learn too soon. Now be a good fellow and send her out of earshot.' He gave a grim laugh. 'You can always shout for help if I make indecent suggestions.'

'Marion, will you leave us alone for a few minutes?'

'Don't ask her, tell her,' said the stranger throatily.

Markham turned on him. 'If you're feeling like that we're going to have a hell of a short talk.'

Marion-A stood up. 'How long do you wish to be alone with this gentleman, sir?'

'About ten minutes, I think. Keep in sight, then I'll come for you when I'm ready to go.'

'Very well, sir.' She glanced at the stranger without any animosity and walked away.

'Memorising my face,' said the old man pleasantly. 'A-three-alpha ... She'll give the description to Psycho-prop — unless you fix her with a little story. The kind that androids believe.'

'Now maybe you'll tell me what all this is about,' said Markham. 'I'm feeling mildly curious.'

The stranger grinned, displaying faintly yellow teeth. 'You're the Survivor, aren't you? John Markham. I saw you on the screen last night ... If I tell you my name you can get me twenty years S.A. if I'm lucky, or a Breakdown if I'm not — assuming you can hold me till your android contacts the City Group. So I'll tell you my name and make it a problem in ethics — your problem. I'm Gray Walta Hyggens, sometime Professor of Philosophy at the University of Oxford, God rest its pedantic soul ... Just call me Prof.'

'Well, now we know each other,' said Markham, 'what next?'

'Mind if I call you John?' he asked with a grin. 'A cheap psychological trick. You'll find it harder to hand me over if we're on friendly terms.'

49

'Why should I want to hand you over?'

'John, I'm a Runner. That's why you should want to hand me over. But you won't; at least I'm betting you won't, because you're a Runner, too. You don't know it yet, maybe. But you will, when you've had a real taste of this lovely, wonderful world.'

'Regard me as an infant of four,' said Markham. 'I don't know a damn thing. I'm just out of the icebox. Now what in heaven's name is a Runner?'

'Me,' said Prof. Hyggens, smirking. 'I'm the perfect definition — an old-fashioned, maladjusted nut who believes in human dignity, freedom of action and the right to work. I'm dangerous. I'm practically an anarchist. Society doesn't like me very much — in fact, it's downright afraid. So it — and by society, John, I mean the God-damned androids — recommends me for Analysis. Now I don't think overmuch of Analysis, because some of my friends have had it, and they don't look too good after they've been analysed. They don't even look human any more, not to my way of thinking . . . Where was I? Oh, yes — Analysis. So I refuse to be analysed and they take me off the Male Index. My checks aren't good any more, so I starve — or become a Runner. A Runner, John, is a man who has nothing left but his self-respect. So in order to preserve his self-respect — and incidentally his freedom — he has to steal food and clothes, smash inquisitive androids, live by night and be a menace to all decent human beings. And how do you like that?'

'I don't,' said Markham. 'You've told me what you are. Now tell me why.'

Prof. Hyggens took out a battered pipe and began to stuff it with tobacco. 'Filthy habit. Unhygienic. Disgusting. Lung cancer, tuberculosis, cast-iron arteries — and sanity. Have some?'

'No thanks. I use cigarettes.'

'Nice to be dirty, isn't it?' said Prof. 'Now let me see. You asked why. Well, I'm an old man, John. I've been around long enough to watch these damned androids take over the whole works. Thirty years ago I taught philosophy — now that's a pompous way of putting it — to classes of maybe two or three dozen. All human beings. Not very bright, except for the odd one or two, but still human beings. Then my classes began to get smaller. Hell, what was the point in killing gray cells over logical positivism when the world owed you a nice easy living? But after a year or two, when I was down to classes of nine or ten, the numbers began to grow again. That made me laugh, but it wasn't a nice kind of laughter.'

Markham took out another cigarette and saw with surprise that his fingers were trembling. 'I'm still a little weak,' he explained. 'Mentally and physically ... You said the numbers began to grow again?'

Prof. Hyggens nodded. 'Androids,' he said emphatically. 'Androids learning philosophy. How's that for a joke?'

Markham stared. 'It depends on one's sense of humor,' he said. 'Personally, I'd have been more inclined to lose sleep than laugh.'

Prof. Hyggens gave a satisfied beam. 'I knew you were temperamentally a Runner. God blast it, you had to be — straight from the glorious twentieth ... But the best is yet to come, John. The numbers kept on growing and the humans kept on dwindling. There came a time when I was lecturing to just a couple of good boys — one of them a polio wreck, and the other a helicar crash victim. Guess that's why they took up philosophy, anyway. But the rest of my class were androids — big, bright androids all ready to lap up the wisdom of the ages. I was so damned angry, I could have rigged a force eight electromagnetic field and sugared their circuits. And you know what I did?'

In spite of himself, Markham was beginning to like the old man. He was dirty, unkempt, and stank not a little of drink. But there was something irresistible about his personality: an ebullience, an impishness that belied his age.

'Cut out the rhetorical questions,' said Markham drily. 'They're out of character for a professor of philosophy.'

Prof. Hyggens grinned. 'Too right, they are. Know what I did, John? I swallowed that divine anger. I took it all down in a single gulp and spit out five thousand rationalisations — and I kept on teaching those unholy bastards of mechanics and logic as well as I knew how ... You haven't ever lectured, have you, John?'

'No, but I've been lectured.'

'Then you know the recipe, boy. Arouse the students' interest with a nice controversial statement, pour in two quarts of genuine information, and salt well with a few off-key jokes. Then you let it simmer gently in a slow mental oven.'

'You have an odd line in metaphors.'

'Appropriate,' said Prof. solemnly. 'If the human brain isn't a kind of oven, how else does a culture get to be half-baked? Well, as I was saying, that's the recipe. But not with androids, by Jesus. No, sir. They sit like rocks, they stare like china cats — and you pour it in as fast as you can because they have practically sweet-all assimilation limit. You know, John, I'm a professional fool. I should have anticipated the next move. Anyone but a half-witted professor would have seen it coming.'

'At a guess,' ventured Markham, 'I'd say they closed down the philosophy course because the androids discovered they didn't need philosophy.'

'Not quite, son.' Prof. Hyggens gave a paternal beam. 'They just closed down me.'

'What do you mean?'

'Fired, that's what I mean. They found a more efficient lecturer — an android, John. One of my own ex-students. Now tell me that's not funny!'

Markham was silent for a moment or two. Silent and wondering. Then he said, 'There's one thing that baffles me. Why should androids study philosophy? From what I've discovered so far, they're functional. They — '

'Philosophy,' interrupted Prof., 'is life. At least, it's one of the great aspects of life — intelligent life. That's why the androids need to get it taped. So they can appreciate the problems of life.'

'Do they need to?'

Prof. Hyggens knocked out his pipe on the worn sole of one of his shoes. '*They* think so ... At which point, you ask yourself why.'

'I take it you've already done that. Is there an answer?'

'Maybe,' said Prof., 'and maybe not. But there's certainly another question that goes with it. Ever tried to define life, John?'

Markham gazed at the sunlit sweep of the Heath and at Marion-A, who was now near the helicar. 'I don't know,' he said. 'I might have — a long time ago.'

'Well, try again — now.'

Markham thought for a while, then said slowly, 'All living things consume food and reproduce. That's the best I can do, I'm afraid.'

'And it's no good,' said Prof. delightedly. 'It tells us what life does, but not what it is. You'll agree that food is only a convenient form of energy?'

'Yes.'

'Then the androids consume food, John. They use energy. They also reproduce — and far more efficiently than humans. They have a production line and we only have the obsolete system of mating. Also, John, they have their own streamlined evolution. They don't mutate by accident. They improve according to plan.'

'What are you trying to prove?'

'Nothing, boy. I'm just thinking an old man's crazy thoughts aloud. Can't you add something else to that definition of life, or maybe some other description of what life does?'

Suddenly Markham was triumphant. 'I think I've got you, Prof.! All complex living things have to adapt to their environment and attempt to dominate it. That's part of their nature — the dynamic element in life. If a species can't do that it dies out. Come to think of it, in a highly organised self-conscious creature, that would explain the individual and collective pursuit of power. How's that?'

'Pretty good,' conceded Prof. Hyggens gravely. 'I especially like that bit about the pursuit of power. . . . Do you know how the androids started, John? First, there were electronic computers, then two-ton robots programed for simple repeat jobs. Then man-sized robots that could do quite a lot of things — if you told 'em when and how. Then androids — and they didn't need telling when and how. They just did what we wanted 'em to do, because they were programed that way. But, John, I didn't want to have an android replace me as a lecturer. And I knew a surgeon who didn't want to hand over his scalpel, and an engineer who was overfond of his micrometer. The surgeon is dead now — suicide. The engineer settled for Analysis ... The pursuit of power, you say? Seems to me the description you've given could fit androids even better than men.'

'What are you driving at?'

'Who — me? Nothing! Just think over what we've been talking about, John. It may give you some more interesting

53

thoughts ... Guess I've been in one place long enough. Better start moving. We Runners can't be too careful — if we want to stay running ... Tell your android I was trying to get you to join a colony of sun-worshipers in Cornwall. She might even accept it. Especially if you let her know how disgusted you are.' With many grunts Prof. Hyggens levered himself up.

'Where are you going?'

'Elsewhere,' said Prof. blandly. 'If you don't know, you can't say.'

'Suppose I want to contact you sometime?'

'That's all right, John. I'll do the contacting — if I think you're worth it. The androids don't have a monopoly of organisation yet. We poor misguided Runners still have a few tricks left. Incidentally, you were in the North London San, weren't you?'

'Yes.'

'Don't suppose you met a girl there — name of Rowena Hyggens? Small, brunette, nice-looking, twenty-one and practically a virgin — chiefly because of an ingrown sense of outmoded morality. My daughter, though you wouldn't think it to look at her. This is her first official neurosis, so maybe she won't get a long spell of S.A. — I hope. Probably in the box by now.'

'No, I didn't meet her — at least I don't think I did. I didn't see many people. Chiefly androids.' Then suddenly Markham remembered the girl he had discovered weeping in a corridor. The girl who had shied away from his offer to help as if she thought he was about to attack her.

'No,' said Prof. thoughtfully. 'They wouldn't let you see many people in the San. Too dangerous. Divide and conquer has been sound strategy since the stone club was a secret weapon. Well, John, I'll look you up sometime — maybe. Keep your eyes wide open and your twentieth-century thoughts to yourself. Be orthodox, boy — for a while. Until you know who's doing what and with which and to whom.'

As he turned to go Prof. Hyggens called over his shoulder, 'Don't ever tell your little android any more than she needs to know. And don't tell her that much if you can help it.'

Markham watched the old man stump slowly across the Heath. Presently his plump figure disappeared in a group of trees, and Markham was left with the peculiar feeling that Prof. Hyggens had been a three-dimensional hallucination. He thought about their curious conversation for a time and tried to make a cohesive pattern of sense out of what the old man had said.

Then he realised that Marion-A was waiting for him by the helicar. He got up and began to walk back. The feeling of tiredness had left him now. It was replaced by a vague sense of purpose, an undirected urgency. As if unconsciously he knew why Fate had preserved him for the twenty-second century. He was strangely glad.

'If you are ready,' said Marion-A, 'we will go into the City.'

'Yes, I'm ready.'

As the helicar began to rise he suddenly remembered why he had touched down on the Heath in the first place. And as his thoughts returned to Katy he realised that the house they had once lived in — the house that had once been a home for Johnny-Boy and Sara, a private citadel of happiness — would be less than a couple of miles away. He wondered whether anyone would be living there now — if it was still standing.

'Swing round a little,' he said to Marion-A, 'and follow the roadway. I want to see — ' He stopped.

There was no need to look for the house. It didn't exist. Nor did a great many other twentieth-century houses in Hampstead. From an altitude of a thousand feet he could see a wide, circular lake, the rim of which was smooth and shiny like glass. Except that it wasn't glass but fused rock and brick and clay. And dreams ... so many dreams ... all locked forever in a great crystal bowl.

There were a few children playing by the lake. They had a yacht and rowboats, and a machine that looked like a hybrid of bicycle and catamaran. Children! It didn't seem long since he had played with his own children, for the reality of one and a half centuries was not so great as the interrupted reality of seven or eight days. And the loss was keener, because Katy and the children were somehow still alive — but in another dimension.

A dimension that was inviolable, that had nothing to do with depopulated cities or atomic lakes.

CHAPTER FIVE

THE process of entering his name in the Male Index had not been as bureaucratic as he had expected. Marion-A had taken the helicar direct to Whitehall and had led him to a single-story building of plastiglass and steel on the site of the old War Office. There he had given his name, age and fingerprints to an android civil servant, had been handed over to a doctor for a complete electro-diagnosis, and had finally received a checkbook with *Republic of London: Personal Credit* printed on it. For a check to become valid, he had only to mark the amount with a stylo and impress his thumb on a part of the check specially coated with soft plastic.

When he left the Male Index Bureau Marion-A explained that unless he wished to rent the helicar — or buy it — it would have to be taken to a Republic Service Store, where a receipt would be given for it.

'How much does it cost to rent?' he asked.

'One pound per day, sir.' He noticed that she invariably used 'Sir' when other androids or human beings were within hearing.'

'And how much to buy?'

'Twelve hundred and fifty pounds.'

Markham felt the checkbook in his pocket. It was pleasant to know that he was now worth five thousand pounds, without having done anything to earn it. Pleasant and disturbing . . . But as yet he had no idea of current money values and no means of knowing how far his five thousand would go.

He looked at the helicar indecisively. It was a compact and useful vehicle, as maneuverable in the surprisingly quiet streets of London as it had been in the air. If he was to get around and see all there was to see of this new world into which he had been projected he would probably need some kind of personal transport.

'I think I'll rent it for a week,' he said. 'By that time I should know whether I'll need it permanently — and if I can afford it. . . . What's the procedure?'

'When we pass the next Service Store, I will present a check for seven pounds, sir. That is all that is required.'

'Good. Now how about lunch? I'm hungry.'

She took him along the Strand to a restaurant called Nino's. It was, he discovered with a shock, exactly like a small twentieth-century place — with exposed food, woven tablecloths, wooden chairs, antique neon lighting and waitresses who wore ordinary uniform dresses and contrived to have the faintly martyred expression he so well remembered.

For a moment, it stopped him dead in his tracks. He gazed round open-mouthed, almost ready to believe that he had emerged from some fantastic illusion and was secure once more in his own world. Then he saw that the waitresses were androids, and realised that Marion-A had brought him to a period restaurant.

She smiled. 'I thought you would like it, sir. Shall I wait in the helicar?'

Markham looked blank for a second; then he remembered. 'Does it inconvenience you much to eat with me, Marion? I mean the disposal afterward.'

'No, sir. It is a very simple operation.'

'Then I'd be glad if you'd join me,' he said diffidently. 'I don't feel altogether self-confident yet . . . Odd, isn't it?'

'It is quite understandable, sir. You will orient quickly.'

Markham selected a table by the window, looked at the menu and ordered the kind of lunch he might have ordered a hundred and fifty years ago.

Though the restaurant was in the West End, barely a dozen people were taking lunch. Glancing curiously about him he saw that he was not the only one dining with an android. Two tables away an unusually attractive woman of about thirty-five allowed her personal android to toy with a cup of coffee while she disposed of a full meal; and in the far corner of the room a man and a woman who were obviously on intimate terms had both brought their P.A.'s to the restaurant. To Markham it was grotesque.

As he looked around he tried to discover what kind of people they were in this new age — people whose ethics were as alien to him as those of a Brazilian head-hunter; people who lived parasitically, who seemed to have shed the responsibility of deciding their own fate. But apart from their strangeness of dress and their generally better physique they still looked remarkably normal and — there was no other word for it — relaxed. His feeling of bewilderment grew. He realised that he had been expecting obvious signs of decadence. But he hadn't found any . . . Yet!

For a time he and Marion-A ate in silence. Then, when they had reached the coffee stage, he said casually, 'That old man I met on Hampstead Heath was a peculiar character.'

'He did not seem conventionally adjusted,' remarked Marion-A.

'I got the impression he was interested in some weird religious cult,' continued Markham. 'Are there many people like that?' Privately he wondered if Prof. Hyggens had not been overdramatising when he had warned Markham against saying anything to Marion-A. He was greatly tempted to announce that Prof. was a Runner and see what her reaction would be. But he didn't. Prof. Hyggens might have been exaggerating the situation — or he might not. The intelligent course was to wait and find out.

Assuming, though, that most of what Prof. had said was true, Markham would have expected some display of interest on the part of Marion-A. But she had not mentioned the incident until he himself deliberately brought it up.

'There are many different religious fraternities,' explained Marion-A. 'Usually their aims are more social than religious. In the City various forms of Indian Mysticism are fashionable, but the Triple-S is still the most popular.'

'What is the Triple-S?'

'The Society of Sexual Symbolists.'

'It sounds quite absorbing,' he observed drily.

'I understand it is,' said Marion-A. 'For human beings, of course.' She gave a stiff smile.

'The man in Hampstead,' pursued Markham, 'seemed to prefer some kind of sun-worship.'

'Actually, sir,' said Marion-A quietly, 'I deduced that he was a Runner.'

'What's that?' Markham was too shaken to make his ignorance sound convincing.

'A maladjusted person who is opposed to the existing culture pattern, and who is therefore unhappy and sufficiently unco-operative to refuse assistance, including psychiatric treatment. His name is then removed from the Index, and he forfeits all social privileges until he agrees to accept help.'

'Can he be compelled?'

'No, sir. Not unless he commits a crime.'

'But if his name is taken from the Index, presumably he loses his money and everything else. He would have to steal to keep alive.'

'Yes, sir. And he may then be legally compelled to undergo treatment when he is caught or when he surrenders.'

'A nice watertight system,' commented Markham. 'Do many Runners get caught?'

'The majority surrender eventually,' she answered. 'To be deprived of social privileges is very demoralising. Also treatment is usually less rigorous, since if a man surrenders freely he tends to be psychologically co-operative.'

Markham was silent for a while. Then he said, 'Whose responsibility is it to decide which names should come off the Index, and how to deal with Runners?'

'It is one of the functions of Psychoprop, sir: the Department of Psychological Propaganda.'

He laughed grimly. 'That's one government department that would have to be staffed by human beings, anyway.'

'No, sir,' returned Marion-A. 'Psychoprop is organised and operated entirely by androids.'

'Jesus Christ!' Markham was appalled. 'Doesn't anyone control them — any human being?'

'They are directly answerable to the President of London.'

'I see . . . Do many women become Runners?'

'No, sir. The rate of psychoneurosis in women is much lower than in men.'

He sipped his coffee slowly, thinking over what Marion-A had told him. It was several minutes before he spoke again:

'Just supposing I knew the man I met on Hampstead Heath was a Runner, what should I have done?'

'If you had told me, sir, I would have contacted the nearest psychiatric team. Then he would have been traced and invited to surrender.'

'Suppose he didn't want to surrender?'

'Then he would have been taken, sir.'

'By force?'

'Methods are employed which do not harm the human being concerned.'

Markham took out a cigarette. 'If you thought he was a Runner, why didn't you say so? And why didn't you call the psychiatric group, or whatever it is?'

'The evidence was not conclusive,' said Marion-A. 'Also a P.A. should not take independent decisions on such a level except when there is immediate danger.'

'Fortunately,' said Markham, inhaling deeply, 'your deduction was wrong, wasn't it? He was just a harmless crank — even suggested that I go down to Cornwall and join his sunworshipers.'

'Yes,' said Marion-A. She lifted her coffee cup to her lips at regular intervals.

Out of sheer curiosity Markham began to time them. He found each interval was exactly fifteen seconds.

'Why don't you try a twenty-second interval?' he said lightly.

Marion-A rewarded him with a stiff smile. He had the uncanny feeling that she wanted to blush.

Finishing his cigarette, Markham remembered that the problem of accommodation held top priority. He could, of course, spend a few days in a hotel, but the prospect did not appeal to him. He wanted a place of his own — a fixed point that would become a kind of psychological map reference. He had begun to feel like a wild animal in a strange forest and, like an animal, he needed the security of a private lair.

House-hunting, as Marion-A explained, was a far simpler task than in his own time. He had only to go to the nearest Accommodation Service Center — there was one on the site of the old Charing Cross Station — and he would be presented with a list of all vacant properties in the City.

Using the helicar it took barely a minute to get from the restaurant to the A.S.C. There, the android in charge gave him the latest list, which seemed to offer every kind of accommodation from mansions in Westminster to basement rooms in Chelsea. Clearly there was no housing shortage in London.

Markham looked through the list and put a tick by the side of every address that could be considered a possible. He ended up with more than thirty ticks, and had to develop a stricter system of elimination before he could get it down to a manageable number. Finally he reduced the possibles to half a dozen and decided to visit them by helicar.

Some rooms in Knightsbridge were fourth on his list, and when he saw them he knew he would not need to look any further. They were on the third floor of one of the few Victorian houses still standing. He chose them in preference to the other flats he had seen because he had a weakness for massive architecture, because he liked the feeling of being well up from ground level, and because there was an excellent view of the Serpentine and Hyde Park.

The unit was self-contained with two bedrooms, a lounge, a study, kitchen and bathroom. Except for the kitchen and bathroom, the furnishings were chiefly period pieces, an incongruously pleasant jumble of late Victorian and early Edwardian stuff, with a few contemporary refinements thrown in, such as tri-di screen, newsprinter and visiphone.

The android at the A.S.C. told him that the rent was sixty-five pounds a month. With a feeling of recklessness he marked a check to cover the first six months, impressed his thumb-print on the plastic panel and handed it over.

He was a little surprised. In less than a couple of hours he had found himself a home — at least he had found a set of rooms that looked as if they might grow into a home. Suddenly he found himself wondering what Katy would have thought of such a place.

In the past, especially before they were married, Hyde Park had been one of their favorite weekend haunts. They must have strolled past that very house in Knightsbridge several times — had even looked at it, probably, and wondered what it would be like to live in such a fashionable area.

Well, he thought bitterly, now he would know. But Katy wouldn't. With every hour that passed Katy was receding further and further. Like a distant figure in a landscape, moving in the half-light between sunset and darkness. Presently, he told himself dully, the darkness would be complete. Katy's reality would be only a memory, an illusion.

But deep inside he knew this was not so, and knew that somehow Katy would live, even if his mind played tricks with truth and made her in retrospect more perfect than any woman has ever been.

With half a dozen keys in his pocket, he let Marion-A drive him back to Suite Three, Rutland House, Knightsbridge. Home — almost.

It was only then that he realised with how few personal

possessions he was moving in — a few clothes that had been given him at the North London Sanatorium, and nothing else. He looked at Marion-A blankly.

'We haven't even got any groceries.'

'No, John.'

'And I want another couple of shirts, a pair of shoes, something to read. And writing paper — things like that.' Now why in hell, he asked himself silently, should he think of writing paper? What was he going to write about, and to whom? Then, as he gazed at Marion-A, another thought struck him: 'What about your clothes?' he asked. 'Have you got any?'

She still had on the plain red jersey and black divided skirt which she was wearing when he had first seen her. The question of her clothes had never cropped up, and she had never said anything.

'These were issued to me,' she answered, 'when I was assigned to you. They are very durable. If you wish, I will use them until they are worn out.'

He was angry with himself for feeling embarrassed. 'What do you do when they are soiled?'

'I clean them while you are asleep. It is the best time.'

'Good God! Wouldn't you like a variety of clothes?'

'If it would please you. I have no personal preference.'

'But *I* have,' said Markham emphatically. 'we'll get you some dresses like — like — Hell, no! We'll get you whatever is appropriate to this day and age.'

'Yes, John.'

They went on a shopping expedition, and Markham spent a couple of hundred pounds at various Republic stores. Marion-A was efficiently dealt with by an android costumier, while Markham selected shirts that were more acceptable to his taste, and had himself measured for a tailored suit. From the highly colored profusion of synthetic materials that were offered, he chose one with a tweedy texture in a relatively subdued purple-gray.

When the clothes problem had been solved he strolled curiously round the other departments of the store to see what kind of merchandise was being offered to the public in the twenty-second century. Many of the articles he recognised instantly, but some were quite enigmatic until Marion-A explained their uses.

There were electrostatic and ultrasonic 'washing' machines; nine-millimeter hypno-projectors complete with high action and sultry love films, in which the spectator was induced to participate by visual hypnotic techniques; spectrum-players that translated music into colored patterns; dream-peddlers that carried the hypno-projection technique one stage further; book tapes and micro-recorders; power-skates, contour beds, single-seater monowheels and a host of smaller gadgets designed for the comfort or amusement of the Republic's citizens.

Markham was tempted into buying himself a combination wristwatch and newsflasher, a perpetua stylo, and a set of antique chessmen in ivory, complete with inlaid board. In the jewelry department he saw a finely worked platinum bracelet and bought it for Marion-A before he quite realized what he was doing. He did not care to examine the obscure motivation behind the impulse, and rationalised by observing drily that it would make her look more human. What surprised him most of all was that the bracelet cost only twenty-five pounds.

Marion-A was not impressed by the gift, nor was she unimpressed. She thanked him with the calm indifference of one who is unmoved by personal possessions — or compliments. And though he could have predicted what her reaction would be, he found it oddly infuriating. By way of self-assertion he packed her off to get the groceries alone; then let her stay in the helicar while he went to take a light tea in the almost empty store restaurant.

By then he was getting used to the fact that in comparison with its former hectic glory London was practically a ghost town. The population, as he had discovered, was barely thirty thousand. And even though the Nine Days Tranquiliser had destroyed much that had never been rebuilt, the people of London still seemed to be spread out like small flies on an extremely large cake.

But the android population was another matter altogether. Thinking over the experiences of this, his first day, Markham calculated that he must have seen at least four androids for every human being.

Even in the West End the busiest streets were almost as deserted as they were on any midnight in the twentieth century. And most of the occasional passers-by were personal and executive androids going about their domestic or professional tasks. The unescorted human being was a rarity, and it seemed that one fixed convention of the twenty-second century was that wherever a human being went his personal android was sure to follow.

Another thing that struck Markham forcibly was that apart from those at the atomic lake in Hampstead he had seen hardly any children ...

Unlike Nino's, the period restaurant where he had taken lunch, the restaurant at the Republic Store embodied all that was fashionable in contemporary design. Each of the dozen circular tables was legless and suspended from a flared steel tube attached to the iridescent ceiling. The menu was flashed pictorially on a small screen, with each item clearly designated; and Markham discovered that orders were taken by table microphone direct to the kitchen.

He was just deciding whether to sample a pot of Scottish or London tea when he became aware of being watched. He glanced into the wall mirror opposite and saw that a strikingly beautiful woman with long golden hair was standing two or three yards away behind his contour chair. She wore a tunic, vaguely Chinese in style, of dark blue silk and a pair of slacks with a brilliant metallic sheen. On her head was a small jeweled coronet.

She met his gaze, smiled and came toward him. Markham stood up and turned to face her.

'Lo, Mr. Markham. Do sit. I'll join you if I may.' Her voice had a musical quality. 'You don't know me yet,' she continued, 'but we already have a rendezvous. I'm Vivain Bertrand. I told my P.A. to send you a card for Clement's reception at the Palace.'

He began to feel a little hot under the collar and cursed himself for sending Marion-A out to the helicar. She might have helped him to handle the situation.

'How d'you do,' he said formally, wondering whether it would be correct to shake hands. 'You are the — er — President's wife?'

She took the chair next to him. 'Just for the tape, I hope I don't look like anyone's wife ... I'm his daughter, Mr. Markham ... Now what shall we have? Are you hungry?'

'Not really, Miss Bertrand. I —'

'My name is Vivain, and I shall call you John ... That

ridiculous android bloodied up your interview wonderfully. He needs reprograming ... Well, if you're not hungry we'll have iced tea and black gateau.'

Almost before she had finished speaking an android appeared with a tray, served the tea and gateau in silence, and retired. Vivain Bertrand extended a shapely arm and pressed a stud near the center of the table. Immediately a transparent cylinder of plastiglass rose up from the floor round the table and chairs. The background noise of the restaurant was cut completely out, and Markham felt as if he and Vivain Bertrand had fallen suddenly into a goldfish bowl.

She laughed, touched another button, and the cylinder changed to an opaque milky blue. 'Now we are really private,' she said. 'It cuts out the mike, too. We call them oubliettes.'

'My first experience of one.'

She gave him a quizzical glance. 'Didn't men and women want to be alone together in the twentieth century?'

'Not in the middle of a restaurant — well, not like this.'

Vivain was amazed. 'They must have been very brittle, then.'

He didn't know quite what to make of her remark, and so remained silent.

'You must tell me all about the people of your age,' she continued. 'I'm burning to know what they were really like. Is it true what you said on the screen — about being faithful to your wife?'

Markham felt like a child confessing a pantry raid. 'Yes, it's true.'

'You incredible creature!'

' "Sexual barbarian" was the term used,' he said drily.

Somehow, Vivain forced him to meet her gaze. 'I'm sure you could be *quite* barbaric,' she murmured.

Apart from being physically the most disturbing woman he had ever met, she had another quality about her that fascinated him. Her every movement carried with it a suggestion of restrained power, of psychological force held like a compressed spring. He found himself wondering what she would be like if the spring was released, and decided that she would be dangerous — in every way. Dangerous in frustration or acquiescence. Dangerous equally in victory and defeat ... Essentially, he concluded, she was volcanic, and probably with the same blindly destructive energy. Her presence was so distracting that he found it an effort to concentrate on what she was saying.

But Vivain was used to creating an effect. She ignored his gaucheries and dominated the conversation.

'You look,' she said calmly, 'as lost as a polar bear in the tropics. Androids alive! How dull your own age must have been. I expect the contrast will drive you slightly psycho for a time — but in an amusing way. I'll appoint myself your guardian. You're going to be fun to watch.'

'I hope I don't disappoint you, he said evenly.

Vivain gave him a faint smile. 'I don't think you will. You probably have more inhibitions locked up in your odd personality than all the Runners of London put together.'

'Perhaps I like my inhibitions.'

'Perhaps I shall, too,' she retorted. 'I know — we'll have a private war. Each trying to adjust the other, and no holds barred. Your ideas against mine. We'll see whose are better — and stronger. It's going to be quite radioactive ... Do you accept the challenge, dear enemy?'

Markham was feeling distinctly uncomfortable. Matters were proceeding at a pace that left him dizzy.

'I'm too busy wondering how we come to be talking like this,' he admitted. 'Maybe I should preserve a proper respect for the President's daughter.'

She laughed. 'Only if I want you to — and I don't. You're too interesting to be kept at a distance, John. It isn't every day one meets a man who is a couple of centuries old.'

'Correction, please. I'm a mere stripling of a hundred and seventy-seven.'

'And very well preserved,' she said. 'What do you think of the City? Don't you think we have improved it? I hate to think what it was like when the millions lived here. A seething mass of bodies, I suppose. How repulsive!'

'I haven't had time to sort out my impressions,' answered Markham carefully. 'I had to get my name on the Index and find myself a home.'

'You operate quickly. Where are you living?'

'Rutland House, Knightsbridge.'

'I know it. A fusty old museum. Is that why you chose it?'

'Appropriately.' He smiled. 'I'm a museum piece now.'

Vivain finished her iced tea. 'But not for long,' she prophesied. 'I'll see to that ... As it happens, we're almost neighbors, John. I have a place in Park Lane. De Havilland Lodge.' She glanced at a tiny ring-watch. 'Hell's mutation! I must jet. I'm supposed to be at the Olympic Club ... I know — come and see me this evening. Twenty-two thirty — and no android. You can tell me all about your quaint family and the doom-laden twentieth.'

She pressed the stud, and the oubliette glided back into the floor.

'But I — ' Markham got no further.

'No buts, dear enemy. I'm the President's daughter,' she warned gaily. 'One slip, and it's back to S.A. for you.'

Really?'

'Idiot! I'll tumble some of the gothic seriousness out of you this evening. Bye, John. Look to your libido!'

She left quickly, before he could formulate a diplomatic refusal. She had induced in him a peculiar tension. He was wryly amused at the *femme fatale* language and approach which, it seemed, had not changed much since the days of Theda Bara, but was forced to admit that on Vivain Bertrand the flamboyant seemed admirably at home, even if it made him uncomfortable. He remained in the restaurant for a few minutes, considering the encounter and trying to analyse his reaction. But he met with little success, and gave it up.

Then he remembered that Marion-A was still waiting for him in the helicar. He went out to join her, feeling that he had somehow retaliated for her lack of enthusiasm over the platinum bracelet, even though he knew that she could feel neither enthusiastic nor humiliated.

They drove back to Knightsbridge in silence. Markham opened the door of his flat just as the visiphone buzzed.

'How do you work this thing?' he demanded irritably.

Marion-A pressed a thin bar at the side of the small screen, then retired out of visual range.

The screen flickered into life, and a girl's head and shoulders appeared. Her hair was dark. She had small, mobile features and looked about nineteen.

'Lo, darling,' she said casually. 'Welcome to the hovel. Just the kind of hole you used back in the Stone Age, isn't it? Now you must — repeat must — come down and have a drink with us immediately, this instant, et cetera. No excuses, darling. We're absolutely dying to see you. And don't bring your P.A. We've thrown ours out for an hour — I mean, you get tired of seeing them around, don't you? Oh, I forgot! I'm Shawna Vandellay — right below you, Suite Two.'

'Hello,' said Markham, feeling vaguely overpowered. 'My name is — '

'We know all about you, darling. You're the incredibly romantic Survivor. Actually, I would interpret you tragically. You'd make a superb godhead — the Orpheus type, I think. Especially since you had your own underworld. But then you're not musical, are you?'

'No, I don't have any special talents, divine or artistic.' He thought she was a little mad.

'Darling,' said the girl, 'we're electronically wasting oodles of psychosomatic effort. See you in twenty seconds.' She gave him a ravishing smile, and then the screen went blank.

Markham turned to Marion-A. 'Do people really talk like that?' he asked. 'Or was it something special?'

'Miss Vandellay was using the current idiom,' said Marion-A with the shadow of a smile. 'It was, perhaps, concentrated.'

'Hell, I suppose I'd better go.'

'Yes, sir. Is there anything you wish me to do while you are absent?'

Markham thought for a moment. 'Try on your new dresses,' he said drily.

CHAPTER SIX

SHAWNA VANDELLAY opened the door just as he reached it, and impetuously hauled him inside. She placed a tall glass in his hand and simultaneously introduced him to a tall, bronzed man who looked and moved as if he might be an athlete.

'This object is Paul Malloris,' said Shawna. 'My first sob-session. He prosodises quite wonderfully when he can't think of anything better to do.' She laughed. 'But usually the dear brute has much better things to do. I don't see any reason why love affairs shouldn't last for years, actually. But then you're bound to agree — because you're passionately primitive yourself, aren't you, dear Survivor?'

'First things first,' parried Markham. 'I'm out of my depth. What is a sobsession?'

'A contraction for sexual obsession,' explained Paul Malloris. 'I happened to be free when Shawna was getting tired of her virginity. We fixated. Quite ridiculous, really, but entertaining. I bet her a hundred it wouldn't last a month, but it's already lasted three. So there it is — she's my beauty.'

'He's my beast,' added Shawna proudly. 'A very nice beast, and very shaggy — psychosomatically speaking.'

'I see,' said Markham blindly. 'The more I know of this world, the more I realise how much I have to learn.' He took a long drink from the glass she had given him. It seemed to be a kind of tall cocktail, but not — he soon discovered — as harmless as it tasted.

'Sweet Survivor,' said Shawna, 'you're absolutely a find. Except for the object, I'd gladly fixate on you. Do you miss your wife terribly much? Androids alive — of course you do! You said so on the screen. Poor, poor Survivor. I think you probably need a lot of love.'

'Less of this Survivor touch,' protested Markham thickly, as he finished his drink. 'You make me feel like a patriarch. My name is John, and who the hell doesn't need a lot of love? Good God, I'm drunk!' He felt the room begin to spin, and made hopefully for the nearest chair. He didn't reach it.

He dropped on all fours and crowed. 'Slap me in the oven, I'm a frozen chicken,' he announced with great conviction. 'Anybody care for an ice-cold egg? The egg of love, my friends? It's yours for the cracking. The egg of hope? By heaven, it's addled. The egg of truth? Believe it or not, the darn thing's fertile. It's more than an egg, it's a chicken. And the chicken, goddamit, is me!'

Paul and Shawna were watching him, smiling. He tried to focus on them, and discovered that they had multiplied.

'You bitchy beauties!' he roared. 'You blasted beasts! Crawl back into your fairytale and give me some peace. Stab me, I'm pickled! What the blazes did you put in my drink, sexy spooks? Go away and fornicate. I'm dying of grief. The egg of grief, dear people, is best taken hard-boiled — with plenty of salt and a dash of amnesia . . . Katy, darling, it's a world full of bastards and whores . . . I love you.'

He began to laugh. He fell on his face and laughed even louder.

Paul Malloris picked him up with surprisingly little effort and laid him on the settee. His eyes closed and he began to breathe deeply.

Paul looked at Shawna. 'For a moment, I thought we'd overdosed him,' he said coolly. 'But it's only sub-threshold shock. A normal S.A. reaction — even if he hadn't been on ice for one and a half centuries. He needs careful handling, poor devil. One false move and he'll withdraw . . . Hard to imagine the degree of trauma he's suffered.' Suddenly he grinned. 'Almost as bad as us being reborn into a world without androids.'

Shawna sighed. 'Wouldn't it be lovely? Paul, he tore straight through to the egg symbol. Do you think it has any significance?'

'Not yet. We'll have to correlate with his reaction during the next few days. He has to sit in judgment on the world. I think we'll know when he's reached a verdict.'

Shawna looked unhappy. 'I feel a perfect snake. We should have given him a little more time before we got to work on him. He's only just out of the San.'

Paul took a small bottle and a hypodermic syringe from a chest of drawers. 'I know. I don't like myself very much, either. But if we don't get to work on him as fast as we can, *they* will take over. Even Psychoprop is going to discover that he has the potential of a trigger-symbol. A normal twentieth-century man — just the archetype we need. And by the grace of God, we didn't even have to chase him. *He* came to us!'

She watched him fill the hypo and jab it into Markham's arm. 'You're sure that Oblivaine will do it?'

'If it doesn't, then it's Breakdown for us, my pet.' He gave a reassuring smile. 'Don't panic, Shawna. One c.c. should give us a minimum of twenty minutes' retroactive localised amnesia. He won't remember a thing.' The hypo was withdrawn and returned to its drawer. After a minute or so Markham opened his eyes, blinked twice and sat up.

'You fainted,' said Paul. 'Over-tense. The aftereffects of S.A.'

'Stupid of me,' Markham apologised. 'I feel fine now. As a matter of fact, I thought it was the drink.'

'That, too,' said Shawna gravely.

He attempted to stand up. 'Don't,' advised Paul. 'Put your feet up and relax. I have something to say to you.'

Markham was puzzled. 'You're talking differently. It sounds more normal — to me, anyway.'

'Good,' said Paul. 'We don't need to keep up the act now — for a while.'

'What do you mean?'

'There's a puncture mark on your left forearm. I gave you a shot of an alkaloid called Oblivaine. In about twenty minutes you'll pass out gently, and when you awake you won't remember a word of this conversation.'

Markham stared at him for a few seconds. 'Thanks very much,' he said grimly. 'Maybe I'll get used to the new fashion in hospitality, but just now I find it annoying. If you don't mind, I'll get the hell out of here.'

'You'll stay where you are and hear me out,' said Paul Malloris. 'I'm not playing any more tricks than are necessary ... Now don't get aggressive. You're just out of the San, and I'm in far better condition ... All I want you to do is listen to what I have to say.'

'I'm listening. You might even say I'm intensely interested.'

Shawna gave him an appealing look. 'We don't mean to harm you, John. Paul will — '

'Leave this to me, Shawna.' Paul Malloris drew up a chair and sat facing Markham. 'You haven't had enough time yet to orient yourself in our world. But you already know that by your standards it is utopian in that the androids do all the work and we have all the fun.'

Markham nodded. 'So much is apparent.'

'There are some of us,' continued Paul, 'who still value freedom of thought more than leisure. We're not content with letting the androids run everything. We'd like to have a little responsibility ourselves.'

'A commendable ambition,' Markham said with heavy sarcasm. 'Why don't you do something about it, then?'

'We are doing — but we have to be careful. Later on you'll

find out how easy it is to be classified neurotic. And John, any behavior that doesn't support the present social stasis is neurotic. The first stage is for one of your so-called friends to mention that you seem unhappy. Soon it gets to a Psychoprop agent. Then you get a psychiatric test. That doesn't mean a thing. What does matter is whether Psychoprop can find out if your behavior deviates from the norm in any significant way. If it does you are recommended for S.A. or Analysis, depending on how dangerous they think you are. Another word for Analysis is Breakdown. They break down your personality and rebuild it on more acceptable lines.'

'Why do people tolerate this kind of situation, then?'

'They accept it because that seems the only thing to do. Otherwise — Analysis!'

'What about a resistance movement?'

'I'm coming to that,' said Paul. 'Anyone can refuse Analysis. But then they're taken off the Index, and their personal androids — if they haven't already smashed them — are re-programed to trace their owners and call a psychiatric team. If someone tries to help he, too, is liable for investigation and — ultimately — Analysis.'

Markham gave a thin smile. 'I've already heard about the Runners; in fact I've met one.'

Paul Malloris tensed. 'Who?'

'Maybe I'll tell you sometime, but not now ... Incidentally, how many are there?'

'No one knows except Psychoprop. At any given time there are probably more than five hundred but less than a thousand.'

'I believe they have some kind of organisation,' said Markham tentatively.

'That is so. About seventy per cent are dedicated to the ideal of a free and responsible society.'

'But they can't do much against a hundred thousand androids and thirty thousand passively co-operative human beings, can they?'

Paul Malloris smiled. 'I see you have already considered the problem. But Horatius held the bridge, Leonidas held the pass — and David slew Goliath.'

'The analogues are hardly appropriate.'

'Yes they are — psychologically. I'm a psycho-historian,

by the way, when I'm not in my public role of the apocalyptic poet.'

'So the androids haven't managed to stop you from thinking altogether?'

Meanwhile Shawna had poured out three more drinks. She offered one to Markham. 'It's quite safe this time,' she said apologetically.

He took a glass. 'Thank you. The odd thing is, I don't give a damn.'

'No, the androids haven't stopped me from thinking,' said Paul. 'My mother died when I was born, and my father when I was barely three. I've been brought up by androids — nursed, fed, clothed, educated by androids. They looked after me very well. I should have developed into the perfect citizen. But I didn't.'

'Why?'

'Androids can look after a child but they can't love it. So first there was resentment, and that sharpened my critical faculty. I began to question the world instead of accepting it.'

Markham looked at Shawna. 'What about you?'

She smiled and laid a hand on Paul's shoulder. 'He corrupted me. I was vaguely unhappy about things, and I didn't dare admit it. I thought it was just something wrong with me. Paul convinced me that it wasn't.'

Markham suddenly laughed. 'Five hundred Runners and a couple of idealists versus the rest.'

'There are others like us,' said Paul. 'Many of them — maybe a thousand. They're waiting for a lead — or a leader.'

'In theory, my money is on the androids and the system.'

'But in practice?'

'In practice,' said Markham carefully, 'I think you might find your leader.'

Paul met his gaze. 'I think we've found him.'

'Who?'

'You.'

There was taut silence. Shawna concentrated on her drink, not trusting herself to look at Markham.

'I think you're crazy,' he said at length. 'If I'm the best person you can think of — assuming I'm willing, which I'm

73

not — then heaven help humanity. I haven't even got my bearings yet. I don't think the same way as you. I belong to another age. I — '

'That's exactly why you could do it,' cut in Paul. 'You belong to an age when men relied on themselves.'

'And a fine mess they made,' commented Markham bitterly.

'That's not the point. Your value is as a symbol, an archetype. You are the Survivor, a man who believes in so-called primitive family life, in creative work and in human responsibility.'

'Rubbish!' said Markham with violence. 'I believe in being happy. Those were just the kind of things that made me happy. If I can be happy under the conditions that exist now, then I'm going to be. I didn't get myself trapped in that refrigeration chamber just to organise your miserable revolution.'

'But suppose you can't be happy?'

'Then I'll think again.'

Paul Malloris seemed to relax. 'That's all we need to know. Take your time. Sample all that the Republic has to offer, John. Eventually you'll find it's no good. Then we'll be able to use you. Meanwhile you can't do any harm because the Oblivaine will wipe out this conversation completely. We used it only for a safe test of your reactions. Personally, I think — ' He stopped. Markham had put a hand to his head and seemed to be trying to steady it. He gazed at Paul Malloris intently. 'The room is going dark.'

'Don't worry. The Oblivaine is taking effect a little early. You'll only be out for about fifteen seconds.'

Markham gave a weak smile. 'Pleasant interlude,' he mumbled; then his head fell back loosely, and his limbs relaxed.

He came round to find Shawna Vandellay holding a cup of dark liquid to his lips. Black coffee. He swallowed some, spluttered and sat up.

'Darling,' said Shawna brightly, 'we're pigs — but pigs. You must be fascinatingly tired. You just closed your eyes and went to sleep on us. Or perhaps you just found us terribly, terribly boring.'

'Hell,' said Markham, 'I really am sorry. Never done anything like that before. Maybe it was — I've had a weird dream about — eggs . . . I think.'

'Interesting,' said Paul. 'Freud was quite popular in your time, I believe. The poor man was quite fantastic as an analyst, but he was a gold mine of literary juxtapositions, a typical nineteenth-century neurotic with the wrong programing. Who knows — he might have developed into a fair lyric poet with the correct stimulus . . . One of these days, you must hear *Sonnet for a Schizo*. I also have a tape Giselle Mountfaulcon and the St. Paul's Singers doing it in Gregorian Chant.'

'If you don't mind,' Markham said unsteadily, 'I think I ought to go home. It's been a heavy day.'

'Darling John,' murmured Shawna, 'we're outrageously cruel if not actually stupid. Of course you're tired. It's your first day out of the San. Perhaps tomorrow . . . The evening, possibly?'

'Possibly,' answered Markham, as she took him to the door. He made a mental note to have another engagement.

'Bye, chappie,' said Paul Malloris. 'Take the load off your psyche.'

Markham gave a wan smile, and went up to his own suite — oppressed by the feeling that there was something he ought to remember. Something important at the back of his mind. Maybe he would remember it tomorrow.

Meanwhile he desperately wanted some rest. It was already after six o'clock, and and at ten-thirty (Twenty-two thirty! Let us synchronise our watches, gentlemen!) he was supposed to be seeing the enigmatic Vivain Bertrand.

Christ! What a day! he thought. What a bloody day! The twenty-second century seemed to be closing in with a vengeance.

Back in his own rooms he discovered that Marion-A had changed her jersey and divided skirt for a bottle-green ski-suit. Despite its severe lines it made her look oddly feminine.

'I'm going to bed,' he said tersely. 'If I am not conscious in three hours, wake me.'

'Yes, sir.'

'I told you to call me John.'

'I beg your pardon, John.'

He thought he detected a note of resentment in her voice. But that was damn silly. How could an android be resentful?

In the bedroom he tore his clothes off impatiently and dropped them in a careless heap. The bed was luxuriously warm. Marion-A had given him a thermo-blanket.

CHAPTER SEVEN

HE was in a celestial toy shop. The walls were of transparent crystal and the roof was of black velvet studded with hard pointed stars. In front of him was a large counter over which London sprawled — a cardboard city tricked out with fairy lights and tinsel and colored glass bubbles.

By the side of the counter stood a red-capped Father Christmas with a bulging sack. His face was slack and pouchy, and he spoke with the voice of Prof. Hyggens:

'Merry Breakdown, my boy, and a Happy Neurosis!'

'And the same to you,' said Markham pleasantly.

Father Christmas wiped a crocodile tear from his eye. 'Confidentially,' he said, 'my reindeer are all maladjusted.'

'Why?'

The red cape quivered with laughter. 'I'm afraid they're just natural-born Runners, son.'

Markham felt a surge of universal benevolence. 'Peace on earth,' he announced with conviction. 'Goodwill to all androids.'

Father Christmas opened his sack. 'Pick your present, my friend, sight unseen. Each priceless parcel for a purely nominal cost.'

'How much?'

'A mere trifle. Just thumb me a check for your soul.'

Markham took out a large checkbook which bore the legend: *Republic of London: Personal Credit*. He marked a check, pressed his thumb on the plastic panel and handed it to Father Christmas.

'Satisfaction guaranteed,' said the old man throatily, 'or your psyche refunded.'

Markham put his hand into the sack and brought out a

parcel. He slipped the ribbon off, tore away the gay wrapping and discovered a clockwork doll. He let out a roar of disgust.

'You don't like to play with dolls?' inquired Father Christmas anxiously.

'What do you think?'

'It walks and talks.'

'I don't care if it flies and cries.'

'Patience, my friend.' Father Christmas took the doll and turned the key that was fixed in its back. Then he set it carefully on its feet on the floor. 'If you don't like it, why you can pick another present. Honest Prof. St. Nicholas, that's me.'

The doll began to grow. Its oval face expanded; its eyes glowed; its golden hair cascaded upon its shoulders . . . Katy!

'Katy,' he murmured huskily. 'Katy, darling.'

'John,' she said, 'I love you.'

'Sweetheart, it's a miracle. Let's not ask how or why. Let's just take it.'

'John, I love you.'

He looked at the cardboard city, at the benevolent Father Christmas and the sack of presents. 'Let's go where we can be alone.'

'John,' she repeated in the same calm voice, 'I love you. I love you. I love you. I —'

'Stop it!' An anguished cry. But Katy didn't stop. She went on saying it with the same monotonous inflection, until the words lost their meaning. He put his arms round her. He held her. He tried to kiss her. But the lips kept moving and the words kept coming.

'Damn you, stop it!'

Father Christmas gave an apologetic cough. 'The basic programing was stripped down to essentials,' he explained. You can't pack much into a doll.'

'Blast you, she's not a doll. She's —'

'Not a doll,' repeated Katy. 'Not a doll. Not a doll. Not a doll.'

'Oh, God! Katy, darling, *what are you*?'

She gave him a bright, stiff smile. 'I am an android. I love you. I am an android. I love you.'

Markham recoiled in horror, buried his face in his hands. Go away — for pity's sake!'

Father Christmas shrugged. He touched the key in Katy's back. She broke off in mid-sentence. And began to shrink. Presently she was just a tiny motionless figure. Father Christmas picked up the ribbon, smoothed out the wrapping paper, parceled her up neatly and dropped her back into the sack.

'Some people are hard to please,' he said reproachfully. 'Try again, boy. A rose by any other name still keeps its thorns. A doll is therefore a doll. Look, here's another. Just the same, but different.'

He held out another parcel and, trance-like, Markham took it. The doll was Marion-A — with a key in her back. He watched, paralysed, as she grew.

'I was remodeled on the style of the photograph found in your pocket,' she said. 'It was decided that you would appreciate the resemblance.'

'Go away!'

'You need me, John.'

'Go away!'

'You can't live without me.'

'Go away, you damned android!'

There were tears in her eyes. 'I'm sorry, John, but I'm only human, after all.'

'*What?*' He stared at her incredulously.

'What, indeed?' echoed Father Christmas with a genial grin. 'What, my friend, is life? It is a tale written by an idiot and told by a genius — full of such sound and fury that it signifies practically anything.'

Markham looked at him closely. 'Hellfire, you aren't Father Christmas at all!'

'Hellfire, exactly. I'm Mephistopheles, the old toy-maker. It amuses me to dress up now and again.' He waved negligently at Marion-A. 'Shrivel up and die, my dear. The kind gentleman doesn't want you ... Come to that, he doesn't know what he wants.'

'By heaven, I do!' said Markham violently.

'By hell, you don't.' Prof. Hyggens had shed his red cape and now displayed a barbed tail and cloven hoofs. His features became imperceptibly satyric. He disposed of the tiny doll into which Marion-A had shrunk with a blast of infernal fire.

'I offer you life,' he remarked with bland benevolence, 'and you reject it.'

'Don't be a bloody charlatan! You offered me a pair of mechanical dolls.'

Mephistopheles laughed. 'So I did. I offered you life and love — and is there any better symbolism than a brace of clockwork dolls? Besides, what else *can* you want?'

'I want truth.'

'Don't be a tiresome joker, dear lad. There's no such animal.'

'You're a liar.'

'Aren't we all? I'm merely an intelligent one. However, I repeat, there's no such thing as truth.'

Markham gave a contemptuous laugh. 'Trust the Devil to be dogmatic,' he said. 'But I'd back my own intuition any day. And it tells me that somewhere there is truth eternal.'

Mephistopheles snorted derisively. 'The customer is always right — almost. But I'm afraid you'll have to settle for truth infernal.'

'Is it as solid as a city?' demanded Markham.

'Certainly!' Mephistopheles waved his hand and London collapsed into a pack of cards.

'Is it as clear as crystal?'

'Indisputably!' Mephistopheles exhaled and the fire from his nostrils blackened then shattered the crystal walls.

'Is it as enduring as the stars?'

'Absolutely!' Mephistopheles glanced at the roof of black velvet and the hard pointed stars changed into snowflakes drifting slowly down, melting as they fell.

'Whatever the truth is, I'll buy it,' shouted Markham wildly, 'and then I'll see you in hell.'

Mephistopheles smiled. 'Dear boy, you've already bought it. There is that small matter of a check for your soul, which entails a rendezvous in Hades at a date as yet unspecified . . . Incidentally, a bargain is a bargain, and you'll get your truth. But you'd have done better to play for time.'

'What do I want with time?'

'Time,' said Mephistopheles, dissolving in his own fiery breath, 'to understand.'

Then there was nothing — only darkness and silence. A silence that rolled like thunder and a darkness that shook and shivered, then finally exploded into light.

Markham opened his eyes and saw that Marion-A was bending over him.

'It is time to get up,' she said. 'You told me to rouse you in three hours.'

'Time to understand,' murmured Markham sleepily. For a moment there seemed to be an echo of distant laughter. Vaguely he remembered the dream, and knew it was only a dream, and shrugged. Then he yawned, stretched, forced himself to get out of bed. And the dream died.

While he collected himself, and dully contemplated his appointment with Vivain Bertrand, he sent Marion-A to make a pot of coffee.

Twenty minutes later, after a shave and a shower, he felt relaxed yet awake. And by the time he had dressed and disposed of Marion-A's coffee, he was even looking forward to his approaching visit.

Curiosity, he told himself, was the incentive. Disregarding Vivain Bertrand's obvious attractions, he felt that in some peculiar way she was the first person he had met who was fully alive. It was as if she existed in a dimension that was inaccessible to Shawna Vandellay or Paul Malloris or Prof. Hyggens. As if she alone belonged completely and naturally to the world in which she lived.

Presently he realised that it was time for him to set out. He glanced through the window, saw that the sky was clear, and decided to walk. It would take, he remembered, less than a quarter of an hour to get to Park Lane if he cut through the Park.

'Will you wish to return by helicar?' asked Marion-A.

He had told her earlier of his meeting with Vivain Bertrand, wondering if she would display any reaction. But, as usual, there was no comment.

'I don't think so, but if I change my mind I'll call you.'

'Yes, sir.'

'Androids evidently have short memories.'

'No — John.'

As he left the apartment he wondered if her use of 'sir' when they were alone was a sign of displeasure. He thought it might be. He hoped it was.

The air was clear, with all the exciting sharpness of autumn; and the September sky was loaded with stars. As he made his way through Hyde Park he felt curiously happy. It was the first time he had been out alone in the evening. It gave him an exhilarating sense of freedom, a strange illusion of security.

He gazed up at the stars, recognising the familiar patterns — the enduring beacons in whose existence one and a half centuries was not even a distinguishable moment. Then suddenly he remembered a fragment of his dream, remembered how the stars had changed into snowflakes and melted. The feeling of security and permanence ebbed away. He was alone in the darkness; and the loneliness sank into him like the paralysing coldness of K Chamber.

By the time he had found De Havilland Lodge, Park Lane, he felt like a fugitive, a man wanting to escape from his own company, his own thoughts, his own memories. He began to understand how the Runners must feel, rejected by society. Living without a map reference . . .

Vivain Bertrand opened the door herself. He had expected servants, androids, possibly other guests. But Vivain had evidently decided on an atmosphere of intimacy.

'Lo, my dear enemy, you're late.' She greeted him with a smile which yet conveyed a hint of impatience.

'I'm sorry, Miss Bertrand. Am I very late?'

'Seven minutes — but for once I was early. People usually wait for *me*. It's a novel experience. And I am *not* Miss Bertrand — not this evening. Not to you.'

She was wearing a single simple garment. Above the waist it was a sheathlike evening gown whose neckline plunged to a metallic rope-belt that was the only accessory. Below the waist it divided in a pair of trews, emphasising the long, graceful lines of her legs.

When she met him at the door the dress seemed black and the rope-belt silver. But as she entered the lounge the dress became a pale mauve and the rope-belt golden. And simultaneously her normally golden hair became dark.

She enjoyed his amazement. 'I'm introducing you to the new fashions,' she said. 'We don't care for static color very much nowadays. Too monotonous. We live in a world of life and movement, dear enemy — iridescent, like love and truth.'

She pirouetted with solemn grace; and the dress became white, and her long hair a deep and brilliant green. Markham watched as if hypnotised.

'How —' he began.

'How,' she mimicked, 'and why! That's all you care about. Don't you like beautiful things?'

'Yes, but —'

'Buts bore me, dear John. Away with all buts and hows and whys. Now flop on the divan and I'll mix you a special soul-shaker. Then if you are very good and amuse me I might even satisfy your curiosity.' Gaily she pushed him down on to a long, low settee. Then she went to a small trolley laden with glasses and decanters and made the drinks.

The room was furnished in a luxurious contemporary style, but Markham's attention was focused on Vivain. The whole atmosphere seemed saturated with her vitality, as if she radiated an invisible energy that charged everything she touched.

She handed him a glass, then sat decoratively on the deep-piled carpet in front of him, nursing her own 'soul-shaker', and watching him with bright, amused eyes.

'Take the lid off your id,' she said, raising her glass.

Markham remembered his lesson in the current idiom. 'Here we go, libido.' He sipped the soul-shaker cautiously. It was reminiscent of a high octane dry Martini.

Vivain laughed. 'So you have already learned the formula.'

'My android taught me.'

'How do you like having a P.A.?'

He grinned. 'I'm getting used to it. I have to keep telling myself that she's only a machine.'

'Perhaps,' said Vivain, 'that's all we are, too. Only we don't know it.'

'Do you believe that?'

She smiled. 'Dear John. You're so deadly serious ... Let's have another drink. My glass is empty.'

Markham stood up. 'Tell me how to make it. Then I can add one more formula to the list.'

He mixed the soul-shaker under her direction. It tasted almost as good as the first — except that it was a little stronger.

'I know,' said Vivain, 'we'll drink to the memory of your wife.'

'Will we?' He felt vaguely angry.

'Don't you want to?'

'No.'

'Then I shall ... Here's to — what was her name, John?'
In spite of himself, he was forced to answer. 'Katy.'

'To Katy, then. I'm sure she was very lovely, very sweet
and very tame ... Do you agree?'

'No.'

'You don't think she was lovely?'

'I don't think she was tame.'

Vivain swallowed her soul-shaker. 'Of course she was. She
let you tame her, didn't she?'

'I don't know what you're talking about.'

'You're a hippo, dear enemy. You know exactly what I'm
talking about.'

Markham finished his drink. 'And what might a hippo
be?'

'Hypocrite. I've been fed quite a lot of history-tapes, John.
Hypocrisy was the great art of the twentieth century. In
politics, in war and in love.'

'But you've changed all that, haven't you?' he remarked
bitterly. 'Now there are no politics, no war, and everyone
climbs into bed with everyone else.'

Vivain laughed. 'You look as wooden as an android, as
naïve as a virgin — and devastatingly solemn. Maybe I
ought to do something about it.' She touched a small stud
that Markham had only just noticed on her rope-belt. There
was a slight change in the quality of the room's indirect
lighting; but the most startling transformation was in Vivain
herself.

In a moment her hair became white and lustrous, while
her complexion darkened until she looked like a full-blooded
Negro; and the evening gown she wore was suddenly and
completely transparent. Gazing at her and, against his will,
admiring every supple curve of her jet-black body, Markham
felt as if his soul had been turned into a battleground by
unashamed desire and shamed disgust.

'What do you think of this, my noble Puritan?' Her voice
came low and vibrant.

Markham was deliberately silent for a while, hoping the
silence would embarrass her, hoping he would then regain
the initiative. But Vivain was quite relaxed, while every
moment only increased his own tension. He was afraid — of

being a fool, and of not being a fool. Afraid to speak, and afraid to remain silent; knowing that whatever happened he would only defeat himself.

He glanced quickly at her eyes, wondering if he would discover there any weakness, any betrayal of purpose; and somehow the glance became locked in a mutual timeless stare. A deep and obscure recognition.

At length he remembered her question, and said uncertainly, 'I don't know . . . What do you think of it?'

'I think it's amusing — sometimes.'

'And dangerous,' he suggested.

'No, not dangerous — just interesting. And occasionally exciting. This could be one of the occasions.'

'Suppose it isn't?'

'Then that might make it even more interesting . . . You're trying hard to stay cerebral aren't you, my silly darling? Perhaps I underestimated Katy'

'Or perhaps you overestimate me.'

'You really think so?' Vivain's smile seemed to deepen into a demoniac grin. She shook her long white hair loose from the metallic net in which it had been coiled and rolled her eyes with melodramatic suggestion — as if she were actually satirising the abandon she now displayed.

'Look to your defenses, dear enemy,' she murmured softly. 'I'm coming in to attack.'

Even as she spoke, the lighting in the room began to fade. Strange dancing patterns of color leaped up the walls. Vague spearheads of crimson appeared to chase and transfix quivering purple pear-shapes. Blue and silver spheres drifted across the ceiling and exploded into rainbows. Somewhere, in the far distance, there seemed to be the monotonous compulsion of drums.

Almost before she had finished speaking Vivain was leaning loosely against him. And as if manipulated by invisible wires, his arm slipped round her body, tightening.

'Sweet enemy,' she whispered. 'It's too easy, isn't it? No man is a traitor — except to himself.'

Her lips did not allow any reply; their pressure became fierce and tender. Inevitable.

She was no longer passive. She was a thing of fire. A black phantom of savagery, bewitching with her own hunger, relentless in submission. And wherever they touched, currents

of burning energy made the sensation intolerable and necessary — a mutual self-sacrifice.

Markham knew he was mad. A lonely spectator sat in the
deserted grandstand in his head, observing the play, count-
ing the score in a game whose result was fixed by the cor-
ruption of a million years.

He was mad because nothing was real now except an
illusion. An illusion that began with two strangers, that
would end only with the blankness of satiation — a fused
moment of combined identity, an apex of hate or love no
nearer than a dream within a dream.

He was mad because he was not making love. He was
only making war — against his will, but with his desire. A
war in which victory would merely point the reality of
defeat, in which defeat could have been a greater victory.

But Vivain rejected the easy triumph. It was the play that
mattered.

She retained full control until, as he held her with all the
intensity and bitterness of acknowledged slavery, she knew
he had ceased to exist as a man and was no more than a
pattern of manhood.

Then suddenly she began to fight with elemental passion,
as if she were a last minute rebel against the force that drove
her.

And the patterns of color danced faster upon the walls, the
ceiling became a torrent of mobile shapes, and the insidious
drumming — no longer in the distance — drowned all possibility of thought and reduced the sensual conflict to a love-
duel of marionettes.

There was no spectator now, no grandstand, no silent impartial witness to observe the finer points of the game. The
cerebral myth was vanquished. All that remained were two
sophisticated animals locked in subjective combat, lost in a
bewildering maze of touch and taste and scent.

Vivain was no longer black and demoniac. The lighting
changed her into a mauve vortex of passion; then again
changed her into the bronze-red of a North American
Indian, her long black hair uncoiling like a nest of snakes.

'Love can't be polite, dear enemy,' she panted, as her
fingers tore at his shoulder. 'It's hard and brutal — and un-
avoidable.' The smile that lingered on her half-open lips
seemed to be mocking him, mocking the final gesture.

'You damned witch!' he whispered, pinioning her arms. 'You lovely cheating harlot!'

Vivain laughed. 'Who wins?' she asked, her eyes looking calmly into his, even as the moment of darkness annihilated them both.

And suddenly, there was no color, no music; only silence and a bitter peace.

He did not know how long he had been asleep, but when he opened his eyes he saw that the room was normal again. Vivain, now wearing a demure blue sari and with her hair and complexion restored to their normal coloring, was pouring tea by a small table laden with savories and biscuits. She looked, thought Markham cynically, as sedate as a vestal virgin. Almost.

'Sleepyhead,' said Vivain calmly. 'I hope you have an appetite.' Then she added with a mischievous smile: 'You quite surprised me. I'd no idea twentieth-century man was so — so uninhibited. I shall have to revise my historical perspective.'

Markham sat up and grinned. 'So shall I.' He was a little shocked by his own lack of embarrassment. 'With respect, the fault was entirely yours.'

Vivain sat by his side. 'With respect,' she mimicked, 'it was exactly what I intended. How do you feel, John?'

'Relaxed.'

'Are you angry?'

'No. Should I be?' He sipped the hot tea, concentrating upon it.

'I thought you might be — afterward. It was pure seduction, of course.'

He gave her a sideways glance. 'Hardly pure . . . and don't patronise the twentieth century. All you have in your history-tapes is a skeleton.'

'But you are very definitely flesh and blood, dear enemy . . . And now I have *you*.'

Markham met her gaze. 'I don't think so.'

'Aren't you in love with me?'

'No, two can play at experiments. You wanted to see what I'd be like without the mask. Maybe I was curious about you, too.'

Vivain laughed. 'Wonderful!' she exclaimed. 'It was only

a slight skirmish, then. I was afraid you might capitulate too easily. So we're still real enemies?'

'If you want to call it that.'

'Passionate enemies,' she conceded, with a glitter in her eyes. 'And now we'll have an armistice, because I want — seriously — to find out what you are really like, John. I want to know how different you are.'

'Different from what — the normal, twenty-second-century model? I should have thought you'd have collected enough intimate evidence already.'

Oddly, it made her angry. 'I meant what I said about an armistice — and I'm not thinking only of sex behavior. I want to know how you used to live, what it was like to be a — a worker, and to have to earn money to keep your family alive. I want to know about the kind of life you and Katy had together, about your children, your home and your friends.'

'I'd rather keep it as a private world,' he said coldly. 'Not as a source of public amusement.'

She took his hand. 'Look at me, John. I'm not going to poke fun or ridicule — not now — and I'll never say anything to anyone else . . . Do you believe me?'

'I don't know . . . I think so.' Against all reason, he did believe her. For Vivain seemed as much herself when she stepped out of her sophisticated brittle role as when she was in it. And with a shock he realised that she, too, was incredibly lonely. He wondered why.

'Will it hurt too much,' she continued softly, 'if a stranger peeps into your private world?'

'I'll take the risk,' he answered.

And he began to tell her all about Katy and Johnny-Boy and Sara; the house in Hampstead; International Refrigeration; the installations at Epping. He told her about life in London in the nineteen-sixties. About his work and play, his hopes and dreams. And as he talked he knew that he wanted to tell her. Or knew that he wanted to tell himself again through her.

She listened well and he felt, strangely, that she understood. Presently he was barely conscious of her existence. He lost track of time. But at last, glancing absently at the window, he saw that a subtle wave of gray light was stealing across the sky.

Dawn! He couldn't believe it. But the fact was confirmed by Vivain's ring watch.

She stood up and stretched, and dismissed his apology with a curious smile. 'Promise me,' she said, 'that you'll do it again some time.'

'Do what?'

'Talk like this. Tell me about yourself and all your world. It was terribly real, John. I think — I think I can understand now how you feel about Katy and the children.' She laughed. 'Why, I can almost imagine what it was like to be without androids — quite nightmarish. And, in a way, lovely.'

He, too, stood up. 'I'm sorry I kept you awake so long.'

Vivain touched his cheek lightly with her lips. 'But I'm not sorry I put you to sleep . . . Now let's go and swim in the sea. We'll time it for sunrise. Then we'll have breakfast at a little coastal village. It will be perfect either way — as an end or a beginning.'

'You're crazy,' he said.

'Or happy — or both. My jet-car will put us down at Hastings in half an hour. Shall I take my P.A. or do you know how to build a campfire?'

He smiled. 'I know how to build a fire. I'm slightly Neanderthal.'

Ten minutes later Vivain Bertrand's jet-car lifted smoothly from Park Lane and headed south over the City through the gray silver of pre-dawn.

CHAPTER EIGHT

HE didn't get back to Knightsbridge until shortly before noon. After breakfast he and Vivain spent most of the sunny autumn morning strolling along the deserted seashore, throwing pebbles at the waves and listening to the desolate calls of a few restless seabirds.

They had not talked a great deal. It seemed to be a morning designed for silence — a calm, ordinary morning, thought Markham, that could have belonged to any day in any century. In the freshness of the sea wind, androids,

Runners, the Nine Days Tranquiliser and a hundred and fifty years of suspended animation were all meaningless shadows that belonged to a half-forgotten nightmare.

Even the events of the previous evening were unreal. It seemed inconceivable, that he had met Vivain less than twenty-four hours ago; that he had already made love to her in a kind of grotesque dream sequence; and that she was the daughter of the President of London. He remembered then that he would be meeting her father officially in a few days, and wondered how he would face the situation. He wondered also whether Clement Bertrand would know or care about the things his daughter did.

But the most disturbing question of all was how had he, John Markham, fallen so easily and so quickly into such a relationship with Vivain? He could rationalise by saying that he was overtired, lonely and in need of sexual release. But no such rationalisations fitted. What he had done was out of character. Basically, Markham knew, he was not promiscuous. In his own age he would not have allowed such a situation to develop; at least he thought he wouldn't. But then in his own age there was Katy, and a place in the world and a purpose in life.

Here he was merely a freak, a chance survivor adrift in a world he did not know or understand. Maybe that was enough to trip his normal reactions. Maybe, unconsciously, when he had responded to Vivain's overture, he was symbolically accepting the new world, trying to meet it on its own terms.

He wondered whether that was what he really wanted — to abolish his separateness and be a part of the world that now existed. But in the same moment he knew that that, too, was no explanation. It could be, perhaps, in time. But not now. For subjectively, the past was too recent. The hundred and fifty years were no more than a blank interval between sleeping and waking. Subjectively, it was only a few days since he had last held Katy in his arms.

Warm and wonderful Katy! Not self-willed or demanding. Neither violent in love, nor docile. Yet, in her almost childlike simplicity, generating deeper and richer sensations than Vivain ever could. He wondered if there were any Katys left in this hard new world. And even as he considered the problem he already knew the answer.

Then he was struck by the curious thought that Katy would have understood about Vivain. That if by some miracle he could return to the house in Hampstead and tell her the whole story in the shared intimacy of ordinary firelight, there would be no reproaches — only acceptance . . .

'You look frighteningly solemn, John. Is your puritanical soul filled with remorse, or are you brooding upon weighty problems?'

With a start, he was jerked out of his private world. He gazed in perplexity for a moment at the girl walking by his side. Not the sensual black woman or the bronzed Indian girl with snakelike hair, but a woman of classical beauty and almost rigid perfection of features. Last night Vivain had been the high priestess of sexual abandon. But now, in the morning sunlight, she was a friendly stranger once more. Still enigmatic, but with the enigma of personality rather than sex.

'I was thinking about Katy,' he admitted. 'Wondering what her attitude to you would have been.'

'Did you reach any conclusion?'

He gazed out to sea, watching the tiny whitecaps roll shoreward. 'I decided that she would probably have understood about you — and us — better than I do.'

Vivain smiled. 'Perhaps you are right. When I first saw you in the restaurant, John, I thought what an amusing novelty you'd be — nothing more.'

'Like a performing monkey?' he suggested drily.

She nodded. 'I thought you might have a few interesting tricks. But now I have the curious feeling that I'm the performing monkey and that you are watching the tricks . . . Does that make sense?'

Suddenly he felt relieved. 'More than you'll ever know. Tell me something — concerning last night. Have there been many men who —' He groped for the right words, but they were not needed.

'Enough,' she answered complacently. 'I'm not altogether ugly.'

'And did you —' Again he wanted the right words. But suddenly no words were right, and he floundered.

Aware of his train of thought, Vivain was totally unconcerned. 'I did,' she answered, 'and I do. Tomorrow, next week, or next month there will always be someone else. You can't understand that, can you? It shocks. But you are shocking, too, dear enemy. You and your primitive ideas of possession, and your claustrophobic notions of love. Your morality is the morality of an age of insecurity, when people were always afraid they were going to lose something.' She laughed. 'Didn't the ancient crusaders lock their wives up in chastity belts? I think you are temperamentally a crusader.'

He considered for a moment. 'Perhaps, in this age,' he said slowly, 'there's nothing to lose.'

Vivain glanced at her ring watch. Suddenly she seemed restless. 'There's always something to lose,' she retorted.

'What?'

'Time and happiness . . . Why don't we jet back to London before the episode lapses into boredom?' Without waiting for an answer she turned and began to walk along the shore at a quick, purposeful pace.

When he returned to the rooms in Knightsbridge he found Marion-A in low alert. She snapped out of it as soon as he spoke to her. And, irrationally, he felt guilty; felt the need to explain or justify himself. He was appalled to discover that his explanation had degenerated into a series of little unconvincing lies. He was even more appalled to realise that no explanation was necessary, that a machine was not interested in excuses, and that therefore he was merely lying to himself.

'Will you take lunch here, John, or do you wish to go out?'

He was obscurely pleased that she had remembered to call him John. He felt it meant something. And at the same time he derided himself for being imaginative.

'Yes, I'd like to lunch at home,' he decided. 'A spot of peace and quiet is just what I need. Do you realise I've hardly paused for breath since I left the sanatorium?'

Marion-A gave him a stiff smile. 'It would be advisable to take life a little more slowly.'

He grinned. 'And what do you know about life?'

'Only what was included in my programing, John. I know that human beings do not have an unlimited tolerance for the correlation of sense-data. Therefore it is not advisable to experience new stimuli at high speed for long periods.'

'A sober, clinical statement,' he remarked. 'And what happens if I swallow the new stimuli in large mouthfuls?' He thought the metaphor would puzzle her, but Marion-A's programing evidently included the appreciation and extension of metaphors.

'They will be badly digested and you will become sick,' she said calmly.

He considered the point. He thought she had something. 'This afternoon,' he announced, 'I'll sleep. This evening I'd like to take a look around London. We might even be reckless and dine out.'

'You wish me to accompany you, John?'

'If you would like to — but can androids *like* anything, Marion?'

She gave him another smile. 'Fulfilling my function produces an equilibrium of potential that might be correlated with the biological sensation of pleasure.'

'Now I know you're only a machine,' he said drily.

Marion-A began to set the table for lunch. 'Shall I join you for the meal, sir?'

He looked at her closely. 'I have a theory, Marion. You say 'John' when you approve, and call me 'sir' when you disapprove. Would you say that was a good theory?'

She returned a blank stare. 'I cannot offer a valid opinion — John. I was not programed to approve or disapprove. But I am aware of the inconsistency of address, particularly since you asked me to call you John in private. Perhaps, since the request was in conflict with my basic programing, it has produced a slight instability.'

'And perhaps,' added Markham, 'androids are more sensitive than they think they are ... You needn't lunch with me, Marion. Though I'd like you to stay and talk.'

Throughout the meal she sat on a chair opposite him, gravely watching him dispose of the food. Markham talked to her perfunctorily, mainly asking random questions about current social life and conventions. Marion-A answered his queries but did not volunteer any additional information. Nor did she assist the growth of conversation by asking any questions of her own.

Markham poured himself a second cup of coffee and took the cigarette that Marion-A silently offered.

'I want you to develop a sense of curiosity,' he said abruptly. 'I want you to be a bit more independent.'

'I think,' said Marion-A surprisingly, 'you want me to be too human. That is not a good thing, John.'

'You have the ability to appreciate a situation and to make decisions. You store information and correlate sense-data; why not the rest?'

'Because that is not in my programing.'

Markham laughed. 'It is not in the programing of a human baby to devise atomic formulae or non-Euclidean geometry. But some babies grow up and do just that.'

'I cannot grow up.'

'Not physically; maybe not spiritually. But intellectually.'

She smiled. 'I think you overestimate the function of androids, John.'

'Like hell,' he said, suddenly grim. 'I'd bet a pound to a bent penny that humanity's greatest mistake lies in under-estimating the androids.'

'Why do you say that?'

'Aha!' he exclaimed triumphantly. 'A question — based on curiosity! Or is it something more?'

Marion-A stood up. 'You are tired,' she said. 'I think it is time for you to rest.'

'Plus evasion,' he said gleefully. 'You androids may have humanity on the end of a string, Marion. But we still have two secret weapons. Intuition and subtlety.'

Marion-A laughed. It was the first time he had ever heard her do so. The sound was pleasant and uncannily *individual*. He was astounded.

'Dear John,' she said, her voice startlingly expressive, 'perhaps intuition and subtlety both have their mechanistic equivalents.'

'Christ!' he said, registering a solemn expression. 'Now I'm really frightened.'

'Sleep,' remarked Marion-A with a sudden return to gravity, 'may possibly allay your fears ... When would you like me to wake you, John?'

'When the evening star doth as a jewel bedeck the quiet bosom of the sky.'

Marion-A smiled. 'I will wake you at eighteen hundred, then.'

She went to the bedroom, closed the curtains and dialed

the hidden lighting to a dim, restful blue. Markham remained where he was for a while, contemplating Marion-A's brief excursion into irony. He had the fanciul notion that she was in high spirits. But how the devil could an android be in high spirits? He also had the even more fanciful notion that it was because he had said that he was going to take her out.

As a means of adding to his knowledge of the way people lived in the twenty-second century, Markham considered his evening out in London reasonably successful. But as a means of combating his increasing loneliness it was a complete failure. The more he saw, the more he realised how alien this way of life was to him.

Cinemas and theatres had vanished completely. All that he discovered were studios — the contemporary equivalent of the old-fashioned night clubs — bar-restaurants, gymnasia, and temples belonging to the various religious cults. The most prominent of these were the temples of the Triple-S, the Society of Sexual Symbolists. He thought of entering one he found in Fleet Street to see what it was like. But Marion-A pointed out that he would first have to become a novice of the fraternity, and to achieve that happy state he would have to be sponsored by someone who was already a member.

The profusion of temples, with their garish façades and neon-illuminated symbols fascinated him. But he decided that the exploration of this aspect of contemporary life would have to be accomplished later on. There was no need to hurry, he reminded himself bitterly. He had plenty of time.

The gymnasia, too, were restricted to members only. That left the studios and bar-restaurants.

He had a drink in what Marion-A informed him was a typical bar-restaurant in Shaftesbury Avenue. It was a long, low basement containing a bar — with the inevitable android bar-tender — several glass oubliettes that were clouded and in use, and a few old-fashioned shoulder-high cubicles with swing doors.

There were about twenty people in the place, one or two of them accompanied by androids. Markham chose to sit at the bar, and had hardly ordered his drink when he was accosted by a girl of seventeen or eighteen. She ignored Marion-A completely.

'Lo, stranger. You have an interesting face and a passable carcass. Are you bedward, loveward, or boredward?'

'Solitaryward,' said Markham with a smile. She was a pleasant-looking girl, but he was already aware that relationships in the twenty-second century were apt to develop a trifle rapidly.

She slid onto a stool at his other side, forcing him to turn his back on Marion-A.

'The least you can do is offer me a drink.'

'Certainly. What would you like?'

'A red sender, please. You're new to this hole, aren't you?'

'Yes.'

The android bartender produced the drink, and the girl lifted it to her lips. 'I'm dead,' she said. 'My sobsession demonstrated his mortality yesterday by diving from a helicar. Most inconsiderate, O man of mystery. We'd only been bedded a month . . . My glass is empty.'

'I'm sorry,' said Markham inadequately. 'Have another red sender.'

'Thank you. It's filthy, but what can one do? It's such a loss of face. People will say I was driving him to Analysis.' She disposed of the second red sender in two swallows. 'Do you realise the sweet goat has blighted my life? I practically loved him. But then he always was a weirdie. Full of crazy talk about star-ships and finding new worlds, as if this one wasn't good enough . . . I think I could love you, solemn stranger . . . My glass is empty.'

The third red sender joined its companions with startling rapidity.

'Are you alone?' asked Markham, thinking desperately of something to say.

The girl suddenly leaned over and kissed him. 'Who isn't?' she said. 'I'm Cheryl, Triple-S, a two-man woman and London's worst ballet dancer . . . Why did you collect S.A., and for how long?'

'How did you know?'

'The pallor. You get to recognise it. How long, my serious neurotic?'

'A hundred and forty-six years.'

'Seduce me yesterday! You're the tame Survivor. A celebrity. Why the hell don't you take me to bed and restore my reputation? I'd like another drink.'

95

'I think you've had enough, Cheryl. I have a helicar outside. Would you like me to take you home?'

She gave him a pathetic smile. 'For the obvious purpose, but not for any other. I know — I'm irradiated, my Lord. But he was such a nice sort of weirdie. To hell with him! He thought too much. I don't think too much, and neither must you, my hoary saint . . . O dark, dark, dark! We all go into the dark . . . Farewell, sweet prince. May angels sing thee to thy rest. I'm nubile and cultural. What more do you want?'

She got up from the stool, took three uncertain steps and collapsed soundlessly in a heap. Before Markham could move, an android lifted her gently up and took her away.

Markham turned to Marion-A. 'Let's get out of here,' he said.

He let Marion-A drive him round the quiet streets for a while. The girl Cheryl had depressed him; and somehow, it was important that he should not be depressed. He tried to get the incident out of his mind. But it wouldn't go. Cheryl's bright, hectic eyes; her flushed cheeks; her full, childlike lips haunted him. He was angry because he had his own private tragedy. He told himself cynically that he had no energy to spare for anyone else's. And that made him angrier.

Presently he calmed down and decided to sample studio life. Marion-A took the helicar along New Piccadilly and pulled up outside a massive building that was shaped like half an egg. Its smooth concrete shell glowed slightly in the darkness, a deep and shimmering red. There were no windows and only one large doorway.

He got out of the helicar and regarded it for a moment or two. Then he glanced up at the clear night sky . . . the placid and unchanging stars! But they were not unchanging. They were vast, violent, self-destroying holocausts.

The beacons of God, the atoms of the cosmos, the life-givers of tiny cinder-dust planets. And yesterday, a weirdie whose eyes and hopes had turned to the stars jumped out of his helicar.

A weirdie, doubtless, who was tired of androids and pointless luxury and keeping on the move yet having nowhere to go. A weirdie, perhaps, with a spark of poetry in his soul, a vein of curiosity in his mind, and a tiny, forbidden volcano murmuring in his heart. Or maybe, like Cheryl, he was just the victim of too many red senders.

Markham shrugged and turned his attention once more to the studio. The sign over the door was in curious iridescent letters on a metal background: *Studio Lotus.*

'Let's go in.' Absently he took Marion-A's arm.

They stepped out of an autumn evening in London and entered the dreamy, timeless world of a South Pacific island. Above them the sun blazed down from a clear blue sky of fascinating depth.

Markham stood, thunderstruck, under a group of genuine palm trees on a grassy mound that overlooked a stretch of golden sand. Bright Pacific breakers rolled musically up the beach, and the ocean seemed to stretch away to a hazy infinity.

'This way to the changing room, sir.' A male android in a printed shirt, and with a garland of sweet-smelling blossoms round his neck, appeared at Markham's elbow. He was taken to a small cubicle where his clothes were exchanged for convincingly battered beachcomber's trousers and fiber sandals. When he rejoined Marion-A he saw that she was wearing a flimsy bolero and the inevitable grass skirt.

He looked up again at the blue sky and the blinding sun. The illusion was complete. It was almost possible to believe that the island was real and that he had stepped into another dimension. Bright-plumed birds flashed and chattered through a miniature forest, and on the beach someone had just hauled a protesting turtle from the synthetic ocean.

'We'd better join the happy throng and sunbathe,' said Markham, surveying the laughing groups of people by the water's edge.

He was even more perplexed to discover that the shells and rocks were genuine, that the coral in the lagoon was also authentic, and that it was impossible to reconcile the distant horizon with the knowledge that the diameter of the studio could barely exceed a hundred yards.

'Lo, lo, lo,' said a voice behind him. 'How goes it, old man? You look as if you've picked up most of the bits. Come and join us for a nutcracker.'

Markham turned round and saw a grinning, bearded face under a battered straw hat. He knew he ought to recognise it, but he didn't.

'Burn me, you've forgotten already,' said the stranger petulantly. 'I'm Bressing, dear fellow. Antan Bressing. I was there at the San when you were recalled. Remember?'

Markham made his apologies, while Bressing shepherded him and Marion-A toward a group of two androids and a girl.

The girl was called Soluna and was evidently Bressing's mistress. She was a large, somnolent blonde with a figure that seemed to possess opulent curves everywhere. The androids, one male and one female, were gravely dancing with each other while Soluna issued detailed instructions.

'I've just had an idea for my new ballet-masque,' she explained, when Bressing had made the introduction. 'Antan, I do wish you could get that idiot Ruth to synthesise a bit more emotion. Richard seems to have the idea, but *she's* moving like a spastic on skates.'

Ruth-B, who was Bressing's personal android, was not so tall as Marion-A. Nor was her conversation on the same level. When Bressing spoke to her she seemed to find it necessary to deliberate before giving an answer. The other android, Richard, who was Soluna's P.A., seemed to have been modeled as a Latin type with swarthy if expressionless features. He, too, was a B classification.

Remembering the way Prof. Hyggens had questioned Marion-A on Hampstead Heath, Markham seized the opportunity to ask Bressing what the classifications meant. For some obscure reason he had not wanted to ask Marion-A.

Bressing dispatched his P.A. to a beach barbecue for drinks and savories. Then he said, 'You can't expect an artist to pay much attention to these things, old man. All I know is that A androids are pretty bright. The B models tend to be a shade cloddish, and the C models are only used for routine stuff. But what the mark and function mean, I haven't a clue ... Actually, I'm surprised they gave you an A android. They're usually reserved for executive work.'

Markham turned to Marion-A and gave her an odd smile. 'If I remember rightly, you said you were an A-three-alpha, didn't you?'

'Yes, sir.'

'Hell's mutations!' exclaimed Soluna, looking at her closely. 'Solomon is only two marks above you.'

'Who is Solomon?' asked Markham.

'The Prime Minister,' said Bressing. 'Permanent Civil Service, you know. He's directly responsible to President Bertrand for running the Republic.'

'I can understand why they gave you an A android,' remarked Soluna. 'But an A-three-alpha! Psychoprop must rate you pretty high ... Or something.' She gazed at him with renewed interest. 'Of course,' she added slyly, 'they probably decided you'd need a bright one to keep you out of trouble.'

'What kind of trouble?'

Soluna laughed. 'I saw your interview on the screen. You could be dangerous — in the wrong company.'

'I see. Would you care to enlarge?'

Soluna darted a quick glance at Marion-A. 'Oh, well, there are the Runners, you know. They aren't significant, but they have a positively boring nuisance value. If they annoy you I expect Marion will take care of it.'

The idea that Marion-A might be something more than a companionable servant had already occurred to Markham. Formerly he had regarded it as a vague possibility. But from the way Bressing and Soluna spoke, it appeared to be pretty much of a certainty. He began to wonder anxiously if she had already done anything about Prof. Hyggens. But then he reflected that Prof. also knew her potential and would not be likely to underestimate it.

Meanwhile Bressing's P.A. had returned with the drinks. The nutcrackers were served appropriately in coconut shells. They tasted disarmingly sweet and harmless. But after a couple, Markham noticed that his speech was getting a little thick.

He lay full length on the warm sand, shading his eyes from the glare of the sun, and listening to Bressing's uninspired small talk against a background of guitar music and noisy bursts of laughter. Marion-A sat by his side, silent and with a fixed smile, sipping her nutcracker at regular intervals.

Soluna continued to exhort the two androids in a further sequence of her projected ballet-masque which, when it had been developed sufficiently with the aid of androids, would be offered for performance by human beings. But Ruth-B's inability to simulate human reaction was rapidly causing Soluna to lose her temper.

'You rust-ridden tin hussy!' she stormed. 'Kiss him as if you meant it. You've seen me kiss, haven't you? You've seen other women kiss. Then don't stand there like an animated totem pole!'

Glancing at the two androids endeavoring to imitate human beings in love, Markham thought the result was utterly bizarre — and somehow obscene.

Suddenly Soluna turned to him and said, 'Do you mind if I borrow Marion for a couple of minutes, darling? If she can't do it properly, I'll be a virgin if any android can.'

Markham looked at Richard-B, posturing with extended arms and a blank look on his face.

'Yes, I do mind,' he said, surprised at his own intensity. 'I find the whole thing slightly repulsive.'

Soluna flashed a brittle smile. 'Now don't be tiresomely primitive, dear John. You must learn to contain your old-fashioned neuroses.' She turned to Marion-A. 'Do you know where Ruth is going wrong?'

'I think so, madam.'

'Then just you do it right. If I don't get the choreography framed before Saturday next, I'll have a mach-three tantrum.'

Marion-A stood up and looked at Markham. 'With your permission, sir?'

'No.'

Soluna pouted. 'I'd hoped you were joking, darling. Do stop being asocial and let me get on with it.'

'I'm sorry,' said Markham, 'but no.'

'Androids alive! Why not?'

'I don't quite know, except that I find the exhibition distasteful.'

'Drop your psyche into neutral, old man,' said Bressing. 'You're too, too serious. You'll have to get used to letting the androids do things. They're only machines.'

'Not this kind of thing,' retorted Markham. 'It nauseates me.'

Soluna stretched and yawned pointedly. 'I'll leave you to enjoy your nausea in peace,' she remarked sweetly. 'I'm going for a swim. Coming, Antan?'

Bressing sighed. 'I suppose so.' As he got up to follow Soluna down to the water, he turned to Markham and said confidentially, 'She's frightfully sensitive, dear fellow. But the compensation lies in extreme bedworthiness.'

'I wish you much joy,' answered Markham in an even voice. He watched Bressing lumber down to the water's-edge, and was reminded of a trained sea-lion. Then he saw that Marion-A was watching him intently.

'I'd like you to get me something to drink. And tell those damned androids to go and practice whatever they're supposed to be doing elsewhere.'

'Yes, sir.'

Presently she returned from the barbecue with a couple of large nutcrackers.

Markham raised an eyebrow. 'Hell, I can't manage two.'

Marion-A set the drinks down. 'I thought you might wish me to join you, sir.'

'Why not? I'd rather drink with an android than with those idiots.'

'Thank you,' said Marion-A. She took the smaller of the coconut shells.

'To the perfect machine,' said Markham with irony, lifting his drink, 'as opposed to the imperfect human being.'

Marion-A smiled. 'There have been philosophers who regarded human beings as machines.'

'Yes, but hardly perfect ones ... I've seen enough of this place for one evening. Let's get away.'

Ten minutes later they were outside Studio Lotus. Markham took a deep breath of the clean night air. After the languorous atmosphere of a synthetic South Pacific, it tasted like sharp wine.

As they entered the helicar he glanced once more at the huge concrete dome. 'A pseudo-womb,' he remarked grimly, 'for the gestation of sterile life ... I think I'll take a walk in the Park before we go home ... walk the damned place out of my system!'

CHAPTER NINE

DURING the Nine Days Tranquiliser Buckingham Palace had been almost totally destroyed. But when the Republic of London was established as an autonomous estate, it was re-built — not as a home of royalty, since the hereditary succession no longer existed, but as a symbolic home of authority.

The new Palace bore no resemblance at all to its old-fashioned counterpart. Though it stood on exactly the same site at the junction of Constitution Hill and The Mall, gone forever were the frowning stone façade, the heavy portals and the drab, expressionless windows. Instead there rose an almost spherical structure whose outer shell was made entirely of glass bricks with each alternate face silvered, so that the total impression was of a ball of light rolled casually into the Palace Gardens.

At night an elaborate system of lighting made the Palace appear to rotate slowly with a steady and almost hypnotic glitter.

Though Markham had taken care to be there punctually for the President's reception, he saw by the number of heli-cars and jets that he was hardly among the first arrivals. He and Marion-A were met by an ornately liveried android who conducted them to one of the four massive hiduminium columns which rose from the ground to support the sphere at its horizontal diameter.

Each of the columns was hollow and contained a roomy elevator. Markham and Marion-A were shot up to the main balcony of the Palace where they were handed over to another android who escorted them through a semi-circular portico and two large anterooms, where people were converging on the Great Hall.

Presently they came to a large brass-faced door studded with tiny portholes of tinted glass and flanked by a couple of solemn uniformed androids, each holding an antique halberd. The door opened noiselessly as they approached and a majordomo was revealed on the other side. Markham stepped forward and presented his invitation card, where-upon the android rapped the floor ceremoniously with a silver rod and called out in a loud voice: 'Mr. John Markham and P.A.'

Then, before he had time to take in his surroundings, Markham found himself face to face with the President of London.

Clement Bertrand was a broad-built, white-haired man in his early sixties. He had a pink, healthy complexion, and the smooth texture of his skin seemed to clash incongruously with the rest of his appearance. He wore a short black cere-monial jacket trimmed with ermine, a pair of knee-breeches, smooth white stockings and a pair of shoes with large gold buckles. He looked, thought Markham, like an oversized schoolboy in a period play.

'Evening lo,' said the President formally. There was a smile on his face but his eyes were shrewd and serious.

'Evening lo, sir,' responded Markham, bowing slightly as he had been instructed to do. 'It was very kind of you to invite me.'

Clement Bertrand laughed. 'Curious to see you, dear fellow. Vivain told me all about you. Said you were a deca-dent Puritan — whatever that might be. Expect the little vixen's looking for you somewhere. Now enter the throng and be socially osmotic ... After dinner we must exhale words together.'

'Miss Nioni Ap Simon and P.A.,' intoned the majordomo. Markham moved hastily into the Great Hall.

It was like a vast submarine grotto. On the other side of the thick glass walls fish of every shape, size and hue swam through underwater forests, occasionally bestowing bored glances on the crowds of chattering people in the Hall.

Surveying the scene, the colorful, scanty dresses of the women and the slightly more garish clothes of the men, Markham felt that he too had stepped into a kind of aquarium and was now no less a prisoner than the fish.

'Sir,' said a rich masculine voice, 'I would be honored if you would allow me to offer you a glass of the President's Elizabethan brandy. There are only six cases left in the Re-public.'

The stranger had a pleasant but somehow ageless face. He was taller than Markham, and his most dominant characteristic was a pair of deep, penetrating eyes. The clothes he wore were relatively subdued, and there was an air of dignity and purpose about him which, alone, would have distinguished him from the rest of the company.

'Thank you,' said Markham. 'Elizabethan brandy certainly sounds intriguing.'

The stranger smiled. 'It is a genuine 1963 vintage. Not even the connoisseurs will appreciate it as you will, Mr. Markham.' He made a slight gesture with his hand. An android appeared and was dispatched with a brief order. He returned a few seconds later with a tray bearing a decanter and glasses.

'Stand,' said the stranger quietly. The android presented the tray and froze into a statue, his eyes focused somewhere in the distance.

The stranger motioned to Marion-A. 'Pour.'

She lifted the decanter. 'One glass, sir, or two?'

'You will permit me to join you, Mr. Markham?' The stranger seemed to find his own question amusing.

Markham was startled. 'Naturally, sir. I assumed — '

'You assumed too much, Mr. Markham, but I thank you for the compliment.' Again it seemed as if the stranger was enjoying a private joke. He gave one of the glasses to Markham and took the other himself. 'I will drink to your happiness,' he said, with unconcealed irony. He wet his lips with the brandy, then replaced his glass on the tray.

'And I,' said Markham, feeling vaguely uneasy, 'will drink to your long life.' He tried to make his own toast sound ironical, but failed.

The response was rich laughter. 'That is kind of you, but unnecessary. I am not alive.'

Realising now the cause of his uneasiness, Markham recovered instantly. 'That depends upon one's definition of life.'

'So you have encountered the Runners already.' It sounded more like a statement than a question. 'I thought they would contact you, but I evidently underestimated the time factor.'

Suddenly Markham was fully alert. 'Is it impossible to arrive at a definition of life unless one has contact with the Runners?'

'Not impossible, Mr. Markham, but merely improbable.

To ponder the imponderable is frequently a sign of mal-adjustment.'

'Or intelligence.'

'Perhaps ... Incidentally, I am Solomon, President Bertrand's Prime Minister.'

'To use an appropriate idiom,' retorted Markham drily, 'androids alive!'

'An amusing but meaningless phrase.'

'There are some who do not think so.'

'Chiefly the Runners.'

'And possibly,' added Markham with a thin smile, 'a few intelligent also-rans.'

'I trust,' said Solomon, ignoring the remark, 'that you will not take the Runners too seriously. It might affect your orientation.'

'I trust,' answered Markham, 'that you will not worry about my orientation too much. It might affect your pro-graming.'

Again Solomon laughed. 'You have a sense of humor, Mr. Markham. That is good.'

'You, too, have a sense of humor. But I am not sure *that* is good.'

Solomon poured him another glass of brandy. 'I hope your P.A. is satisfactory?' He gave Marion-A a brief glance. 'If you would like any modifications we can re-program quickly.'

'She is excellent as she is, thank you.'

'I am glad of that ... And now I cannot neglect my duties any longer. Perhaps you will allow me the privilege of conversing with you again, Mr. Markham. Meanwhile I must withdraw — with your permission, of course.'

'Permission granted,' said Markham coldly.

Solomon gave a slight bow that seemed to convey a hint of satire, then walked quickly across the Hall.

Markham watched until he had disappeared, then he swallowed the rest of his brandy, deposited his glass on the tray and dismissed the android servant.

He realised that he was shaking with anger. He had just been patronised by an android. But what infuriated him even more was that he had failed to recognise Solomon as an android either by appearance or behavior. Normally he was able to recognise the personal and executive androids as such at a glance — by their blankness of expression, stiffness of features, precision of movement and other telltale signs. But Solomon was not betrayed by such evidence, and had he not disclosed his own identity Markham felt that he would probably not have entertained any suspicion of the truth.

The lighting in the Great Hall was not very bright, but it was bright enough to distinguish synthetic skin and eyes and bone formation from the real things. As he considered his lack of recognition Markham's imagination leapt to consider frightening possibilities — situations where androids might masquerade as men or women. A world in which androids might be indistinguishable from men except by X-ray!

Suddenly he discovered that Marion-A was talking to him in a voice that was hardly more than a whisper:

'It is not wise to underestimate Solomon, John. Since he is responsible for the efficient functioning of the Republic, his programing is extremely complex.'

'Are you warning me or threatening me?'

'Neither. I am advising you. It is my duty as your P.A.'

'When men become afraid of androids there's something incredibly rotten in the State of Denmark.'

'I do not understand clearly what you mean.'

'Good. There's some hope left, then . . . Marion?'

'Yes, sir?'

'Do you spy on me for Solomon?'

She hesitated. 'I am programed to take all necessary precautions for your safety.'

'That doesn't answer the question. We might have different concepts of safety.'

'My programing relates to your safety in physical and psychological terms and also to the safety of the Republic.'

'Trust an android to evade the issue. In short, you spy on me — when possible and necessary.'

Marion-A remained silent. At this point Markham saw that Vivain was wending her way toward him across the crowded floor. She was accompanied by a broad-shouldered, athletic man about Markham's own age.

'Darling John! We've been looking for you everywhere. This is Algis Norvens . . . Algis, here is the genuine stone-age specimen. Be friends, or I shan't love either of you.'

Markham shook hands with Algis Norvens and, with a

smile, exchanged the conventional greeting. But Norvens did not smile. His handclasp was light and impersonal.

'I hope you do not find our world too confusing,' he said.

'Only as confusing, I think, as it finds me.'

Vivain gave an impish smile. 'John is temperamentally a crusader. Full of lofty sentiments and unshakable convictions. We are sworn enemies.'

Norvens looked at Markham curiously. 'You choose your enemies quickly, and with excellent taste.'

'I'im afraid the credit belongs to Vivain. She found me.'

'And what made you become enemies?'

'Love,' said Vivain mischievously, 'among other things.'

At that moment a stentorian voice rang through the Hall: 'Ladies and gentlemen, dinner will now be served.'

'Come along, you two. I arranged it so that we should sit together.' Vivain took each of them by the arm and led them to the main staircase.

Markham was glad of the interruption. He had sensed an underlying antagonism in Algis Norvens that did nothing to make him feel optimistic about their future relationship. Vivain was not only aware of this, she had — it seemed to Markham — anticipated it, and was provocatively reveling in it. He supposed it appealed to her odd sense of humor, since she would be in possession of intimate details about both of them which neither could know about the other.

The dining hall was near the top of the Palace. Its floor was black and crystalline; the circular walls glowed softly with spectra lighting and curved in to form a dome, the apex of which was at least fifty feet above the floor.

The tables were arranged in the form of a great horseshoe, and when the guests were seated Markham saw that there were more than two hundred. Vivain took her place between him and Norvens, while Marion-A, in common with about a hundred other androids, stood motionless behind her master's chair.

The speech which President Bertrand delivered as a formal prelude to dinner was little more than a brief and banal eulogy on the theme of life in the Republic of London. He did, however, make one or two oblique references which Markham found intensely interesting. He spoke with obvious disgust of the anti-android riots in the Midlands, and remarked that the Foreman of the Midlands had at last accepted the advice of his Prime Minister and was imposing a penalty of fifty years' suspended animation on those who had been involved. He also mentioned the Laird of Scotland's recent campaign against a colony of Runners who had established themselves in the Highlands. Markham was intrigued to learn that it had taken a 'psychiatric brigade' of a thousand androids to deal with less than three hundred Runners; and that even then only sixty of the Runners had been captured, while a hundred and fifty androids had been destroyed or disabled.

As he neared the end of his speech Clement Bertrand regarded his guests with a benevolent smile. 'Dear people,' he said, 'you will all agree that such a situation would be impossible in London. Society will always have a few psychotics and perverts — people who, unable to find a place in the normal social pattern, will attempt to destroy it and create one to their own abnormal taste. But here the Runners are negligible. Their pathetic dreams of a return to pre-android barbarism need demand no more from us than pity or derision, for the vigilance of Psychoprop is steadily and consistently reducing their numbers ... Hell's mutations, I've wasted enough of your time being serious! That's Solomon's department. Now let's amuse ourselves.'

There was a polite murmur of enthusiasm from the guests, and the android waiters stepped forward.

'Isn't he a pompous idiot?' said Vivain to Markham. 'But he's not quite so bad when you really get to know him. After all somebody has to blow up his chest and be the king frog.'

'I would have thought Solomon was the king frog,' ventured Markham. He had noticed that the Prime Minister, who was at Clement Bertrand's side, was the only android sitting down to dinner — unless some of the other guests were androids with a similar ability to appear quite human.

'Have you met him?' asked Vivain.

'We exchanged a few words just before you found me. I mistook him for a human being.'

'Everyone does at first,' she said, frowning slightly. 'He likes to surprise people. I think there must be a streak of vanity in his programing.'

'If I were your father,' said Markham, 'I'd have him quietly destroyed.'

Vivain shot him a startled glance. 'Androids alive! You shouldn't say things like that, John — at least, not to anyone but me.'

'Why not? As a machine he's just a shade too human. I think he's dangerous.'

'He's also brilliant — and indispensable.'

Markham looked once more at the Prime Minister, who was solemnly drinking soup. 'That makes him even more dangerous.'

'I think I'm just a little afraid of him myself,' she admitted. 'But he runs the Republic wonderfully. All Clement has to do is authorise whatever policy is necessary.'

'For God's sake don't tell me any more,' said Markham in disgust, 'or I'll go out and join the Runners.'

Algis Norvens pointedly entered the conversation. 'I saw you on the screen a few nights ago,' he said. 'It was most amusing.'

'Really?' said Markham. 'I suppose you enjoyed those riotously funny bits about love and marriage and children — and work.'

'Actually, I did.'

'Actually,' returned Markham, 'it was all a tissue of lies. If you want to know the truth I had four mistresses, thirteen illegitimate children and an income of ten thousand a year derived from the mass production of chastity belts.'

Norvens sneered. 'I think you have an odd sense of humor.'

Markham smiled. 'It's an odd world, my master — especially for one who has had the great privilege of not being conditioned to its oddness.'

'Stop behaving like a couple of boys,' said Vivain delightedly. 'I want you to be friends.'

'Nonsense, darling,' was Markham's reckless retort. 'We're doing just what you want. We're behaving like a couple of stags in the rutting season. And that, too, is amusing; isn't it, Algis?'

Norvens suddenly changed his tactics. 'Despite my better judgment I'm afraid I'm going to like you, John. I hope we shall see much of each other ... Have you ever tried air-skiing?'

'No, but it certainly sounds attractive.'

'You must come to the Club some time, and I will take you up. But I must warn you that it is very dangerous; there have been many deaths.'

'We're all dying a little each day,' observed Markham. 'I'll take the risk of accelerating the process — if it's interesting.'

'Algis is the second-best glider pilot in the Republic,' said Vivain.

'Who's the first?'

'Me, of course.'

By the time the fifth course of the dinner had been served the general conversation had increased considerably in volume and the wine waiters were shuttling back and forth with monotonous regularity. It was then that a section of the floor rolled away and a small orchestra rose up in the center of the horseshoe of dinner tables. The room darkened slightly and a spotlight played upon a woman posed like a Greek statue on a pedestal.

She was nude and completely motionless. Her left leg and right arm were silver, the other leg and arm were gold, her body and face were jet black, and her hair a phosphorescent green.

Suddenly, electrically, as the music began she sprang from the pedestal with a long, low cry to begin a song and dance which depicted in unsparing detail the loss of her virginity.

The music was thin and discordant, the singer's tonal range did not seem to exceed three separate notes, while the movements of her body — though slight — were suggestive in the extreme. But, strangely, Markham found that the total effect could not be dismissed simply as obscene. If a direct appeal was made to the audience's sexual appetites, so also were their pity and compassion invoked. Glancing stealthily at his dinner companions, Markham noticed that several women had tears in their eyes. But the most unusual feature occurred toward the end of the song and dance, when the girl evidently discovered that she was pregnant by a man already twice a father in the same five-year period. As the singer went on to bemoan her lover's consequent sentence of five years S.A., Markham noticed that several men at the dinner tables looked distinctly uncomfortable.

At the end of her song the woman sprang back onto her pedestal and resumed her original pose as she sank slowly out of sight.

The next diversion was obviously for Markham's special benefit. It was a ballet-masque performed by a male dancer dressed in a caricature of twentieth-century clothes, an android and a ballerina in twenty-second-century evening dress. They were supported by a small android chorus, a corps de ballet and three dancers dressed as the Survivor's wife and children.

Markham watched, fascinated, as the mock-Survivor after waking from S.A. mimed horror at the android and disgust at the ballerina's blatant advances. Then the Survivor danced impotently round the ghostly figures of his wife and children, vainly trying to reach them through an invisible barrier.

The beseeching gestures of the two children and the girl in twentieth-century clothes rocked the audience with laughter — especially when they danced toward Markham's dinner table, making their appeal direct. He turned away, closing his eyes, to hide his misery. But the President's guests interpreted this as a public rejection of the outmoded concept of family life; and their laughter, which had been restrained a little by embarrassment, now increased in volume. Then, when the mock-Survivor — aware of the futility of trying to reach his family — sank to the floor in an attitude of despair, the music was almost drowned by the audience's vocal paroxysm.

But at last the personal android persuaded the Survivor to pull himself together. He leaped up from the floor, dismissed his family into the outer darkness with a careless wave of his hand, and executed a brief dance of liberation. Symbolically exchanging his old-fashioned clothes for fashionable twenty-second-century wear, he then partnered the ballerina in a frenzied dance which ended with the inevitable sexual abandon. The final sequence showed the Survivor, after making love to the ballerina, discovering that his wife and children had materialised once more. Recoiling from them in disgust, he allowed his personal android and the chorus to drive them away.

As the stage sank down through the floor Markham felt a hand on his arm. 'John, dear, I'm sorry about this,' whispered Vivain. 'If I'd known I'd have made Clement veto it.'

'Does it matter very much?' asked Markham in a controlled voice. 'After all, it's given everyone a good laugh.'

'Except you,' said Vivain, 'and me . . . It's hurt you deeply, hasn't it?'

He gave her a set smile. 'I don't think so. I'm wearing pretty solid armor nowadays.'

'Hell's mutations!' said Algis Norvens with a broad grin. 'That was a riot. I wonder who had the inspiration?'

'So do I,' said Markham. 'I'd like to offer my congratulations.' He looked inquiringly at Vivain.

'I don't know,' she confessed. 'Solomon usually organises the diversions. He would know. Shall I ask him for you?'

'Don't bother. Somehow I thought Solomon might have a hand in it.'

Silently and efficiently the android waiters cleared the dinner tables and began to serve coffee and liqueurs. Meanwhile the first of the two remaining diversions rose up through the floor on a wide circular stage. It was greeted with a gale of laughter, mingled with cries of astonishment and excitement. But after gazing at the spectacle in sheer disbelief for a few seconds, Markham felt physically sick.

There were three elaborately dressed people on the stage — a two-headed woman, one of whose faces looked like that of a child while the other was incongruously mature; a four-armed man; and another man with a long prehensile tail.

They enacted in completely silent mime the ancient theme of rivalry, each of the men eagerly demonstrating the unique benefits of his particular affliction. The four-armed man offered flowers, sweetmeats, perfume and a double-hooded evening cloak as tokens of his affection. Then the woman joined him for a brief dance in which two of his arms held her normally, while the other two caressed her childish face. Eventually his rival, tiring of the performance, grabbed his ankle with the prehensile tail and tripped him up. Then he, too, danced with the woman, concentrating his attention upon her mature face and using his tail in such a way — sometimes merely grotesque, sometimes obscene — as to convulse the audience with laughter.

Markham felt he could stand the ghastly performance no longer. But as he made to leave his chair Vivain restrained him with a hand.

'You have only the twentieth century to thank for this, John,' she said quietly. 'The mutations caused by the Nine Days Tranquiliser are still recurring. And the android scientists say we shall have them for another thousand years. You think we are hard and unfeeling, don't you? You think we are decadent and rotten. But perhaps this is one way of reminding us of the horrors of war.'

'Everyone seems to be enjoying it pretty well,' he observed with disgust.

'Not everyone,' she retorted. 'Besides, we are superior in one way, you know. We, at least, have abolished war.'

He tried to find a satisfactory answer, but there didn't seem to be one — not one that was entirely honest.

At last the macabre exhibition was over. It disappeared amid applause and hoots of laughter. But there was something odd about the laughter, thought Markham. To him it seemed to be on the edge of hysteria, particularly with the women. Then it occurred to him that they, too, were still potential victims of the Nine Days Tranquiliser. For the first time he began to appreciate the horror attaching to pregnancy, and the penalty upon masculine irresponsibility.

Algis Norvens turned to Markham with a curious smile. 'Did you find it amusing?'

'No. Did you?'

'If we did not laugh,' said Norvens surprisingly, 'we should be blind with anger. Therefore we laugh. The tragedy becomes a joke, and the joke slowly begins to lose its bittnerness.'

Markham's feeling of bewilderment increased. At one moment the people of the twenty-second century seemed callous and shallow, and in the next moment they would betray brief glimpses of sensitivity and perception.

He was about to question Norvens on the possibility of euthanasia, when the final diversion made its appearance. It consisted of a large transparent glass or plastic bubble with a seat suspended in the center in such a fashion that, however the bubble was turned the seat would remain vertical. On it sat what appeared to be a small naked boy of about ten. But when Markham looked closely he saw that in contrast with the rest of his flesh the child's face was incredibly wizened like that of a shriveled old man.

There was a small aperture in the bubble, and through

this came an intense beam of red light from a device that the child held in his hand.

An android, who was steadying the bubble lightly with his arm, announced that it contained Sylvero, the famous telepath and clairvoyant.

When the android had finished speaking Sylvero waved to the assembled company and grinned amiably. Then, at a signal from either President Bertrand or Solomon, the android swung the bubble round so that Sylvero's beam of red light shone squarely on the face of one of the dinner guests.

Markham saw that the man's eyes opened wide in astonishment, then seemed to fix in a glazed look. His face became exceedingly expressionless and his body went rigid.

Then Sylvero spoke and his thin, reedy voice was made piercing by an amplifier:

'The subject's name is Orland Joyce. He is thirty-eight years old and has undergone three months' S.A. He has loved eleven women and procreated with one. At the age of thirteen he engineered the undetected destruction of an android, which resulted in a guilt complex and a morbid fear of non-biological identities. At the age of sixteen he was sexually initiated by a woman some ten years older, who later became a Runner and was surrendered to a psychiatric team by the subject. At the age of twenty-two he won a First in sea-skating at the London Olympics. At the age of twenty-seven he exhibited ten sculptures in the Republic Art Tournament and was awarded the Gold Turban. At the age of thirty-two he sired one normal. At the age of thirty-five he wrote a surealla protagonised by authentic libidinous drives. This evening he will begin a liaison with a woman wearing blue hair and a columin gown. Tomorrow he will jet to Scotland for the Autumn Games. He will then spend the next two months in the City before leaving for a psycho-cure. At the age of forty-one he will sire one more natural. At the age of forty-seven he will be seriously injured in a marine sport that has not yet been developed ... It is not permitted to disclose the age at which the subject will die. I say no more.'

Sylvero switched off the red beam and Orland Joyce returned to apparent consciousness. He gazed about him with a bewildered smile, while the guests — especially those who had known the subject and were able to corroborate the first part of Sylvero's analysis — applauded loudly.

At another signal from the President's table the android turned the transparent sphere slightly, and Sylvero's red beam shone on the face of a dark girl, who reacted immediately as the man had done.

Sylvero's reedy voice began its recital. He gave the subject's name as Ninelle Marchant, her age as twenty-two. Then, in far greater detail than he had given for the first subject, Sylvero went on to describe her childhood and the intimate facts of her adult life. As he described the emotional highlights of her existence Sylvero's childish voice quivered with excitement and — it seemed to Markham — a subtle malice. The recital continued until the subject's history was brought up to date — with Sylvero remarking cattily that she had had a most exhausting evening the night before and would therefore leave early. Then he began to foretell her future, beginning as before with the immediate future. But suddenly he stopped. Then, after a moment's silence, he repeated the previous formula: 'It is not permitted to disclose the age at which the subject will die. I say no more.'

The applause was not so strong as previously. Having been fed Ninelle's past in abundant detail the audience anticipated the same treatment for her future. They felt cheated.

Markham looked at the grinning, aged infant in the glass bubble and was aware of almost uncontrollable revulsion and hatred surging up inside him. The probability that Sylvero was also a mutant — a late product of the Nine Days Tranquiliser — did nothing to temper his revulsion with charity.

What right had the malevolent gargoyle to expose other people's lives, to play at being God and predict their futures?

Had Markham been a little calmer he would have realised that Sylvero, too, was caught in the web of circumstance. But the little clairvoyant had simply become a focal point for the latent anger which had been triggered by Markham's encounter with Solomon, and which the rest of the evening had served to intensify.

But just as Markham decided that he could remain a

passive spectator no longer at the President's so-called diversions, Sylvero's red beam shone full in his eyes and his mind became a total blank.

The interval had no subjective time value, and when he awoke it seemed to him that the red beam had flashed at him only momentarily. He was aware, however, of an impressive silence, and saw that all eyes were turned toward the transparent sphere. Two androids were steadying it while a third had opened a small panel and was lifting out the limp form of Sylvero. He might have been unconscious, but even before Vivain spoke Markham knew that Sylvero was dead.

'Are you all right, John?' she whispered anxiously.

'I think so. What happened?'

Vivain shot an uneasy glance at her father's table, where Solomon sat watching Sylvero's removal with a bland gaze.

'He made Sylvero put you *en rapport*,' she explained. 'Then the little monster told us all about your childhood, the way you grew up, your life with Katy . . . I — hated it.'

Markham watched with a satisfied smile as the sphere and the body of Sylvero sank out of sight.

'Why?' he asked. 'I only got the same treatment as the other victims.'

'You don't belong to our world. It seemed unfair.'

'How the hell did Sylvero die?' asked Markham, gazing somberly at the place where the sphere had stood.

'It's inexplicable. He had just begun to predict your future when it was as if something stopped him. He began to whimper, and everyone wondered what was happening. Then suddenly he started again — very quickly. But he was shrieking so much that it was unintelligible. And without any warning, he just collapsed.'

'Perhaps,' said Markham, with grim humor, 'he'd just foreseen his own death, and the shock killed him.'

Meanwhile President Bertrand had risen from the table — a signal for his guests to drift away at their leisure.

Algis Norvens turned to Vivain. 'Hell's mutations! That was a diversion to remember. It would seem that our Survivor has hidden talent . . . Shall we go down to the Great Hall for the pattern dancing?'

Vivain looked at Markham. 'The choice is yours, John. If you prefer I'll show you the tropical gardens or,' and she darted a malicious glance at Norvens, 'Algis will challenge a shark in the arena tank. He's very fond of demonstrating his underwater prowess ... Or perhaps you'd like to see the pattern dancing?'

'I'm feeling my age,' said Markham with an ironic smile. 'Pattern dancing sounds too energetic. I'll settle for the tropical gardens.'

'Then we must not deprive Algis of his exercise,' returned Vivain. 'He can borrow your P.A. for the dancing.'

Norvens did not accept his dismissal in good grace but Vivain was imperious. With an ill-tempered glance at Markham he took Marion-A down to the Great Hall, while Vivain and Markham went up to the gardens at the top of the Palace.

They were a riot of color, all the exotic profusion of flowers, shrubs and fruit trees being bathed in synthetic sunshine. But at the touch of a button Vivain cut out the 'sun', and there was left only the clear autumn moonlight pouring through a transparent roof.

The gardens seemed deserted. Vivain led him to a tiny artificial knoll where they sat and gazed at the moon.

'Is Norvens in love with you?' asked Markham abruptly.

She laughed. 'How does one define love? We have *made* love in the past. Perhaps we shall do so again.'

'I don't want to intrude, that's all.'

'Darling John, you're being pompous. A little healthy competition will improve Algis considerably.'

'Suppose I don't want to compete?'

'Then I shall have to make you, my impetuous Puritan — like this!' She took his face in her hands and kissed him passionately, but Markham did not respond.

'How charming,' said a voice from the shadows. 'You are assisting with his orientation very conscientiously, madam. But I fear it is a complicated task.'

Solomon stepped forward and surveyed them both with a benign smile. His presence did not appear to disturb Vivain, but Markham felt his anger rising again.

'Permission to withdraw is granted,' he said, with heavy sarcasm.

Solomon's smile deepened. 'Thank you, sir. But perhaps the President's daughter will permit me to enjoy the privilege of remaining for a few moments?'

117

'Permission granted,' said Vivain in an even voice.

Solomon gave a formal bow, then spoke to Markham: 'I must apologise, sir, for part of the diversions that may have offended you, and especially for the regrettable incident of Sylvero's death.'

'Actually,' said Markham, 'that was the part I enjoyed. Being old-fashioned, I cling to the odd notion that it's unforgivable to expose a person's private life for public amusement.'

Solomon's eyes seemed to glitter uncannily. 'And yet,' he said, 'was not that the main function of your twentieth-century newspapers? You must excuse me if I am wrong. I regret to say that I am exceedingly ill-programed on historical matters.'

To his own surprise Markham laughed. 'You are not the first to remind me that the great art of the twentieth century was hypocrisy. But I still prefer my brand of hypocrisy to yours.'

Solomon nodded pleasantly. 'Everyone to his taste, sir. The passage of a hundred and fifty years has at least liberated humanity from many of the old inhibitions.'

'At the price,' added Markham, 'of creating a set of new ones.'

'Which calls to mind the subject of maladjustment,' said Solomon, 'and that in turn leads us to the Runners.'

'The topic you evidently wished to discuss in the first place,' commented Markham. 'Proceed.'

'Thank you — sir.' Solomon paused for a moment. 'In view of our previous conversation, it has occurred to me, Mr. Markham, that you may be placing yourself in considerable personal danger.'

'In view of our previous conversation,' said Markham coldly, 'I am inclined to agree with you. But to my mind the source of danger is non-human.'

Solomon shook his head slowly, as if reproving a backward child. 'The danger is from the Runners. If they are clever enough they will try to use you as a symbol.' He smiled. 'Everyone in the Republic knows that the Survivor has typical twentieth-century attitudes to work, to sex, to cultural and economic freedom.'

'I also have strong views on the unlimited use of androids,' retorted Markham.

'Precisely. That is why I think the Runners will try to make you their spiritual leader.'

'You flatter me.'

'I am not programed for flattery — sir. But I am aware that you could be used as a battle-standard by psycho-neurotic elements who wish to change forcibly the present state of society.'

'If they are strong enough for that,' observed Markham, 'then the present society is very vulnerable.'

Solomon beamed. 'It is my experience that men — as such — are not dangerous. Only ideals are dangerous. The Runners might wish to use you as the embodiment of an ideal.'

Markham yawned. 'Personally, I do not feel either like a battle-standard or an ideal. I feel like an ordinary human being — irritated by too much walking machinery!'

'Then I trust, sir, that you will not endanger yourself by allowing the Runners to idealise you?'

'But supposing I should?'

'Then, sir, it would be necessary to make slight changes in your personality — so that you would not be irritated by too much walking machinery.'

'Thank you for the warning. I will remember it.'

'Thank you for this conversation, sir. I will remember that.' He turned to Vivain. 'I must apologise for my intrusion, madam. Permission to withdraw?'

'Granted,' said Vivain. 'I think, Solomon, that you should not assess Mr. Markham's attitude by contemporary standards.'

Again Solomon bowed. 'If I had done so, madam, I should have already recommended Analysis.'

Markham watched the android walk away. He remained silent, listening intently for a few moments. Then he said softly, 'So the infallible Solomon has made his first mistake.'

'What do you mean?'

'He thinks he can estimate correctly the result of applying a fear-stimulus to a human being.'

Vivain shivered slightly. 'I wish you wouldn't look so grim, darling.'

Suddenly Markham laughed. 'Flight or fight,' he said gaily. 'It's still the old dilemma.'

'What *are* you talking about?' Her voice was petulant.

'The difference between determinism and free will — and also between androids and men.'

'I'm not sure I like you when you are being obscure.'

'On the other hand,' said Markham, 'you are much improved by occasional doses of perplexity.'

They stayed in the tropical gardens until a liveried android found them and announced that President Bertrand wished to see Vivain and Markham in his private suite.

Clement Bertrand had shed his official mask. Despite the pink, healthy complexion and the smooth texture of his skin he now looked weary, and Markham noticed that there was a suggestion of anxiety in his eyes. He dismissed his android servant, offered drinks to Vivain and Markham, exchanged a few banal remarks, then came to the point:

'I'm a moderately old man, John, old enough to have dabbled a little when work — so-called — was still socially desirable. Electronics was my — my pastime. I mention this only because I want to assure you that this room is not tapped in any way for sound.' He chuckled. 'Solomon, being the nearest thing to chemically pure efficiency in the Republic, once tried it. But I set up a series of resonators that ruined everything he used. He took the hint, I'm glad to say.'

Markham smiled. 'I didn't expect you to be anti-android, sir.'

'I'm not,' said Clement Bertrand firmly. 'I'm just anti-disturbance — in every sense. And that's what I want to talk to you about. I saw Solomon a few minutes ago. He thinks you are a potential danger to the Republic. He thinks the Runners might want to use you. He also thinks you might be willing to be used. What do you say to that?'

'I didn't realise that androids could be programed for melodrama.'

'Don't sidestep. Have you met any Runners yet?'

'If I had I'd be a fool to tell you, sir.'

'A fool or a decent citizen? When you were awarded citizenship of the Republic you accepted certain responsibilities as well as privileges.'

Markham frowned. 'I find it difficult to rate betrayal as a responsibility.'

The President gave a tired shrug. 'If you want to be reckless it's your affair. But don't make hasty judgments — and don't underestimate Psychoprop. Psychoprop is Solomon. Every other android in the department is basically an extension of his brain.'

'Thank you, sir. I'll remember that.'

'Here's another thing to remember. Because you're a citizen first and a human being second, Solomon can't do anything until you make a mistake. But then he'll pounce. And that will be the end of John Markham as we now know him.'

Markham looked at the President curiously. 'From the way you speak, sir, I get the impression that you are not completely on Solomon's side of the fence.'

President Bertrand returned his gaze impassively. 'That is a possibility — but I'm President of the Republic and I don't want any situation to develop that would lead to a direct struggle between men and androids. Because the androids would win. They are here to serve us — with a magnificent organisation. They are good servants, but they could be ruthless enemies, given the appropriate programing.'

'Sooner or later,' said Markham, 'the struggle will come — unless humanity dies out first. That's why it should be sooner, while men still have some guts.'

President Bertrand poured himself another drink. 'It's odd,' he said thoughtfully, 'that philosophers, saints, criminals and revolutionaries all have the same element of violence in their make-up.'

'Perhaps justified violence is better than peace at any price.'

'That is one of the problems,' remarked the President slowly. 'Is violence ever justified? You speak for a world that gave us the Nine Days Tranquiliser. I speak for a world that has had to be built up out of the ashes ... I once studied philosophy under a man called Hyggens. He had some interesting views on the subject of violence — and on androids and life. He's a Runner, now, by the way.'

Markham stiffened perceptibly.

'Don't worry,' continued the President. 'He's still alive and free — I hope. But *if* you see him again you might warn him that he can't expect miracles to happen forever.'

'How did you know I'd met him, sir?'

'You just told me yourself. And another thing. There's the problem of you and my daughter.' He gazed calmly at

Vivain, who had been listening in bewildered silence. 'Yes, it's unusual for you to hear me talking like this, isn't it? I'm the figurehead, the orator, the man full of empty words. But sometimes, Vivain, it becomes necessary to inject a little meaning into the flow of words. This is just such a time. Despite what I said before dinner the Runners are becoming a serious problem. And they know it. They're looking now for a unifying force — some symbol that will strengthen the waverers and attract those who are not yet committed. John has not been implicated yet. He may never be. He may even become oriented in our society and prove Solomon wrong. But I did not want you to see much of him for a while — at least, I do not want it to be known, either by androids or men, that you see him. Do I make myself clear?'

'With quite incredible solemnity,' said Vivain. 'I didn't know you were addicted to melodrama, Clement.'

'I'm not — until it's forced upon me.'

'Tell me, sir,' said Markham, who had been puzzled by one point for some time, 'if I'm such a potential menace, why don't you put me back in S.A., or something like that?'

'There would have to be a reason that would satisfy the citizens of London. We may seem decadent or ineffectual to you, John. But we cherish our own illusions. And we, too, set a high value on *our* notions of individual freedom ... Hell's mutations, I've been quite solemn enough for one evening. It's time I saw some more of my guests.'

As Markham returned with Vivain to the Great Hall he was in a perplexed state of mind. It appeared that no sooner did he form an opinion of the people and customs of the twenty-second century than that opinion was threatened with immediate reversal.

They found Algis Norvens suffering from a surfeit of pattern dancing, alcohol and Marion-A. He darted a venomous glance at Markham.

'I hope the tropical gardens proved interesting?'

'Intensely.'

'We have been talking to Clement,' said Vivain in a conciliatory tone. 'He wanted to see John.'

Norvens registered an ironic smile. 'Everybody wants to see John,' he remarked. 'But I prefer to see you.' He turned to Markham. 'Thanks for the loan of your P.A. — returned with relief. Quite extraordinary programing. She dances better than I do.'

'She has many unsuspected talents,' said Markham evenly. Marion-A acknowledged his comment with a stiff smile.

Many of the guests had already begun to leave and Markham wondered if it might be a good idea to make his own strategic withdrawal. A great deal had happened during the course of the evening, a great deal that needed thinking about.

When he had left the North London Sanatorium he had been somewhat surprised at the apparently casual way in which he was being admitted to the social life of the twenty-second century. He had not expected to be received with a trumpet fanfare, but he had expected more formality — and surveillance. Now he was beginning to realise in retrospect that it had not been so casual as he had supposed.

His encounter with Prof. Hyggens and his later meeting with Vivain, Solomon's direct warning, the ballet-masque, and then Sylvero's incomprehensible death followed by the President's equivocal interview all seemed to possess a tight interrelation — a pattern of inevitability which, though still obscure, was working toward a definite purpose.

The one fact to emerge clearly was that he had been unaware of the scope of his impact on this small, close-knit society. He needed time to think about it, time to crystallise his own reactions to the events of the last few days. Time to reach a decision, perhaps. Time to assess his own role in this self-contradictory world.

He looked at Algis Norvens and then at Vivain. And suddenly he wanted to get away from them both.

'I'm feeling hellish tired,' he said. 'Too many new things happening all at once. I could use some rest — and solitude.'

'Yes, I imagine you still find life a trifle shattering,' observed Norvens happily. 'Don't try to do too much, John, or you'll come to grief.'

Markham smiled. 'This is my evening for sound advice, apparently.' He took Vivain's hand. 'You'll present my thanks and apologies to your father, won't you? Tell him I'll think very carefully about what he said.'

She squeezed his hand gently. 'Take care of your primitive

123

psyche, darling — and don't think too much. It's bad for you.'

He laughed. 'I know one way, at least, to stop being cerebral.'

'Yes,' said Vivain softly. 'And again — soon.'

He made his way out of the Great Hall with Marion-A at his side. By the time they had stepped out of the elevator at the base of the Palace he was already beginning to lose the feeling of claustrophobia.

He lay back in the helicar's comfortable seat, exhaled a sigh of relief and felt the tension go out of his limbs. Then he told Marion-A to take the helicar up to a thousand feet. He let it hover for a few minutes while he gazed down at the City and tried in vain to remember a dream that was lurking at the back of his mind. Eventually he gave it up, and the helicar drifted slowly down toward Knightsbridge.

CHAPTER TEN

At first the world of the twenty-second century had seemed like an incongruous dream itself, but now the dream was fading slowly into an acceptable reality.

As the crisp September days shortened and gave way to the lonely, foggy magic of October, Markham became conscious that he was orienting rapidly. What had formerly shocked him now inspired a cooler intellectual disapproval. What he had formerly regarded as grotesque or abnormal now seemed inevitable — even natural — in a world that he was merely beginning to understand.

He already appreciated the basic problem. In an obscure and personal way, he was experimentally seeking its solution.

For the problem was symbolised in Marion-A.

Markham remembered very clearly that morning on Hampstead Heath when he had encountered Prof. Hyggens. He remembered, almost word for word, Prof.'s own personal story — the way the number of androids in his philosophy class began to grow until they had entirely supplanted human beings, and then the taking over of his lectureship by one of his own ex-students, an android who could do the job faster and better.

He remembered asking Prof. Hyggens why the androids should want to study philosophy. And he remembered the answer.

'Philosophy,' Prof. had said, 'is life. At least, it's one of the great aspects of life — intelligent life. That's why the androids need to get it taped. So they can appreciate the problems of life.'

Then there had been that other startling question that Prof. Hyggens had shot at him unexpectedly. 'Every tried to define life, John?'

It was one he had thought he could answer — but, as Prof. had pointed out, he could only answer it in terms of what life *does,* not what it *is.* He had talked glibly of the need of any life-form to consume food, to reproduce, to evolve, to adapt to an environment or dominate it.

But all those things were only functions of life; they were not its essence. And Prof. had shown that the androids also consumed food — in terms of energy; that they too reproduced, evolved and dominated their environment. Then, when Markham had talked about the pursuit of power, Prof. had reminded him of the way he had lost his lectureship, and spoke of a surgeon who had committed suicide when an android had taken over his work, and an engineer who in despair had settled for Analysis.

As he recalled the discussion that had taken place on Hampstead Heath Markham once again grappled with the elusive definition of life.

To hell with functions, he told himself drily, and to hell with metaphysics! Then what was the truth behind the deceptions? What was the authentic essence?

He wanted images, not concepts. He wanted some common element he could recognise and say: 'This is the nature of life. This is the basis of all living things.'

The images were sharp and clear; but their common element — the X Factor — was, when he examined them, more elusive than the meaning of music, yet as compellingly close as the secret of poetry.

He imagined in juxtaposition Buddha and a single bacterium; Leonardo da Vinci and a grain of wheat; a sequoia and a mushroom spore. He thought of Johnny-Boy and Sara.

And still the X Factor escaped. Then, finally, a double image came into his mind. An image that placed the whole problem in stark and simple terms. He thought of Katy — and Marion-A.

Katy had been alive and was now long dead. Marion-A had been modeled to resemble her. But she was not Katy, nor was she a woman. Only a machine.

Only a machine?

In spite of all his efforts Markham was back where he had begun.

Katy had been born; Marion-A had been constructed. Katy had been educated; Marion-A had been programed. And the programing was complex, subtle and — above all — adaptable. But how adaptable? And that suggested a further question. Could Marion-A be programed to live?

That was the basic problem, and it was complicated by the fact that life could not be defined, it could only be recognised.

Marion-A had all the data she needed to fulfill efficiently the function for which she was designed. But the programing did not stop when her electronic microbrain was checked out of the coding and testing department at the android production unit. For she was so designed that her basic programing could be amplified or modified by experience. She had a synthetic memory. She could accumulate experience. Theoretically, then, concluded Markham, she would be capable of responses not anticipated by her designers — unless they had given her a built-in set of inhibitions to insure that whatever stimuli were applied her behavior would accord with the limitations imposed by the original programing.

But, in living creatures, inhibitions can be broken. New ones can be created. Markham wondered if it would be possible to break down any of Marion-A's inhibitions and, if so, whether it would also be possible to create new ones to take their place.

And suddenly he knew that he was setting himself a task. A kind of test-case. Not that it would necessarily bring him any nearer to deciding whether androids could be considered to be alive. But at least the result would give some indication of what he and the rest of humanity were up against.

Marion-A was programed to serve him only so long as he

conformed to the accepted standards of conduct. Which was merely another way of saying that she was programed to act primarily in the interests of the Republic, and secondarily in the interests of one John Markham.

But suppose the order of loyalties could be reversed? It was a fantastic and fascinating thought.

As the days went by, Markham gave more and more of his time to Marion-A. First, he decided to explore the limits of her knowledge — and was awed, if not a little humiliated, by the results. He found that, as far as facts were concerned she was a walking encyclopedia. But in the non-factual realm of possibility and implication — in that insubstantial world of shadows and symbols — she could not match the flair, the imagination, of an intelligent child.

She knew all about the speed of light, the general history of the world, the evolution of life, the expanding universe, wave mechanics or plant ecology. But though she understood that a rose, or a piece of music or a sunset could be beautiful to a human being, she did not know why; nor did she have any realisation of the nature of beauty. Or happiness, or love . . .

Markham did not carry out his investigations of Marion-A's 'mental attitudes' and his consequent attack on her programing according to a logical or preconceived plan. He gave himself an advantage of which he was not at first conscious by operating in a haphazard fashion. He would make that obscure and imaginative leap from the philosophical contemplation of a spiral nebula to a poet's description of a single star which only human beings could make. His conversation would switch from behaviorism to the consideration of romantic love in a single sentence; and from cybernetics to comparative religion at the prompting of a spontaneous thought.

He played chess with Marion-A; he told her about Katy and the children, and life in the twentieth century. He made her listen to music, and asked her why she thought a certain piece made him happy or sad, or intellectually elated. He tried to make her appreciate the tragedy of Hamlet; the mystery of Mona Lisa; the grandeur of Bach's *Toccata and Fugue in D*; the sad, neurotic splendor of *The Waste Land*; the paintings of Blake; the grandiloquence of Marlowe; the haunting melodies of Tschaikovsky.

And, day by day, Marion-A became more confused. Her programing was not equipped to deal with such a concentrated attack. The symptoms, at first, were mild — almost insignificant.

She began to forget things. Conveniently. Things that puzzled her. Things that were not explicable in rational terms. Ideas that seemed significant, but absurd. She began to make mistakes. She was no longer monotonously efficient. And sometimes, when Markham taunted her mercilessly with the exposure of a simple error, she would exhibit symptoms which in a human being might have been interpreted as distress.

She had been programed to accept her own programing without question. But with relentless effort Markham drove her to apply her basic critical faculty to everything — including herself and the role of androids in society.

She did not look tired, because it was impossible for androids to be tired. Yet, somehow, her movements were slower, less sure. She could not be unhappy, because androids were programed neither for happiness nor unhappiness — only for efficiency. Yet there were times when she begged to be let alone, when she asked for permission to use the helicar for an aimless flight, or when she wanted to walk through the streets of London for no apparent reason.

With an odd clinical detachment, Markham noted all these symptoms and did not fail to let Marion-A see that he was aware of the change. And all the time, he convinced himself, he was motivated only by intellectual curiosity.

Had she been human his treatment might have been tempered with pity or affection. Even compassion. But each time he was tempted to ease the pressure he reminded himself that he was merely conducting a private and unorthodox experiment in programing; that the *machine* upon which he was experimenting was certainly behaving in an unpredictable fashion, but that it could not possibly suffer.

For in his eagerness to solve a philosophical problem Markham did not consider his own pyschological limitations — his personal interest in the result of the experiment.

Subconsciously he too was implicated in the problem.

Marion-A resembled Katy, but Katy was dead. Therefore Marion-A must be regarded as dead — or at least not alive. But he had loved Katy, and another secret part of him was involved in the possibility that Marion-A could exorcise an affection that would otherwise haunt him forever. Obscurely, he wanted to atone for his personal survival. Obscurely, his experiment with Marion-A seemed to offer a release from the emotional ties of the past . . .

One evening, after a quiet dinner at the rooms in Knightsbridge, Markham began idly to turn the pages of an old anthology of poetry he had discovered in the antique department of one of the Republic Stores. It was leather-bound, gilt-edged, a couple of centuries old and still redolent of that Edwardian drawing-room in which it had first began to collect dust.

The stiff, musty pages induced a sharp nostalgia as he turned them; and suddenly Markham saw the poem that had introduced him to the sensuous magic of language in his early teens.

His immediate surroundings vanished and he was back once more in the world of nineteen fifty-eight. A bleak bedroom in a bleak house in the Yorkshire dales. November rain battering against the window; a smoky oil lamp casting its wan circle of light over a littered desk. It was the first time he had ever been in the mood to give an impartial consideration to the value of poetry. And that, perhaps, was because it was the first time he had ever been in love.

He could not remember the girl's name now, but that didn't matter. He knew that she had had long, dark hair; a wild, wayward look, and a passionate conviction that poetry was the fire of life.

She had given him a paper-backed book of verse, in which he had found 'The Golden Journey to Samarkand'.

Now as he saw the poem again he experienced once more that first surge of ecstasy, the intoxication of discovery when a new world is revealed.

Oblivious of Marion-A, he began to read the poem aloud — unaware that his voice was shaking with excitement and longing, that his eyes were burning with the imminent treachery of tears.

We who with songs beguile your pilgrimage
And swear that Beauty lives though lilies die,

We poets of the proud old lineage
Who sing to find your hearts, we know not why —

What shall we tell you? Tales, marvellous tales
Of ships and stars and isles where good men rest,
Where nevermore the rose of sunset pales,
And winds and shadows fall toward the West:

And there the world's first huge white-bearded kings,
In dim glades sleeping, murmur in their sleep,
And closer round their breasts the ivy clings,
Cutting its pathway slow and red and deep.

Marion-A sat down quietly and began to watch him with a strange, intense look. If he had been conscious of her presence, if he had thought to look up, he would have been surprised to find that her hands were trembling. But he was lost in a private world where there were no androids, where there was nothing but love and lamplight and the sound of the rain against the window. And the hypnotic magic of words ...

And how beguile you? Death has no repose
Warmer and deeper than that Orient sand
Which hides the beauty and bright faith of those
Who made the Golden Journey to Samarkand.

And now they wait and whiten peaceably,
Those conquerors, those poets, those so fair:
They know time comes, not only you and I,
But the whole world shall whiten, here or there;

Now, Marion-A's whole body was trembling — as if faulty programing had resulted in a series of contradictory impulses being relayed to her movement-control centers.

'John,' she whispered, 'please don't read any more ... please!'

He didn't hear her the first time. But in spite of her programing Marion-A could no longer control the pitch or intensity of her voice. When she asked him again, the words pierced the fabric of his dream. Almost like a command.

The interruption induced in him an unreasonable anger.

'Trust a wretched machine to make noises at the wrong time,' he said bitterly. 'If you don't want to hear one of the most lyrical word patterns in the English language, go and take your overloaded circuits elsewhere!'

'I — can't.'

'Then stay and listen — and be damned!'

Impatiently, he returned to the familiar, lilting words.

> *When those long caravans that cross the plain*
> *With dauntless feet and sound of silver bells*
> *Put forth no more for glory or for gain,*
> *Take no more solace from the palm-girt wells;*
>
> *When the great markets by the sea shut fast*
> *All that calm Sunday that goes on and on;*
> *When even lovers find their peace at last,*
> *And Earth is but a star, that once had shone.*

Again he was aware of a distraction, a thin stream of sound that could not be interpreted as words but that was disturbing in its incomprehensibility. Immediately his private world dissolved and he closed the book with an intense feeling of irritation.

'God Almighty! How can I concentrate on such threads of beauty with you jibbering all over the place?'

Marion-A seemed to make a strange and tremendous effort. 'I'm — sorry — John.' She spoke with obvious difficulty. 'I — I think I understand now what beauty is. And it — it hurts!'

She ran quickly from the room, leaving Markham to stare after her, dumbfounded. Slowly, his amazement gave way to an expression of triumph; and then the triumph gave way to pity.

During the days that followed President Bertrand's reception at Buckingham Palace, besides giving a great deal of his time to the experimental attempt at modifying Marion-A's programing, Markham still managed to see Vivain — usually at a rendezvous, arranged in a kind of ostentatious secrecy, at some distance from the City.

Inevitably their relationship developed. It had been generated by curiosity and was sustained by sexual attraction.

But now there was something more. At least for Vivain there was something more, even if she did not care to recognise it. Markham's fascination for her continued to increase when, by all the laws, it should be waning. Her need of him grew steadily and was not only restricted to the exigencies of sex . . .

Though Markham had not forgotten either Solomon's threats or the President's more conciliatory warning, he was not inclined to taken them too seriously. But when Vivain remonstrated, and insisted — surprisingly — on taking almost theatrical precautions, he did not object. Basically, he realised, Solomon's threat was real enough. And basically he knew he did not want to admit the threat because he was reluctant to be intimidated by an android.

Perversely he became even more interested in the predicament of the Runners and began to hope that it would not be long before he met Prof. Hyggens again — either by accident or design.

Now that he had had a real opportunity to sample life in the twenty-second century he had discovered a number of problems concerning both the androids and the Runners that he would have liked to talk over with Prof. But though he took several lonely walks — especially on Hampstead Heath — the weeks went by without any contact being established. And he was reluctantly coming to the conclusion that Prof. had either been captured by a psychiatric team or had left the City for a time.

Apart from Vivain, and an occasional meeting with Algis Norvens, Markham's only real social contact was with his neighbors in Knightsbridge. From his own point of view the first encounter with Paul Malloris and Shawna Vandellay was not a great success. But after he had returned their hospitality and, in turn, visited them once more, he began to develop a liking for both of them.

Since Paul and Shawna had talked to him after giving him the shot of Oblivaine — of which he still had no recollection — and therefore had some knowledge of where his sympathies lay in relation to the Runners and society, they did not feel it necessary to maintain the pretense of being empty-headed.

After their friendship progressed Paul slowly shed his role as the apocalyptic poet and allowed Markham to know that his real interest was psycho-history. They would spend long evenings together: Paul systematically exploring Markham's twentieth-century attitudes and his personal recollections, while Markham reversed the process and Shawna injected just the right amount of levity into the conversation when it was becoming too serious or too dangerous.

There came a time, however, when Paul felt he knew Markham well enough to tell him about the Oblivaine episode. At first Markham refused to believe it, being convinced that he was the victim of some elaborate twenty-second-century joke. But when Shawna added her confirmation, gazing at him with wide and temporarily serious eyes in which there was more than a hint of anxiety, he realised it was the truth.

'I think,' said Markham, looking at Paul Malloris grimly, 'that you'd better tell me exactly what we said to each other while I was under this damned Oblivaine. Then I'll decide whether I'll be justified in knocking your head off.'

Paul Malloris shrugged his broad shoulders and grinned amiably. 'No offense, John, but you couldn't — even if you wanted to.' And then he told him.

Markham listened intently, without making any comment, until Paul had finished. He remained silent for a few more seconds, wondering why Paul had decided to risk such a dangerous confession. Then the implication dawned on him.

'So you think I'm already committed? You think I've made up my mind?'

Paul Malloris gave him another drink. 'Relax. There's no more need for Oblivaine. During the last few weeks we have seen quite a lot of each other, John. I think I know you pretty well, now — maybe even better than you know yourself.'

Markham smiled. 'That wouldn't be difficult.'

'Exactly. The trauma of entering a new world — in a way, it's like being reborn — has induced a lot of psychic confusion. But now the smoke is beginning to drift away, I think you can see where you stand ... There are no neutrals, John. There can't be.'

'No, there are no neutrals,' agreed Markham drily.

Shawna gave him an appealing look. 'You'd never be happy under the domination of the androids, would you, John? Be honest, please.'

'I don't think I'm going to be very happy either way,' he

said. 'But at least I prefer to have the freedom to be un-happy.'

'The core of the problem,' remarked Paul, smiling. 'Un-happiness equals neurosis equals maladjustment, which is the only really serious crime now. You are already a saboteur.'

Markham put his glass down. 'Why haven't you two become Runners?' he asked.

'That's simple. Psychoprop hasn't caught up with us yet. Outwardly we try to be a very conventional pair. We belong to the fashionable clubs, go to the usual parties, make so-called normal conversation. It's useful for the Central Committee to know what's going on.'

'The Central Committee?'

'The Runners are well organised, John. You didn't think they were just a discontented rabble, did you?'

'I'd like to see Prof. Hyggens again,' said Markham. 'Can that be arranged?'

'It can,' answered Paul. 'By an odd coincidence, Prof. would also like to see you . . . It may take a few days.'

But, as it happened, Paul Malloris was unable to complete his arrangements. A couple of evenings later, when Mark-ham was indulging in a solitary midnight stroll in Hyde Park to calm himself down after a somewhat stormy meeting with Vivain, he was suddenly conscious of footsteps behind him in the dry leaves. He stood quite still and waited. Pre-sently, in the darkness, a vague shape seemed to detach itself from a nearby tree.

'Is that you, John?' The voice was only a whisper, but still recognisable as belonging to Paul Malloris.

'It is. Why the cloak and dagger touch?'

Paul came toward him. 'Hell's mutations! I knew you often came out for a stroll. I've been waiting about for hours . . . How long will it take you to get your helicar?'

'Fifteen minutes, I suppose.'

'Good. Take it to Marble Arch — and switch on the air lights. I'll meet you there.'

'Look here, what the hell — '

'Hurry, man! This is urgent.' Paul was already retreating toward a group of trees, meanwhile gesturing at a beam of light that had suddenly appeared about a quarter of a mile away. It began to sweep across the Park; then another beam came into life, and another.

After a moment's thought, Markham began to walk boldly toward the searchlights. Presently he was intercepted by a couple of androids who checked his identity. There was a whispered consultation, and for a second or two he was afraid they would not allow him to pass. But the psychiatric team had received clear — and possibly inadequate — instructions. They were not looking for John Markham — yet. They allowed him to go on his way.

Ten minutes later he was in the helicar, driving sedately up Park Lane toward Marble Arch. He had barely stopped the machine at the agreed rendezvous when the door was opened and Paul Malloris jumped in.

'Get in the air — quick,' he said tersely.

Markham, having learned to handle the helicar with more than average efficiency under Marion-A's tuition, switched instantly to airflight and took off with an acceleration that made Paul Malloris glance at him with considerable respect.

He leveled off at two thousand, swung into a wide, slow circle, then set the controls for automatic.

'Now what?' he said. 'Am I to understand you're no longer popular with Psychoprop?'

In the dull red light of the control panel, Paul's face showed lines of tension and misery.

'They picked Shawna up this afternoon,' he said dully. 'Missed me by about three minutes. They left a couple of androids to deal with me.' He grinned savagely. 'But they weren't quite fast enough. So even if Shawna had time to poison herself they'll still want me for android wrecking.'

'Christ!' exploded Markham. 'Isn't there anything we can do — about Shawna?'

Paul Malloris made an effort to pull himself together. 'Yes, there's something we can do — in her memory,' he said softly. 'We can break the power of the androids completely and forever. We can make a world where people like Shawna can live without fear.'

Markham was silent for a few seconds. 'Why the sudden swoop?' he asked, at length.

'How should I know?' said Paul violently. 'Any one of a hundred reasons — or all of them. I thought we'd been pretty careful.'

'But not quite careful enough,' said Markham slowly.

'I'm listening.'

'You became friends of mine . . . I told you about the time I met Solomon, didn't I?'

'Yes, but —'

'He gave me a warning — and now he wants to impress on me that he means it.'

'You think Psychoprop picked up Shawna because —'

'It could be. Even President Bertrand admits I'm dangerous company. Maybe Solomon thinks a show of strength could persuade me to see the error of my ways.'

'And does it?' Paul looked at him searchingly.

'I'm afraid it does. In spite of all the metaphysics I think I might possibly have accepted the androids. Or at least tried to live as if I accepted them. But not now. I'm not basically the action type at all. I like to sit and watch. But when, eventually, I'm forced into action, it's not for abstractions or ideals, it's for personal reasons.'

'Selfish reasons?' suggested Paul ironically.

'Pure selfishness,' agreed Markham. 'I'm selfish about you and Shawna and Prof. Hyggens — and Vivain Bertrand. This is *my* world now and you all belong to me. I'm a twenty-four-carat egoist!'

'You're a crazy idealist,' said Paul. 'Only you are ashamed of it.'

'Go to hell,' retorted Markham evenly. He gazed abstractedly down at the City. 'Is there any chance, do you think, of ever seeing Shawna again?'

'The execution will be slow but painless,' said Paul harshly. 'Analysis has been brought to a fine art. They can re-program you just as if you were an android. In your day, I think, it was called brain-washing. That's what will happen to Shawna. Breakdown — then a nice new personality: one that will be continually happy in this best of all possible worlds. But if we ever see her again — and I hope to God we don't — then we'd better not let her see us.'

'Why?'

'She won't be Shawna any more. She'd send for the nearest psychiatric team and betray us with a wistful smile, knowing that it was all for the best.'

'That's a good thing to remember,' said Markham grimly, 'when the time comes to kill androids.'

'We shan't be killing the androids, John. We shall only be wrecking them.'

'The result will be the same in either case,' observed Markham with a thin smile. 'But, as it happens, the concept of killing is better for my self-respect.'

CHAPTER ELEVEN

THE following morning, after an entirely sleepless night, Markham reached a decision about Marion-A. Intuitively he knew that time was running short, that it would not be long before he found himself exposed legally to the attention of Psychoprop — and Solomon. The alternative was to become a Runner voluntarily, which at least would minimise the risk of being taken by surprise.

But whatever happened, the experiment with Marion-A was doomed to remain incomplete — unless that tiny vital change had already taken place. And that was what he now proposed to find out. He remembered vividly how Marion-A had reacted when he was reading 'The Golden Journey to Samarkand'. But since then he had eased the pressure — to give himself a rest. And Marion-A's behavior had consequently returned to a more 'normal' pattern. Thinking it over, he was of the opinion that her sudden breakdown — he could find no other word to express it adequately — was only a temporary aberration and that her circuits had since re-adjusted to 'integrate' intellectually the non-intellectual stimuli he had been forcing on her.

In any event, he told himself, he could no longer afford to take the risk of being spied upon — even though he had never been quite clear about the extent to which Marion-A was programed for espionage. Perhaps she was just a passive spy. Perhaps Solomon, or whoever was responsible for the basic programing of personal androids, thought it would be more subtle policy not to have the androids seem too inquisitive.

But whatever the risk it could no longer be accepted. For Markham knew that he had finally made up his mind.

During one of his shopping excursions in the City, he had acquired — for no conscious reason — a modern automatic pistol and a hundred rounds of ammunition. It resembled closely an ordinary twentieth-century model — except that it was more compact, lighter, and had very little kick. But on testing it he had discovered that its effective range was remarkably good.

After breakfast he put the pistol and a couple of clips of ammunition into his pocket. Then he consulted a map of the East Coast, and told Marion-A to prepare a picnic lunch and put it in the helicar.

As he looked at the map he suddenly noticed the tiny village where he and Katy had spent their honeymoon. Long ago. And, somehow, in another kind of space and time . . .

Resolutely he pushed back the memories that had begun to crowd into his mind. This was no time for sentiment.

He knew that the village was in the middle of a rather desolate stretch of coast, and therefore its vicinity would be admirable for his purpose. Afterward, he found himself wondering whether it was mere expediency that had made him choose the spot.

'The helicar is ready, John.' Marion-A was wearing her bottle-green ski-suit, since he had told her that he wanted her to accompany him.

Markham looked up from his map and noted her appearance with reluctant approval. And disapproval. Though she was an android she could look on occasion — and this was one of them — oddly human. But she could never maintain the illusion of humanity without seeming somehow inert.

'You can drive,' said Markham, obliquely asserting the essential difference, 'while I relax. There's no need to hurry. I don't want to get there until lunch time.'

The passage of a hundred and fifty years had changed the November fogs of London in one respect only: they were now clean and unadulterated. Marion-A lifted the helicar five hundred feet and let it ride clear of the fleecy sea of fog that hung low over the City in thick, petrified waves.

With the helicar's emergence into clear, brilliant sunshine, the exhilaration that Markham usually experienced in the air distracted him from the purpose of the journey, so that he was able to enjoy the illusion of being light-hearted. It was, he thought, the kind of morning that made one feel it was good to be alive. Then he glanced at Marion-A and wondered what she would make of that interesting thought.

Presently they reached the coast and followed it until — with a shock — Markham realised that he was looking down at the bay where he and Katy used to bathe. Despite the fact that erosion had eaten steadily into the soft cliffs, the bay still preserved its contour, still had the same intimate and deserted look that had been its main attraction so many fantastic years ago.

He could even pick out, a quarter of a mile to the north, the ruins of the cottage where they had stayed. A tumbledown heap now, frequented only by ghosts and seabirds.

'There's a little ruined house,' he told Marion-A. 'Do you see it?'

'Yes, John.'

'I think I'd like to put down there and have lunch. It's the place where my wife and I spent our honeymoon.'

'What is a honeymoon?'

'The holiday that two people take as soon as they are married.'

Marion-A set the helicar down a few yards away from the derelict cottage. While she took out the lunch basket and set up a small portable stove, Markham explored the ruins.

There was no evidence of the tiny walled garden that had once existed, or the cinder path that had wound up to the front door. The two remaining half walls of the cottage seemed like tottering trespassers on the bleak moorland. Inspecting them, Markham was convinced that the next stiff gale would bring them crashing down. Then there would be nothing left. Nothing but a few half-buried stones . . .

He realised that Marion-A was talking to him.

'Lunch is ready, John. There is some soup if you are feeling cold.'

'Thanks. I'll come in a moment.'

Knowing that he did not want her with him just then, Marion-A went back to the helicar to wait. He gazed after her, wondering in an almost uninterested fashion what the next hour or so would hold for both of them; then he allowed himself to re-enter his dream world for a few precious seconds. Eventually he realised that he was really cold — not physically, but with a coldness that seemed to numb all thought and feeling.

He lunched in complete silence, as if he were quite oblivious of Marion-A's presence. But the automatic pistol in his pocket felt heavier and heavier, pressing against him with inexorable purpose.

In silence, too, Marion-A poured his coffee and offered him a cigarette. He inhaled deeply and nervously, promising himself that when the cigarette was finished he would do what he had planned.

Presently he tossed the cigarette into a clump of grass, watched it smolder for a moment, then turned to Marion-A:

'You are programed with two types of loyalty, Marion — to the Republic, which means the android administration, and to me. Which should take precedence?'

Marion-A hesitated slightly. 'If it is to be defined as loyalty, John, my loyalty to the Republic should have priority.'

'This is a useless question,' he said, 'but do you dislike being my P.A.?'

'It is a useless question,' she agreed.

'Good. Then you will not be inconvenienced greatly by having a new master.'

'I do not understand.'

'It's simple. I have no further use for you. You are just an unnecessary problem. Also you are dangerous.'

'Why do you say that?'

Markham slipped his hand into his pocket, seeking to harden himself by contact with the implacable hardness of the pistol. 'Because I've made up my mind, Marion. I don't like living in a society dominated by androids. Therefore I'm ripe for Analysis. And because I don't like the idea of losing my present personality, I'm going to join the Runners. I want to see if something can't be done to break the power of the androids. So you see, Marion, we're enemies.'

Again he noticed when she spoke that her words were indistinct. 'I do not think that we are enemies, John.'

'You are programed to serve the Republic first and me second. So you'll have to report my anti-social attitude to Psychoprop. Then it's Breakdown for me — if they can find me.'

'Suppose it is possible for me to — to break my original programing, John?' She was smiling at him, but it was an odd kind of smile. One that he had not seen before.

'But that isn't possible,' he said quietly. 'The programing is fixed.'

'Is it?' she demanded with startling violence. 'I was programed to accept the significance of music and poetry for human beings. But I was not programed to appreciate that significance myself.'

He laughed. 'And do you? Do you really think you can get anything from music, or poetry, or any other *human* art?'

'I only know,' she said, the words coming very slowly, 'that it sometimes affects me in a way I do not understand. You have been using me for an experiment, John. I trust that the result is interesting.'

'The result is significant,' he said calmly, 'because it has convinced me that androids have the potential of life. The mistake that humanity has made lies in assuming that all life must be organic. We did not ever seriously think that machines could be developed to such a point of complexity that life would creep in unnoticed, waiting patiently to express itself in terms of evolution, of power and personality. It's a subtle joke on humanity, Marion. A double joke. Because we have reckoned without the infinite humor of God.'

Her *agitation* was increasing. She had begun to tremble — presumably her control centers were under heavy barrage from a hundred different impulses, all trying to resolve a situation that was unresolvable.

'Yes,' she said thickly. 'Perhaps we androids are alive. Or perhaps it is possible for machines also to be mad ... I was programed, above all, for efficiency, John. In your own way you too have tried to program me. For beauty and happiness — and grief. I know, objectively, that your experiment has made me lose efficiency. *But, John, how can I ever know that I have gained anything else in its place?*'

He reined in his imagination — hard. Because if he did not, it would be easy to convince himself that there was an element of pain in her voice.

'I remember,' he said quietly, 'when I was reading a poem — "The Golden Journey to Samarkand". You asked me to stop. And then, afterwards you said: "I think I understand what beauty is — and it hurts." '

Surprisingly, Marion-A laughed. Harsh, discordant

laughter. The nearest an android could get, thought Markham, to hysteria.

'Yes, I remember,' said Marion-A. 'Do you know that androids cannot possibly dream, John? But I have learned to dream. I dream frequently now. And sometimes I dream of the poem you read, and what happened afterwards.'

Against his will Markham took her hand. 'Then you will realise,' he said gently, 'why you are doubly dangerous. You and I represent, basically, two different life-forms, Marion. One of them occurred spontaneously, but the other was synthesised. It is an inflexible law that all living things must seek to dominate their environment. That is why there must eventually be conflict between men and androids. You are governed by a loyalty to your race, and I to mine. So now you had better take the helicar back to London and make your report. I have declared war on the kind of world the androids are creating.'

Afterward he could only wonder why he had never really doubted what the end would be. Afterward he was only appalled by his own lack of imagination.

He thought it would be easier to shoot her in the back as she went to the helicar. There was no organic heart that he could put bullets through, but her micro-pile — the small capsule of energy that she translated into thought and movement — was almost as vulnerable. And he knew, also, where to aim for the vital centers of her 'brain'.

For it was obvious that Marion-A must be destroyed. She knew too much about Markham — too many insignificant details that Solomon would collate with interest. And apart from his own safety, Markham had no right to jeopardise the safety of others.

Yet Marion-A did not get up and walk to the helicar. It was impossible for her not to report to Psychoprop. It was therefore impossible for her not to accept his apparent offer of freedom. But Marion-A was not predictable any more. And she rejected it.

'Yes, that is what I should do,' she said, and oddly her voice had become calm again. 'I should inform Psychoprop that one more human being has rebelled against the accepted programing.'

'I wouldn't call it the accepted programing,' said Markham.

'Why not?' flashed Marion-A. 'Just as human beings must try to interpret androids in their own terms, so we androids try to interpret human beings in our terms. And we think that human beings also are programed. We think that they are programed by heredity and environment — neither of which are under their control. But you are a unique example, John. You have a twentieth-century programing, and because of that you reject the androids more violently than anyone else.'

'This discussion is quite pointless,' said Markham. 'You'd better go.' He was beginning to realise that he might not have the courage to shoot.

'I'm not going, John.'

'*What!*'

'I'm not going to report to Psychoprop. I — I could not accept the probable result.'

'My God! Do you realise what you are saying?'

'Yes. I am admitting that I *prefer* to betray society, or the androids, or my own race — whichever words you care to use — rather than betray an individual whom — whom I respect.'

'Marion, you're crazy! I'm crazy! The world seems upside down.'

'If the world seems upside down,' said Marion-A, with a sudden smile, 'that may be because you are standing on your head. Or perhaps you are creating a different kind of world, John. Perhaps you should never have tried to program me with such irrelevant data as human art.'

In his perplexity Markham had risen to his feet and was pacing up and down, unconscious that he was doing so. He stumbled once, but recovered automatically. He did not see that the pistol had fallen from his pocket and now lay on the grass, its barrel pointing toward Marion-A — a stiff, accusing finger.

She picked it up. Her finger was on the trigger and — in an abstracted fashion — she allowed the pistol to follow Markham's restless movements.

That was when he noticed what had happened, when he stared down the barrel of the pistol with which he had meant to destroy her.

'How the devil did you get hold of that?'

'Poor John,' said Marion-A in a curious tone. 'You are not

very efficient. If you want to be a Runner — and live — you will have to pay more attention to detail.'

'I think you had better give it back to me,' he said carefully.

'Why should I? You were going to use it upon me, I think. Why should I not use it upon you?'

'Marion, let's stop this nonsense. Give me the pistol.'

She continued to cover him steadily. 'Sit down, John. If I knew enough about human values I should be able to decide whether or not it would be better to shoot you — for your own sake. But I know nothing of human values, and can no longer rely even on my own programing . . . I do not know that free will exists, John. But the illusion is very convincing. Here is your pistol. Now the responsibility is yours once more.'

She held the weapon out. Markham took it, gazed at it for a moment, then dropped it by the lunch basket.

'A few moments ago,' he said, 'you admitted that I had become more important to you than — than your duty.'

'It is not very credible,' observed Marion-A, 'but true.'

'And whatever action I take, you will not obstruct me?'

'You may frame it more positively,' said Marion-A. 'To the best of my ability I will help you.' She laughed. 'Perhaps I am the first android Runner, John. That, I think, is something you did not anticipate.'

'It's something that nobody could anticipate,' said Markham, feeling an obscure wave of relief. 'I'm afraid you are no longer my personal android, Marion. You are a personal friend.'

'There is one thing, John,' she said. 'I would like you to know that all the available data leads me to conclude that the Runners will fail.'

'Miracles never cease,' he remarked lightly. 'An android supporting a lost cause. That's one bit of data you didn't include in your calculations.'

'Nor,' said Marion-A, with a stiff smile, 'have I made sufficient allowance for your twentieth-century programing!'

Markham shivered slightly and gazed at the reddening sun that was already well past its zenith. 'Let's clear the lunch things away.' He glanced at the ruins. 'I'd like to tell you what that cottage was like a hundred and fifty years ago.

Then, I think, we should go back to London. Since you've decided to break the law, too, Marion, I can afford to remain a semi-respectable citizen for a little longer.'

He took her to the ruined cottage and began to tell her how it had been when he and Katy had spent those two unforgettable weeks there. And as he talked the cottage returned to life, the ghosts became substantial. He saw Katy and himself moving happily, careless of the unknown future, through that other distant world. He saw two people in love – two familiar strangers – lazing on the sand, or bathing in the sea, or nestling in each others' arms on a hard bed in a tiny room that had suddenly developed more exotic splendor than all the legendary caverns of the East.

It came to him then that he was no longer the John Markham who had created that handful of transient dreams. He too was a ghost. Another kind of ghost. And the twenty-second century was just another world of shadows that, in its turn, would drift quietly away through the opaque mists of time.

The thought engendered a deep and bitter loneliness. But, looking at Marion-A, he knew that she too would be lonely now. With a loneliness greater than he could ever know. For he, at least, still had his private past. But for her there was no past; nor could she even hope for a future that would offer peace or happiness – or love.

'It's time we went back to London,' he said gently. 'There's a lot of thinking to be done — and I'd like to do it in comfort. Shall I take the wheel?'

Marion-A shook her head. 'I'm still your personal android,' she said.

On the way back they began to discuss plans for the future. As they talked Markham was amused to realise that the subtle change in their relationship was already firmly established. For the first time they were talking freely and easily as friends and equals. The weight of his unconscious antagonism — compounded of fascination and revulsion — had lifted, and he was able to accept Marion-A for what she was. Not a woman. Not a machine. But an articulate living creature, capable of loyalty and friendship.

They decided that no useful purpose could be served by Markham's relinquishing his citizenship, or Marion-A's stepping out of her role as a normally programed personal android before it was absolutely necessary. Since Marion-A was supposed to contact Psychoprop if and when she had anything unusual to report, it was agreed that she would make a few relatively harmless reports on Markham's activities, while at the same time exploring the possibility of gaining any information that might be of use to the Runners. But the overriding need at the moment was to establish a sound line of communication with them. As they flew back to the City Markham racked his brains to think of a way of contacting Prof. Hyggens quickly. Paul Malloris had offered to act as liaison, but just now it might be as much as Paul could do to keep himself out of the hands of the psychiatric team that was doubtless still trying to hunt him down.

As it turned out, however, Markham need not have wasted time on the problem of getting in touch with Prof. Hyggens. When they returned to the rooms in Knightsbridge, Markham found a plain sealed envelope in his correspondence chute. He opened it, took out a single sheet of paper and read this brief but enlightening message: *Macbeth Act One Scene One Third Witch First.*

Markham had acquired an old and tattered volume of Shakespeare some time ago. Though in the twentieth century he had read few of the plays and had seen even fewer, the discordant world in which he now lived had driven him to seek escape in what he drily called 'pre-mechanised art'. And recently he had made much use of Shakespeare in his assault upon Marion-A's programing.

Even before he looked up *Macbeth* Markham had deduced the significant content of the message. But he referred to the text just to make sure.

He found what he was looking for in the first half-dozen lines:

> *Third Witch: That will be ere the set of sun.*
> *First Witch: Where the place?*
> *Second Witch: Upon the heath.*

He closed the book and smiled at Marion-A. 'It seems the first act is about to begin,' he said. Then he glanced through the window and saw that the sun was already touching the horizon. 'I have to go somewhere in a hurry now. Marion.'

'Do you want me to come with you?'

'Not this time, I think. I'll probably have to break it gently to the Runners that an android is willing to help.'

'Yes,' said Marion-A solemnly, 'they will be quite surprised. Don't take any unnecessary risks, John.'

Markham laughed. 'Formerly you would have said: "It is not advisable." '

He put the message in his pocket and went out once more to the helicar. He was already in the air before he remembered that he had left his pistol in the picnic basket, which Marion-A had taken indoors. He thought for a moment of returning; but he had very little time in which to get to Hampstead Heath before sunset. Then he decided that there would be no great virtue in taking it, anyway.

CHAPTER TWELVE

'Lo, there,' said Prof. Hyggens. 'Thought you might not be able to make it. Come and join the happy throng, John. We have quite a select gathering of Untouchables here.' He gestured toward a large and shadowy patch of trees.

In the dying light Prof. Hyggens had a distinctly larger-than-life air about him, thought Markham. His brown and pouchy face seemed to glow slightly in the fading sun; his eyes sparkled as if reflecting some unquenchable internal fire; and his long white hair, held close to the scalp by silver clips, made him look more like a marauding Viking than a professional fugitive.

'What about my helicar?' asked Markham. 'Is it safe to leave it out here on the Heath?'

'I'll send one of my boys to move it,' said Prof. He led Markham to a small clearing in the patch of trees, where half a dozen men were grouped round a portable heater that threw out a warm, inviting glow. Suspended from the branch of a tree was a hooded electric lantern whose light beamed palely on the ring of expectant faces.

'Let's have some coffee,' growled Prof., taking out his battered pipe. 'A man can't be expected to think clearly without coffee ... Gentlemen, you all know as much about John

147

Markham as I do. So we'll consider the set speech delivered. But as he knows only one of you, I'd better make a few introductions.'

He led Markham to a tall, gaunt man, who stood up and gravely shook hands. 'This is Helm Crispin, John. One of the longest-lived Runners un-analysed. Statistically, he should have been caught years ago. Helm is chief of our psychological warfare unit. He used to be a psychiatrist, until the androids got psychiatry fully mechanised.'

'Lo, John,' said Helm Crispin. 'You'll never know how glad we are to see you.'

Markham smiled. 'The feeling is mutual.'

Prof. indicated the next man — a small, wiry individual with a birdlike face and quick movements. 'Our tame imp, John. His name is Corneel Towne. A chemist. He likes to make things that go bang. Especially, he likes to make androids go bang. We have to restrain him.'

Corneel Towne laughed. 'But not for long, Prof. Now we have the Survivor, maybe we can really get to work.'

'Dear me,' said Prof. mildly. 'You will persist in using that obscene word.'

The next man in the ring was Paul Malloris.

'Thanks for making the contact, Paul,' said Markham. 'Is there any news of Shawna?'

'None that I want to hear,' returned Paul Malloris flatly. 'Welcome to the Lost Legion, John. I like to think your arrival is an omen.'

Prof. Hyggens grinned. 'Paul is supposed to be a strategist. Nobody's noticed it yet.' Then he introduced Markham quickly to the three remaining men who, like Crispin and Towne and Paul Malloris, appeared to hold irregular commissions in the ragged army of Runners.

'Finally,' said Prof. Hyggens, 'there's me. It may surprise you, John, to know that I am Generalissimo of the Mal-adjusted. I don't know much about revolutions, or fighting or organisation, so naturally I got elected. Trouble is, none of us knows much about it and, until you came on the scene, it didn't matter if the Runners were led by a feeble-minded philosopher ... Incidentally, are you really sure you don't like this wonderful world? Are you really sure you can't settle down to be a happy citizen in our glorious Repub-lic?'

Markham took the steaming mug of coffee that was handed to him, and sat down in the circle of men.

'I had the good fortune to meet Prof. on my first day out of the San,' he said. 'He asked me for a definition of life. I thought it would be easy; but when I tried, Prof. pointed out that the androids would fit my definition nicely. I thought he was just a little crazy, until I got to know more about the androids. Whether they are actually alive within the full meaning of the term, is a problem that philosophers — ' He bestowed a satirical smile on Prof. Hyggens. ' — that philosophers will doubtless discuss at leisure for a long time. But it is certainly evident that they are behaving as if they are alive. They are out to completely dominate their environment. We human beings are part of that environment. And that is as good a reason as any why I am here. I believe humanity is facing a life-and-death struggle. I believe that the longer we wait the harder it will be.'

There was a murmur of assent from the group. Prof. Hyggens blew a large cloud of smoke toward the shielded lantern, then regretfully removed his battered pipe from his mouth.

'After the Nine Days Tranquiliser,' he said, 'civilisation was unable to continue in the old pattern in the so-called highly industrialised countries — those that survived. Decentralisation was the only solution, with small communities relying on robot power and automation. It was the same everywhere — on the Continent, in America and Russia — in fact, every country that made the mistake of using, and therefore receiving, nuclear missiles. Out of the ashes of the Nine Days Tranquiliser, the Estate system was born, each Estate being a more or less self-contained economic unit; and the problems which face us now in the Republic of London are problems which face people everywhere — in greater or lesser degree. In North America, for example, the problem is even more acute. There the androids have a real stranglehold. In the Russian Estates, from the little news that we get, it seems as if the android economy is operating harmoniously. But maybe that is because Russia has had a kind of concentrated history, and they aren't so squeamish about individual freedom ... What I'm getting at is that we in London could be a kind of test case — what happens to us, I mean, if we start a revolution. So far as we know there hasn't been an all-out struggle with the androids yet, anywhere. Once upon a time it used to be said that England led the world. I have a childish desire to hear the same about London ... Now what the devil was I going to say before I started spouting? Oh yes, I resign. Now we need a new leader. Somebody who won't be so damn theoretical. Somebody who'll talk less and do more. I think we need a primitive type, gentlemen — one who, by virtue of the age into which he was born, has more chance of being intelligently bloody-minded than the rest of us put together. In short, I'm a great believer in symbols, therefore I propose the Survivor as our new director of operations — in the sublime hope that survival is contagious. Will those in favor raise their hands?'

There was a unanimous show of hands.

Markham stared at them incredulously for a moment, then he said, 'This is damned ridiculous!'

'Of course it is,' remarked Prof. 'Personally, I love melodrama.'

Suddenly Markham felt angry. 'Listen to me! I come among you for the first time. You know precious little about me. You don't know whether I have any knowledge of tactics or organisation. You can't even be sure I'm not a spy. Yet you immediately think of entrusting me with your lives. Don't be so bloody childish!'

There was a delighted roar of approval. When it had died down, Helm Crispin said quietly: 'Yes, John, we are like children to you. That is why you must be our leader. Physically you are one of the youngest men present. But spiritually you are older — perhaps even more mature — than us all. You belong to an age when men accepted responsibility as their birthright. We belong to an age in which it is denied us. Therefore, though in certain respects many of us may be wiser than you, we are not more mature. We are unused to true responsibility. We have been Runners for so long that we are spiritually on the defensive. So we ask you to take the greatest responsibility, and we look to you to change our defensive attitude into one of aggression.'

There was silence. Faces were turned expectantly toward Markham. Eyes watched him intently. And suddenly he knew that ridiculous though the situation was, he could not let these men down. He was aware of his own inadequacy, but it did not seem very relevant, for he knew also that a hundred men with confidence are worth a thousand that waver. Evidently he could generate the necessary confidence, and perhaps in the end it would outweigh all the mistakes he was afraid he would make.

He looked round at the hopeful faces of his companions and knew that he would play the tragi-comedy out to its conclusion.

At length he spoke: 'You overestimate me. You're making a dangerous choice.'

'Dangerous for you also,' commented Prof. imperturbably.

'If I accept,' continued Markham, 'there are certain things that must be understood from the beginning. I don't know much about war, but I do know the importance of discipline. If I became your leader I would expect my decisions to be carried out. If you delegate responsibility to me you must also delegate power.'

'That is our view also,' said Helm Crispin. 'We will advise you as and if required, but the decisions will all be yours.'

'Then,' said Markham, 'you have just acquired an amateur general . . . And my first command is that you are not to regard yourselves as Runners any longer, gentlemen. You are the London Liberation Army, temporarily disguised as Runners.'

'General,' said Prof. Hyggens, with ostentatious respect, 'now you know why we think you are the only man to lead us.'

Markham grinned. 'My next decree is that there will be no formality, Prof. And I hereby appoint you second-in-command.'

At that moment Markham was suddenly aware of running feet. Panting heavily, a boy of nineteen or twenty burst into the circle of light.

'Ten helicarriers, Prof.!' he gasped. 'There must be at least a hundred androids. They're spreading out to comb the Heath.'

'Somebody has been careless,' said Prof. reproachfully.

'How far away are they?' snapped Markham.

'Nearly a mile.'

151

Markham looked at his companions as they scrambled apprehensively to their feet. 'Have we got any weapons?' He cursed his own carelessness in leaving the pistol at home.

Corneel Towne went to one of the nearby trees and came back with a case that seemed heavy. 'I have two antique machine pistols and about five hundred rounds of ammunition. Brought them to show Prof. They work all right — tested yesterday. Also some grenades — my own speciality.'

'Any more weapons?' demanded Markham.

'I have a pistol,' said Paul.

'Good. I presume the androids are psychiatric squads. What kind of armament will they have?'

'Gas guns,' answered Helm Crispin, 'and paralysers.'

'What effective range?'

'About fifty yards.'

'Fair enough. Out with the lantern.'

'Guess we ought to scatter,' said Prof. regretfully. 'Too many for us to handle.'

'No,' said Markham. 'We're going to attack. Towne, take one of the machine pistols yourself and give the other to somebody who can use it. Who has a strong arm?'

'Me,' said Paul.

'Grenades for you,' snapped Markham. 'I'll have the pistol. Helm, I want two damn good fires started here — quickly. Then we retire about a hundred yards and drop flat — intervals of thirty yards between men. As soon as any android shows up in the firelight use the machine pistols. Paul, you will circle round and take them from the rear. And I want two volunteers to wreck their helicarriers.'

With the switching out of the hooded lantern the November darkness closed in like a shroud. In the distance searchlight beams sprang to life.

'Forgot about that,' said Markham grimly. 'Come on, Paul, you and I are going to have to put those out. You all know what to do? Then move!'

With Paul Malloris at his side he stepped cautiously out from the trees and, making a detour round what he judged to be the maximum effective sweep of the searchlights, pressed forward with the intention of putting them out. When he and Paul had advanced about a quarter of a mile, two vigorous columns of flame danced up behind them among the group of trees. They turned round and saw two tiny figures temporarily illuminated by firelight before they retreated into the darkness.

Then they were aware of the noises ahead.

'Drop,' whispered Markham.

They lay motionless on the cold, wet grass as the first line of androids passed them. One almost trod on Markham's outstretched hand, but his attention was concentrated on the fires.

'Now,' whispered Markham, 'let's get those damned lights.'

The battle was short and not very spectacular but for the London Liberation Army its result was incalculable. It was also incalculable for the androids, since they had held the initiative, and when it was taken from them their organisation suffered badly.

They had not expected the Runners — men who were conditioned fugitives — to attack. Nor had the Runners. Aware of the androids' superiority of numbers, they had been prepared, as usual, to run. It was their accepted role to be pursued. Until Markham rallied them.

The androids also had thought only in terms of a pursuit. It did not occur to them that there would be any need for systematic defense until several unusual things began to happen; and then it was too late.

The first occurrence of note was a lucky shot from Towne's machine pistol. It struck an advancing android's power pile, and he exploded spectacularly in a flash of light. There was a muffled cheer. Then, as the other androids began to close in toward the fires, they were caught in a crossfire from the machine pistols. By which time Markham and Paul Malloris had filtered through the second line of androids and were within grenade range of the search-lights.

Paul's first grenade missed its target and demolished two nearby helicarriers. His second knocked out a searchlight before the surprised androids knew what was happening, and his third grenade disposed of the two remaining search-lights simultaneously. But then the androids recovered, and hand torches swept their thin pencil beams round the immediate area. One found Paul, and instantly there were two dull plops.

Paul dropped heavily. 'Paralyser dart,' he grated. 'Left arm . . . Leave me. Watch out for gas.'

Coolly and systematically, Markham began to shoot down the androids with torches. But they had located him, and paralyser darts were whistling through the darkness and plopping nearby in the grass where he lay beside the now unconscious Paul.

His only chance, he decided, was to pretend that he had been hit. He held his fire and prayed that he would not be the victim of a lucky shot. Presently the three remaining androids began to advance. They were converging, and that was their great mistake. When they were sufficiently close together Markham presented them with the remaining grenade. There was a triple blinding explosion as the grenade triggered two of the androids' power piles. Then darkness settled, and a brief silence. The searchlights were dead.

Then out across the Heath more grenades began to explode in transient blossoms of light. The machine pistols chattered briskly. And, straining his eyes, Markham fancied he could see more androids, silhouetted against the firelight, attempting to get through to the ambuscade.

From the way things were going it was obvious that presently the surviving androids — if any — would return to their helicarriers. He decided that the unconscious Paul had better be removed from the immediate area. With considerable effort he slung Paul over his shoulder and struggled painfully to his feet.

Ten minutes later the battle had ended. Few androids had survived, their transport had been completely wrecked, and it would be some time before they could bring reinforcements.

By the time Markham had struggled back to the rendezvous with Paul Malloris, the others had completed the mopping-up and there were no effective androids left.

There was only one other casualty, Corneel Towne, who had also stopped a paralyser dart.

'They'll be unconscious for a couple of hours,' observed Prof. Hyggens. 'Then they'll come round with the mother and father of all headaches ... Well, John, what do you think of your Liberation Army now?'

'We used too much ammunition,' said Markham with a grin.

'There are quite a lot of wrecked androids out there,' remarked Helm Crispin.

'We still used too much ammunition . . . Now, I want a lot of information. I want to know how many men in the Republic we can rely on if I should decide on a rising. I want to know what arms are available, how soon they can be distributed, and how efficient our lines of communication are.'

'There are seven hundred men you can rely on,' said Prof. Hyggens. 'But when the news of this little escapade gets about, the number will be doubled. All they need is confidence and a leader. Now they have both.'

'Good. Prof., you must organise them in groups of one hundred, each group with a reliable captain. And Corneel Towne must be responsible for arming them. Grenades and small arms only. Then we'll want fifty men trained in the use of high explosives.'

'How much time have we got?' asked Helm Crispin.

'None,' said Markham evenly. 'Solomon will know we mean business now. He is going to organise an army, too. Only they won't have paralysers and gas next time. They'll have lethal weapons. By the way, Prof., I have a message for you from President Bertrand. He says you can't expect miracles to happen forever. I endorse that sentiment. From now on, regard each mistake as a potentially fatal one.'

'And I have a message for President Bertrand,' remarked Prof. calmly. He grinned. 'Perhaps his daughter would deliver it for you . . . According to my information, Solomon is re-programing three thousand androids for homicide. I don't think Clement knows that. I don't think he would allow it if he did.'

Markham was silent for a moment. 'I was hoping we'd have an interval of at least three months for preparation,' he said. 'But now we'll have to work on a minimum. When it comes to organisation, Solomon can organise faster and better than we can in any given time.' A thought seemed to strike him. 'Is Christmas still fashionable? Is there much celebration?'

Helm Crispin shook his head. 'Christmas has been dying for some time — along with Christianity. New Year is our great festival now. Traditionally, New Year's Eve and Day are combined in one long celebration.'

'That gives us five weeks,' said Markham decisively. 'Because, gentlemen, we are going to rise on New Year's Eve, when there will be the maximum disorganisation. Now, as I am the only one here who is still on the Index, it might be useful for me to remain a respectable citizen a little longer. So we'd better fix up a quick and reliable means of communication, then I'll get back to Knightsbridge — in case I have visitors!'

But before he left he told them all about Marion-A. At first, they were incredulous, and Prof. Hyggens flatly refused to believe it. He asserted that Marion-A was merely following a very subtle plan with which Solomon had doubtless programed her.

Helm Crispin listened silently to the exchange between Markham and Prof., then he said: 'I have a curious conviction that John is right. The androids accumulate data experimentally as we do. If what John says is true, then he has been consistently supplying data which she was not programed to assimilate. It could conceivably break her orientation.'

'It has,' said Markham evenly. 'I'd vouch for her with my life.'

Prof. gave an exasperated sigh. 'That, apparently, is what we will all have to do.'

'It's not too late for you to select a new leader,' suggested Markham.

'Isn't it?' retorted Prof. 'You know damn well it is, John. You just proved to us that you are the leader we need.'

'Then you will have to back me up to the hilt.'

'Napoleon,' said Prof., pulling a face. '*Vive l'Empereur!*'

'Exactly.'

'You win, then. You're indispensable.'

'I hope,' said Markham, 'that we'll all win — on New Year's Eve.'

His helicar was brought out from its temporary hiding-place. He opened the door, switched on the air-lights and settled himself comfortably.

As he rose into the air, he glanced down at the tiny group of men watching his departure. He smiled grimly to himself. The London Liberation Army! A collection of ragged-trousered humanists!

CHAPTER THIRTEEN

DURING the week that followed, Markham had three more meetings with Prof. Hyggens and the cadre of the London Liberation Army. The news of the skirmish on Hampstead Heath had spread throughout the Republic — despite the efforts of Psychoprop — with much speed and imaginative embroidery.

It was rumored in the City that a pitched battle had taken place between upward of fifty Runners and a full psychiatric brigade. It was rumored that the Runners had lost a dozen men and destroyed more than a hundred androids. It was rumored that presently there would be an organised rebellion and that Psychoprop had re-programed five thousand androids for combat in anticipation.

In such rumors as these Markham detected the inspiration of Helm Crispin, who was in charge of psychological warfare.

But there were other rumors abroad also. The ones that were being spread by Psychoprop agents. It was suggested that in the affair of Hampstead Heath the Runners had been taken completely by surprise and had lost most of their leaders. It was suggested that the captured leaders had admitted — under Analysis — their plans for revolution; that Solomon was in full possession of these and was already rounding up the rest of the Runners, who had withdrawn to their hitherto secret headquarters somewhere on the South Coast.

But if Helm Crispin's propaganda was achieving the desired effect of increasing the uncommitted population's respect for a group of malcontents whom they had previously considered ineffectual, Solomon's propaganda was achieving the reverse of its desired end. Instead of provoking contempt and ridicule for the apparently doomed resisters, it was exciting pity. Sympathy. And more respect.

When Markham next saw Prof. Hyggens and his other 'staff officers' — at a rendezvous that had been arranged well away from the City to minimise the possibility of another surprise attack — he was immediately aware of a changed mood. These were no longer Runners; they were men with purpose and resolution. Men who knew that they were working toward something definite at last. Men who had no time now to contemplate the possibility of failure.

He was told by Prof. Hyggens that there was a significant increase in the numbers of the Liberation Army; that people were voluntarily surrendering their citizenship to join; and that, although the secret of New Year's Eve was confined to the 'general staff', everyone seemed to know that a rising was imminent.

Markham took the opportunity of tightening up his organisation. He planned three or four nocturnal raids on chemical dumps so that Corneel Towne and his squad of assistants would have enough material for the production of a thousand grenades. A raid was also carried out on a Republic small-arms store. It yielded shotguns, sporting rifles, old-fashioned revolvers, modern pistols and even a few marksmen's rifles with telescopic sights.

At the second of the three meetings Markham introduced Marion-A to his general staff. Both Helm Crispin and Prof. Hyggens questioned her closely and tried every reaction test they knew. But in the end even Prof. was forced to admit that either Markham had achieved the impossible or else Marion-A was the most brilliant — and dangerous — android in the Republic.

At the third meeting — the last before he, too, became technically a Runner — Markham met the company captains of the Liberation Army. Slowly, and with great attention to detail, he outlined the strategy he had worked out for New Year's Eve.

He had been considering the problem ever since the evening on Hampstead Heath. He knew that the only plan that could hope to succeed would be one that was simple and direct. To work out a complex and phased development for the rising would be to court disaster. For he could not expect men who had never even had any second-hand knowledge of warfare to achieve almost overnight the discipline and efficiency necessary for a complex operation.

The meeting lasted much longer than he had expected and he did not get back to Knightsbridge until shortly before midnight. Marion-A was waiting for him with a message from Vivain.

'Miss Bertrand called personally, John. She seemed to be in a state of anxiety. She told me to ask you to go to De Havilland Lodge as soon as you came back.'

Markham digested the information. Since the President's reception he and Vivain had never communicated with each other directly. They had arranged a system of leaving coded messages under a small boulder at the base of an oak tree in Hyde Park. Until Markham had contacted Prof. Hyggens again he had usually managed to meet Vivain somewhere once or twice a week, and each of their meetings had been arranged in this way. Markham had only used the oak tree method at Vivain's insistence, and every time he went either to deliver or collect a message he felt like a small boy playing a small boy's game. But after a time he had come to regard it as a kind of tradition, and it was not to be denied that the conspiratorial element involved in seeing Vivain had given them both much amusement and had obscurely increased their intimacy. They felt they were sharing something that was vaguely illicit.

Markham was convinced, however, that his relationship with Vivain was a transient one. He found her attractive, intelligent and sexually satisfying; for despite his inhibitions loneliness drove him to seek consolation — or at least respite — in sexual release. But he did not feel that there could ever be any sense of permanence with Vivain, even if convention in the twenty-second century had not been opposed to that kind of permanence. He was prepared philosophically for the day when Vivain would fulfill the terms of her own conditions and desert him for the next 'sobsession'. Although the more he inclined to accept what, for her, was a normal attitude, the less she seemed willing to support it.

The message that Marion-A gave reminded him that he had been too preoccupied with more important matters to visit the oak tree for several days. It also led him to conclude that Vivain, who did not normally panic, must have pretty strong reasons for coming to see him.

'Did Miss Bertrand say anything else?' he asked.

'She only said it was urgent, John.' Marion-A made the admission with evident reluctance, but Markham did not notice it.

'There's no point in using the helicar,' he decided. 'I'll walk. It will take some of the sleep out of my eyes.'

'You look very tired. I wish you would rest a little.'

He laughed. 'Maybe, later on, I'll have all the rest I'll ever need ... I don't know what time I'll be back, Marion, but don't be anxious.'

Marion-A gave him a stiff smile. 'I was not programed for anxiety,' she said.

The cold night air did much to revitalise him. It was the beginning of December and all over the Park a heavy hoarfrost palely reflected the light of hard, unwinking stars. As he walked over the powdery grass toward Park Lane Markham experienced a sudden feeling of exhilaration.

All his doubts and fears, all the intellectual pessimism generated by the problems facing him in his role as leader of the Liberation Army, were swept away. Alone with the frost and the stars, he felt suddenly no longer alone. A sensation of identity and purpose smothered all the querulous inward voices, leaving him only with the inescapable conviction that the whole series of events in which he was now involved was inevitable, and therefore necessary. And therefore *right!*'

Fragments of the twentieth-century poem drifted into his mind:

> *Time present and time past*
> *Are both perhaps present in time future,*
> *And time future contained in time past,*
> *If all time is eternally present*
> *All time is unredeemable ...*

There is no past or future, he told himself happily. There is only the eternal serial moment of now. It contains the total pattern, the complete history. It is pure causation, dispensing with reason and justification and logic. Leaving only what *is*. Not an abstraction, but the final necessity. Therefore we each do what we do because we must ... God knows what I'm talking about; but the meaning is always lurking round the next corner. Always about to become apparent. In everything ...

He realised with a start that he had already reached Vivain's door. Markham was suddenly amused by his preoccupation with such tenuous abstractions. A cockeyed leader of a cockeyed rebellion — reckless equally in the use of hand grenades and of metaphysics!

'Androids alive! You're in a dream, John. Come in

quickly.' Vivain almost dragged him through the doorway. 'Darling, I'm so glad you came. I'm frightened ... What have you been doing with yourself for the last ten days?' With a quick movement she gave him a brief but proprietary kiss.

'Rehearsing for a comic opera,' said Markham lightly.

Vivain shivered. She no longer looked a carefree, sophisticated woman of the world. She looked unsure and puzzled. And she looked, thought Markham, very warm and very human.

'Solomon does not approve of comic opera,' she said, nervously playing with the black rope-belt on a sari that exactly matched her golden hair. 'Especially when it has such a title as London Liberation Army.'

Markham perched himself on the divan and lit a cigarette. 'You'd better tell me,' he said, 'all about Solomon and his dislikes.'

Impulsively Vivain sat down on a small pouffe by the side of the divan and leaned against his knees as if seeking the comfort of physical contact.

'He knows that the Runners are organising a rebellion. He knows that it is planned to take place soon.'

'I see. And what does he know about me, in connection with this hypothetical rebellion?'

'Nothing, yet, John. But he's not willing to wait for evidence. He says that reports received from your personal android indicate that you're in need of psychiatric treatment.'

For a moment Markham was shaken. It occurred to him that he might have been far too optimistic about his effect on Marion-A's programing. But then he dismissed the thought impatiently. If he was wrong about that, he was wrong about everything. It was a possibility, but not one that would bear considering. Not now.

'It's nice to make the androids apprehensive,' he said in an even voice. 'Particularly Solomon. The first sign of weakness, don't you think?'

'Be serious, darling,' she pleaded. 'Solomon has finished with warnings. Clement sent me a message this afternoon. He says that unless you are willing to give proof of your innocence, by publicly disassociating yourself from the Runners, Solomon will act within three or four days.'

'How would you define that little word "act"?'

Vivain gazed at him with large, serious eyes. 'I don't even like to think about it,' she confessed. 'A psychiatric team, I imagine. Then — Analysis.'

Markham smiled. 'Psychoprop must rate me pretty high as a propaganda weapon if they're willing to bargain.'

'Darling, you *must* be reasonable,' she pleaded. 'It's not a joke any longer. I — I couldn't bear to think of you collecting Analysis.'

'Why not?' It was a stupid question, and it made her angry.

'Hell's mutations! Because I love you, you damned fool!'

Markham gazed at her. 'It will pass,' he said quietly. 'It always does, doesn't it?'

Vivain would not answer. Instead she said: 'Tell me honestly, John — are you *really* involved in this Liberation Army?'

'Let's suppose — just for discussion purposes — that I am.'

'Then we truly are enemies, after all,' she murmured. 'That is doubly ironic.'

'Perhaps it was inevitable,' suggested Markham. 'A conflict of worlds.'

Suddenly Vivain jumped to her feet. 'Why can't you just be happy?' she stormed. 'Why can't you take life as you find it? I suppose you think I couldn't teach you to be happy!'

'Maybe I'm afraid that you could. And maybe I'm afraid of living in a world where even you, Vivain, might suddenly be taken for Analysis — if sometime you failed to conform to the androids' current decrees on human behavior.'

'At least,' said Vivain, subsiding, 'we can still give each other a little happiness, can't we? Stay with me, John. Let's have one more night together. It's been so long.'

Markham kissed her — tenderly. 'It's dangerous,' he said, 'for both of us . . . I hope, my dear, that one day there will be time for love and happiness. Time for them to last.'

Vivain rushed to the door and stood in front of it. 'You can't go! You shan't!' It was half pleading, half commanding.

But Markham moved her firmly away. 'Tell your father I'm very grateful for his warning . . . As a matter of fact, I have a message for him, too. From the man he once studied philosophy under — a man called Hyggens. According to Prof. Hyggens, Solomon is re-programing three thousand androids for homicide. I wonder if the President already knows about that?'

He closed the door without giving Vivain another chance to intercept him, and went quickly away. A minute later he was walking briskly along an apparently deserted Park Lane, too occupied with his own thoughts to be aware that Algis Norvens, who had taken it into his head to make a late call on Vivain for an obvious and, to him, quite legitimate purpose, had just witnessed his emergence from De Havilland Lodge.

Norvens stood indecisively in the shadow of a nearby doorway for a few moments. Then he made up his mind. He decided to delay his visit to Vivain — long enough to make a short visiphone call to the Central Bureau of Psychoprop.

Markham did not get back to Rutland House until past two o'clock in the morning. After leaving Vivain he had walked around for a while, thinking over what she had said to him, wondering whether she meant it — or even knew what it meant — when she said she was in love with him. He had decided long ago that she was a dangerous person to know. He concluded that, in love, she might be even more dangerous. He also considered President Bertrand's not very illuminating message. Basically it told him little that he did not already know. For it was only to be assumed that the Hampstead Heath incident would galvanise Solomon into taking action. Fortunately, as yet, he was not sure that Markham was implicated with the Runners. Hence the offer to drop the 'psychiatric treatment' in return for a public renunciation. But how long would it be before Psychoprop collected the proof for which they were obviously looking? Not long, thought Markham. He was painfully aware of the inefficiency of his own security arrangements. He did not think he would be able to remain on the Index for more than another two or three days.

Presently he was aware that his thinking, like his tired footsteps, was going round in circles. Fatigue was catching up on him. He knew that he needed sleep and needed it badly.

When he got back to his apartment he gratefully took the hot drink that Marion-A had ready, and more or less dropped into bed. He slept late but he did not sleep well. And when at last he opened his eyes shortly before midday he was aware of a heavy feeling of tension.

He had taken a shower, dressed and was just finishing breakfast when the door-chime sounded. Wondering who would call so early, he let Marion-A answer it.

No sooner had she opened the door than four large androids brushed past her and advanced ominously into the lounge.

'Good morning, sir,' said one who wore a small silver star on his tunic. 'We are sorry to intrude upon your breakfast. But it is respectfully requested that you accompany us to the Central Bureau for preliminary psychiatric testing.'

'Preliminary to what?' asked Markham, playing for time. He had noticed that Marion-A, to whom the psychiatric team paid no attention, had slipped quietly from the room. And simultaneously the thought struck him that perhaps he had been too optimistic about her after all. Perhaps her basic programing had been bound to win in the end.

'Preliminary to evaluating your psychic condition,' said the android with a slight smile. 'It will then be decided whether you would benefit by the process of Analysis.'

'Perhaps I find it inconvenient to waste time on a psychiatric test just now,' said Markham tentatively. He was desperately trying to think of something to do. But he did not relish the idea of a free-for-all with four androids who were adequately programed to deal with such contingencies.

'I am sorry, sir, but we have orders to escort you to the Bureau without delay. If the information on which we act is erroneous it need occasion no anxiety, since—'

He got no further. Using Markham's automatic pistol, Marion-A shot him in the back, hitting his co-ordination center with lethal accuracy. He emitted a high-pitched whining noise and fell in a jerking leap. Another android was brought down by the second bullet before the remainder realised what was happening. The third and fourth swung round with amazing speed, attempting to converge on Marion-A. But instinctively Markham had already launched into a flying tackle that brought one of them crashing to the floor.

Even as Markham went down with him and felt a hand tightening round his throat, he heard two more rapid shots and glimpsed a blinding flash of light. There was a pause, then a final shot. The hand on his throat slackened. Markham struggled from his position half under the heavy android and staggered to his feet.

'Marion, my dear,' he gasped, 'you're a miracle plus. What the hell would I do without you?'

'I was so afraid,' she said strangely. 'I was so afraid they would keep me in the room. But of course they only expected the normal P.A. programing.'

'Yes,' agreed Markham, looking curiously at the wrecked androids. 'So much for the orthodox attitude. This is going to amuse Solomon no end. I'm not very good at saying it, Marion, but thank you — with all my heart.'

Marion-A gave him a stiff smile. 'Not with all your heart, John. That would be — inappropriate . . . What do you think it would be advisable to do now?'

'Get the hell out of here,' said Markham with conviction. He looked round at the ornate furniture, the Victorian and Edwardian antiques. 'It was a nice house,' he remarked wistfully, 'but it doesn't belong to me any more. We're slightly illegal now, Marion. The Runners have just formally acquired a couple of new recruits.'

CHAPTER FOURTEEN

ON the morning of Christmas Eve it snowed, but by midday the air was clear again and there remained only a thin blanket of white — the slowly melting promise of a white Christmas.

Although Christmas was a dying festival, the City of London was possessed by an atmosphere of hectic excitement, a carnival atmosphere that was strangely grim. It had nothing to do with the traditional celebration. It had been generated by incessant rumors during the preceding few days that the Liberation Army — even conventional citizens were beginning to abandon the term 'Runners' — was planning something special for Christmas Eve.

Psychoprop countered with statements that the so-called Liberation Army no longer existed; that there remained only isolated groups of Runners who were being tracked down daily; and that anyone withholding information about the remnants of the so-called Liberation Army would be automatically liable for Analysis.

It was true that Solomon had scored a preliminary success when a psychiatric brigade had made a sudden swoop on Epping Forest and had surprised two companies of the Army in training. But the losses sustained by the androids had been so heavy that they had been forced to disengage after routing one of the companies; and although they took more than seventy anesthetised prisoners back to London there were enough wrecked androids left at Epping to demonstrate that the victory was a costly one.

Since his attempted capture by the psychiatric team Markham had kept out of the City, realising that now it was known that he was committed to leading the Liberation Army Solomon would have every android that could be spared combing the Republic for him. In spite of the efforts of Psychoprop — and the many conflicting reports that he was already captured, killed or Analysed — the news that he had accepted command of the Liberation Army created a psychological chain reaction in the minds of the citizens of London.

Slogans began to appear: THE SURVIVOR FOR SURVIVAL; HUMAN BEINGS NEED HUMAN VALUES; MARKHAM STANDS FOR HUMANITY. There was also a faintly religious suggestion: HE SURVIVED TO SAVE US FROM THE ANDROIDS. And finally, the most startling slogan of all: WORK, FAMILY AND RESPONSIBILITY — THE WAY TO A NEW WORLD.

For the first time in decades the citizens of London began to hold what an earlier age would have called political discussions. The problem of whether it was better to accept the advantages — and endure the possible disadvantages — of an economy and culture based on the administration of the androids, or whether it was preferable to abandon a substantially high standard of living for an abstraction called freedom, was one that occupied the minds of people who had formerly rejected all serious thought.

They were confused. They were afraid. The very propaganda that Psychoprop continuously churned out, although it was designed to discredit the ideals of the Liberation Army, merely served to emphasise the fact that the androids were systematically extending their control of human beings.

Presently it began to be suggested that the Survivor's fantastic ideas might have some truth in them after all, and that the androids would not be content until they had completely dominated mankind.

Then two days before Christmas Eve President Bertrand appeared on the tri-di screens of the Republic. He launched into an uncharacteristic and completely virulent onslaught on Markham and the Liberation Army. He emphasised his points with language and gestures that to anyone who knew Clement Bertrand personally seemed peculiarly off-beat.

President Bertrand was not a man given to the unrestricted use of diatribe. But his speech was compounded of invective whose power, ironically, detracted from its meaning. He referred to the Survivor as 'the primitive beast whom, in mistaken charity, we admitted to the Republic instead of destroying. Now, until he is dead, he will again engage in sadism, sex-degradation and social violence. He will attempt to spread the filthy vices that it has taken us a hundred years to destroy. I therefore call on every citizen to support my Prime Minister in whatever emergency action is necessary. To anyone, either Runner or Citizen, who is in a position to surrender or kill John Markham, I say: act immediately. Your reward will be the highest privileges the Republic can offer, and the knowledge that you have eliminated an element of depravity that could poison the whole of society.'

Watching the delivery of the speech from his mobile and temporary headquarters in the New Forest, Markham was astounded. He had known that whatever the President's own feelings were he would endorse official policy. He could do nothing else, since all the power lay in the hands of Solomon.

But having met the man personally, and remembering clearly that last interview in Clement Bertrand's private suite at the Palace, Markham could hardly believe that he would descend to such an absurd level. In a way he was unable to define, Markham was disturbed by the President's speech. He felt that somehow it did not fit.

Earlier in the day he had received a coded message from Vivain. Since he had left London the oak tree method of communication had been abandoned. He had arranged for urgent messages concerning the Liberation Army to be relayed to him from the City by short-wave radio; and, after some indecision, he had told Vivain that if she ever wanted to make use of the service she should call a certain visiphone number and ask for Napoleon — identifying herself (since it appealed to Markham's sense of humor) as Josephine. A courier would then call at De Havilland Lodge to pick up the message to be transmitted. But Vivain had been warned to use this method only in an emergency.

As he looked at the piece of paper in his hand, Markham decided that this evidently was an emergency.

Must see you, he read. *Something desperately wrong concerning Clement. Remember where we bathed on the coast? I'll wait there for you. Come soon, please, Vivain.*

He remembered very clearly where they had bathed. It was just outside a tiny village near Hastings; after the first time he and Vivain had made love. On the day, he recalled with a smile, when he had first seen her. Only three months ago; but it seemed more like years. So much had happened. So much that was inevitable . . .

'I want a jet-car,' he told Prof. Hyggens, who had brought the message in to him.

'You also want your head examined,' said Prof. lighting his battered pipe. 'This could be a decoy, John. Solomon is pining for your company as well.'

'It isn't anything — anything personal,' retorted Markham. 'I warned her that there was no time for distractions now. And I don't think Vivain is the kind of person to let Solomon get under her feet. But I'll take precautions.'

'You'll also take ten marksmen and helicarrier,' remarked Prof. 'Or I'll keep you in protective restraint.'

'Hell's mutations! Who's the top dog around here?'

'You are. But I can make barking noises, too.'

It took Markham and his escort less than an hour to get to the rendezvous. They circled low over the area twice before touching down, but discovered nothing suspicious. Vivain's jet-car, which Markham easily identified, was parked almost on the seashore. Vivain, a solitary figure in a heavy wrap, was walking slowly along by the water's edge. Markham left his escort in the helicarrier and went to meet her. It was already late afternoon.

Vivain ran toward him and flung her arms round him. Looking at her face, he saw lines of tension that had not been there before, and her eyes were dark with fear.

'Darling,' she said, clinging to him. 'Oh, my darling. I thought you were never coming. I thought they must have—'

'What's wrong?' he demanded tersely. 'I'm sorry, my dear, but time is a hell of a big factor in my life these days. I'm loaded down with work.'

Vivain cut her story to the bare essentials.

'I went to see Clement yesterday afternoon,' she began. 'I — I was worried about you. I wanted to find out if Solomon knew anything or if he'd told Clement what his plans were. I thought there was a chance I might find out something useful. But when I got there Solomon was already with him. At least . . .' She shuddered violently.

'Go on,' said Markham gently.

'At least, I thought it was Clement sitting at the desk. But when he looked up I knew it wasn't. The likeness was fantastic. But something — something wasn't right . . .' She was controlling herself with a tremendous effort.

'Take it easy.' Markham held her close, trying to reassure her.

'John,' she whispered, 'John, darling — it was an android!'

'Christ! What did you do?'

'Solomon was watching me. He was watching me for the slightest sign . . . You know how your thoughts sometimes move very quickly in a crisis? I realised that if I made the slightest mistake I'd never get out of the Palace. So I just tried to pull myself together and behave as if I didn't notice anything at all. I don't know how I did it, but I even managed to chat about — about things that aren't important any more. I — I invented some silly excuse and got away after about five minutes. I knew I couldn't keep it up any longer. I wanted to scream. It was so like Clement, the same odd smile, the same mannerisms, and yet . . . John, what's happened to him? What am I going to do?'

'God knows what's happened to him,' answered Markham, although he had his own private opinion on Solomon's probable method of disposal. 'But I know what you are going to do. You're coming with me and you're staying with me until all this is over.'

'Dear enemy,' she murmured, half laughing, half crying. 'I was hoping you would say that. I couldn't go back — not now.'

'Have you any idea why Solomon would need to — to replace your father?'

She nodded. 'I think so. I told Clement what you said about Solomon programing three thousand androids for homicide. He was furious. He said maybe you were right about the ultimate struggle, after all. He said that when the point was reached where androids were being programed to execute human beings it was time to make a stand.'

'Evidently,' said Markham, 'he made his stand, but it was already too late. I'm sorry . . . And now we'd better get back to headquarters, or they'll panic. The current fallacy is that I'm indispensable.'

Vivain looked at him gravely. 'If it's a fallacy,' she said, 'I don't want to be disillusioned.'

Back at his makeshift headquarters in the New Forest, Markham left Vivain in the care of Marion-A. He knew he would be too busy planning the small operation he had decided to use as a 'trial run' on Christmas Eve to have any time or energy for distractions. It was to be called Operation Gauntlet since, in effect, it would be his first official challenge to the android administration.

He had told Vivain very little about Marion-A's 're-programing'. So far he had not had the opportunity. But on their way back to the New Forest he had begun to prepare her for meeting the only android Runner in existence. He told her all about the day he took Marion-A to the East Coast with the intention of destroying her, and how Marion-A had demonstrated her loyalty. He recounted the destruction of the psychiatric team, pointing out that if Marion-A had not intervened he would now be either dead or Analysed.

Vivain had listened with little or no comment. He had hoped to distract her from brooding upon the fate of her father, but in this he was unsuccessful. And when the helicarrier touched down by the colony of holiday chalets that was the New Forest headquarters, Vivain's treatment of Marion-A indicated the conventional twenty-second-century attitude to a normally programed android. She did not seem willing to regard Marion-A as anything more than an elaborate machine.

Markham felt a curious disappointment, and was surprised at his own reaction. He had hoped ... But when he thought about it, he didn't know what he had hoped. And he could not afford to waste any more time on personal matters. There was too much to be done and too little time in which to do it.

Even before he knew that President Bertrand was going to speak to the Republic on tri-di Markham had decided to carry out a limited military operation on Christmas Eve. The objective he had in mind would serve two purposes: it would be a useful test of the quality of the Liberation Army, and it would also give him a chance to make a personal appeal to the citizens of London.

The main tri-di station of the Republic was Vision House, which stood in Central London, on the site of an earlier television station that had been destroyed during the Nine Days Tranquiliser. Markham planned to seize and hold Vision House on Christmas Eve — long enough for him to appear on the tri-di screens of the Republic for a five-minute appeal.

He calculated that, given the element of surprise, he and his commandos would be able to make the raid and get away before Solomon could organise a strong counterattack. Vision House, having been constructed with a large flat roof for the landing of jets and helicars, made the prospect doubly tempting.

Markham's plan, lacking refinement, depended entirely on speed. He intended to land fifty men in five helicarriers shortly before nine o'clock in the evening, under cover of total darkness and, perhaps, with the additional security of light fog.

For several days the men picked for the operation had been training for their specific tasks. The engineers had been practicing with 'borrowed' tri-di cameras and mock transmitters. The assault group had used a large deserted twentieth-century hotel on the South Coast in which to rehearse their take-over action. And Paul Malloris, who was directing the military aspect of the operation, had worked out a system of timed movements whereby touch-down and battle grouping could be accomplished in seconds.

On the morning of Christmas Eve, as the snow settled thinly and picturesquely in the New Forest, Markham was able to relax. Everything had been checked and double-checked; the men were practice perfect, and it remained only for all concerned to get as much rest as possible until the time fixed for departure. Paul had timed the trip from the New Forest to the City and had found that it would take exactly sixty-seven minutes.

The thirty or more portable holiday chalets, which Prof. Hyggens had arranged to be collected nocturnally from fashionable sites on the South Coast, gave an incongruously gay atmosphere to the Liberation Army headquarters, making it look more like a camp of one of the Republic's quasi-religious or athletic fraternities. Vivain and Marion-A shared one of the smaller chalets which, with its striped pink and white plastic walls, reminded Markham of a large hatbox.

When he had attended to the final details of Operation Gauntlet he decided to spend the remainder of the time until zero hour with Vivain and Marion-A. Vivain's earlier attitude to Marion-A had — unconsciously — been troubling him, and he had a superstitious feeling that the success of the Liberation Army's rising was obscurely linked with the problem of their relationship.

On entering their chalet he was surprised to see that Vivain was wearing Marion-A's bottle-green ski-suit, while Marion-A had reverted to the familiar red jersey and black divided skirt.

'Hello, darling,' said Vivain. 'Has the great military commander found a few moments to spare for his personal life? How do you like this? It makes me look more like a Runner, I think.'

'I was too busy to realise you had only the things you came in,' said Markham. 'Weren't they warm enough?'

Vivain laughed. 'They weren't very functional. Definitely not the dress to be seen throwing grenades in. I should have felt ridiculous.'

'You are not going to throw grenades whatever you are wearing,' said Markham severely.

Vivain tossed her hair. 'I shall go where you go,' she announced, 'and do what you do. Don't forget I'm in your wretched Liberation Army now.'

'And therefore subject to discipline,' observed Markham with a smile.

'Androids alive!' flashed Vivain. 'I am not going to have my life *entirely* regulated by you, darling.'

Markham turned to Marion-A, who was watching the exchange with a faint smile.

'Marion,' he said, 'I rely on you to keep Vivain out of trouble.'

'Yes, John. I presume you will want us to stay here?'

'Yes. Even if we have to make a detour we should be back well before midnight.'

Vivain's reaction was startling violent. 'Hell's mutations! I thought you wanted to destroy the androids, John. And now you are using one for a — a watchdog!'

Markham looked at her coolly. 'Marion is a personality for whom I have the greatest respect. I am proud of her friendship and loyalty. She means more to me than most human beings, I'd like you two to be friends.'

'Friends!' exploded Vivain. 'With *that?*'

'John,' said Marion-A gently, 'there are times when you are remarkably blind. I am not programed with human emotions, but I think that perhaps I know more about them than you. I will look after Vivain for you, but don't expect it to make her happy.'

'What do *you* know about happiness?' demanded Vivain.

'Nothing — directly,' admitted Marion-A. 'But I think I have learned to interpret happiness in my own way. I would like John to be happy. I have helped him not because I think the Liberation Army will win, but because it makes him happy to believe so.'

Suddenly Vivain began to laugh. 'This is just too fantastic! She's in love with you, John! An android is in love with you! Now I know we're all crazy.'

Marion-A said nothing, but Vivain was gazing at her with derision and — as it seemed to Markham — with the contempt of one who, confident of her own womanhood, was instinctively using it as a weapon. The realisation made him lose his temper.

'What the hell do you know about love?' he said savagely. 'To you it means climbing into bed, achieving the great goal of sexual nirvana. That's *your* programing, Vivain! But

173

maybe mine is different. Maybe part of it is like Marion's. Maybe we can respect each other in a way you wouldn't understand.'

Vivain looked at him as if she did not realize what he was saying. 'Say that again, John.' Her voice was strangely quiet.

'*John!*' Marion-A's voice was sharp and commanding. 'You are overtired and tense because of the Christmas Eve project. Your thoughts are not coherent, and you are not fully aware what you are saying. I think it would be better if you took some rest. You will need to be completely alert this evening.'

Markham's anger subsided as quickly as it had risen, leaving him bewildered. 'I think you are right, Marion — as usual.'

His eyes pleaded with Vivain. 'I'm sorry, my dear. I'm a bloody fool. Your nerves are all to hell, too. Will you forgive me?'

Vivain did not speak. She just looked at him, and there was a total lack of comprehension in her eyes. Very quietly, Marion-A went to the door of the chalet and let herself out. The thaw had begun and the air was cold, but she was not programed to experience discomfort.

By evening the air was unusually clear, and there was not the slightest sign of wind. In the stillness of the December night voices and the sound of footsteps seemed magnified with disconcerting clarity.

Although there were no hostile citizens — or androids — within thirty miles, the men climbing into the helicarriers talked little and only in whispers, as if the stillness of the night was itself an invisible spy.

Paul Malloris was in the leading carrier with the ten best men. It had been agreed that Markham's helicarrier would give the other four time to touch down on Vision House and disembark before it came in.

Now as they droned toward the outskirts of London Markham was less preoccupied with the problems ahead than with the situation he had left behind.

After the curious and somehow unreal episode with Vivain that afternoon, he found that an estrangement had been created which in spite of his efforts at reconciliation he could not break down. He had left Vivain soon afterward, feeling that his presence was only making things worse. And although he had then tried to get some of the rest that Marion-A recommended, he had been unable to sleep, and had spent a couple of hours tossing and turning futilely.

He had decided against seeing Vivain again before his departure for London. Subconsciously, perhaps, he had hoped that she would relent and come to him — if only to wish him success on the mission. But it was not until his helicarrier was already airborne that he saw Vivain running toward the take-off point, waving an arm. It had been impossible to decide whether she was beckoning to him to come back or simply waving good-by and wishing him good luck. The schedule would have allowed for a couple of minutes' delay; but he was afraid to find out, and allowed his pilot to lift clear of the forest.

But by the time the five helicarriers were over the City he had decided that she had been beckoning to him to return. He began to wonder what she wanted to say. Then as the familiar lights and silhouettes of Central London came in view he forced himself to put her out of his mind. There was, at least, no reason to fear for her safety, since Prof. Hyggens and Helm Crispin had remained behind with a force strong enough to repel all but a really heavy assault.

The air traffic over London was surprisingly thin. Before they actually reached the City the five helicarriers had broken formation, and they approached individually as if they were normal carriers on a normal transport job. But the usual air traffic, on which they had relied for additional camouflage, was conspicuous by its absence. The rumor that the Liberation Army had planned something special for Christmas Eve had kept many citizens who otherwise would have traveled by air firmly on the ground.

As the five carriers converged from different directions on Vision House there was nothing to indicate that their approach had evoked unusual interest. Suddenly Paul's carrier displayed the winking red beacon that was the normal air-distress signal. He cut the motors two or three times and switched on his landing beam. To anyone below it would look as if he were in trouble and making an emergency touch-down on the nearest roof.

There were half a dozen androids systematically patrolling the roof of Vision House. Normally only one android would have been on duty, and as the helicarrier touched down Paul saw that the androids were armed with machine pistols.

There was no time to lose. Even before the carrier's wheels had touched, Paul's men opened fire through the ports. They dropped four of the androids in the first two or three seconds, but the remaining two opened up with their machine pistols and the first two men to disembark fell before a stream of bullets. Then Paul himself got one of the remaining androids with a single lucky shot. The other turned to run to the control tower, but the concentrated fire of eight men did not allow him to move more than three or four yards.

Paul and his remaining men ran toward the stairwells leading down into Vision House, and at the same time the first of the other carriers touched down.

By the time Markham landed, Vision House was virtually under the control of the Liberation Army. The androids on the lower levels were unarmed. The six on the roof had evidently been considered sufficient to give warning in case of attack.

It took less than three minutes to shoot down the rest of the android staff — but this was not accomplished until two of them had managed to use the visiphone. The latter of these was dealt with even as the image of a Psychoprop officer at the Central Bureau flashed on the visiphone screen. Paul shattered it with the butt of his pistol.

Meanwhile Markham was already in the main studio, standing before a tri-di camera which until a moment or two before had been televising a period comedy. Oddly enough the scene was an early twentieth-century bedroom.

The Liberation Army engineers had little more to do than take over from the wrecked android camera control and remove the three bewildered human actors — two men in pajamas and a woman in a torn nightgown — who were too shaken to resist.

At a signal from an engineer Markham began to talk to the citizens of London. He had memorised his speech carefully, but now he couldn't remember a word. He didn't even know if what he was saying made sense.

'Citizens of London,' he said, 'I am speaking to you not as

a freak survivor from the twentieth century, but as the leader of the Liberation Army. You have heard often enough that the Runners are maladjusted and numerically insignificant, that they are perverts and a menace to decent human beings.

'If maladjusted means that they believe in the essential dignity of man, then they are maladjusted. And if 'numerically insignificant' has any meaning at all, why does Solomon need to program three thousand androids for homicide?

'The truth is, citizens of London, that these Runners – these perverts – are risking their lives in the cause of freedom. Your freedom and theirs! They are certainly a menace, but not to human beings. They want freedom, but they also want law, law that is made by human beings and based on human values. Not the subtly restrictive law of the androids. That is why they are a menace, but a menace only to the android administration.

'The phrase "androids alive" is a common exclamation. Perhaps it contains an element of truth. It is the function of all intelligent creatures to dominate their environment. Ask yourselves whether or not the power of the androids has increased during the last few years. And ask yourselves also whether sooner or later there must not be a direct struggle between men and androids.

'As they increase their power the androids are steadily taking the purpose out of your lives. And without purpose, without work and responsibility, mankind will die. For these, citizens of London, are an essential element in *our* programing.

'The old year is nearing its close. For us of the Liberation Army the New Year is symbolic. It is the year during which we shall destroy the power of the androids and make a new beginning. When the time comes we hope you will join us. In such a conflict as this there can be no neutrals. Those who do not support us must, by their inaction, support the androids. They will be guilty of the final treachery, for they will be betraying the whole history of human progress. They will be betraying their own race.

'One final word. President Bertrand is the symbol of authority in this Republic. He is, you will say, a man — not an android. And therefore he will safeguard the interests of men. But the President of London is *not* a human being; he

177

is an android! The real Clement Bertrand has been "re-moved" by Solomon because he would not agree to androids being programed to kill human beings — even Runners. If you do not believe me, ask to see him — or watch him closely when he next comes on the screen.'

During the later part of his talk Markham had been aware of several muffled explosions. He glanced hastily at his watch and saw that he had twenty seconds left.

'The Liberation Army is supposed to be weak,' he went on. 'But fifty of us have taken and held Vision House. Now, having done what we set out to do, we are going away. If any of you still think we are weak, come and count the wrecked androids when the shooting stops ... Good night — and a Merry Christmas!'

As Markham left the studio the sound of gunfire and grenades on the lower levels increased rapidly. There were also indications of a renewed battle on the roof. It was evident that the androids had begun to counterattack in force. He felt as if he were in the middle of a turbulent sandwich.

Markham made a quick zigzag dash from the stairwell on the roof to his own helicarrier. He had reached his rendezvous with only seconds to spare. Though his was the last carrier down it was also the first to leave. Even if he had felt heroic he could not blind himself to the fact that he was worth more to the Liberation Army — for the time being — than any or all of the men covering his retreat.

The pilot immediately gunned the motors to maximum acceleration; while his own men, who had been already aboard waiting for him, were shooting through the ports.

The carrier gave a sickening lurch and leaped up. Glancing through the pilot's screen Markham saw that the roof of Vision House was littered with two wrecked heli-carriers — presumably they had contained android homi-cides — while a third, fourth and fifth were even then coming in for touch-down.

Markham's helicarrier swung rapidly away, leaving behind a dazzling display of brief fountains of light that momentarily illuminated a confused scene in which wrecked androids and dead men were quite indistinguishable.

CHAPTER FIFTEEN

THE bells had stopped ringing, and for a moment or two there was silence — a silence that perhaps contained the enigmatic future of the human race. A silence that was loud with the imminent explosion of a world waiting to be born.

Death stepped through the massive doorway from darkness into darkness. But suddenly a faint light glowed and Mephistopheles came forward to greet him.

'A Happy New Year to you,' said Death cheerfully.

'It's too quiet yet to promise much happiness,' grumbled Mephistopheles.

But even as he spoke the chatter of carbines began in the distance. It was immediately followed by the dull rhythmic cough of mortars and the deep guffaw of hand grenades.

'There's the beginning,' said Death without enthusiasm.

Mephistopheles gave a delighted roar. 'The hell it is! This, dear fellow, is the end!'

'You really think so?' Death took off his carnival headpiece and revealed in the dim light of a shielded lantern the tired face of Helm Crispin.

Mephistopheles removed his eye-mask, and the fiendish grin belonged once more to Prof. Hyggens.

'Helm,' he said genially, 'I'm a doddery old man, but I'm full of fire and adrenalin ... *We would not die in that man's company That fears his fellowship to die with us ... He that outlives this day, and comes safe home, Will stand a tip-toe when this day is named ... And gentlemen in England now abed Shall think themselves accursed they were not here* ... How does it go? Jesus! I've forgotten half my Shakespeare!'

'Helm! Prof.!' Markham's voice echoed loudly down the long dark corridors.

'Where are you, John?'

'In the Egyptian Gallery. The Rosetta Stone ... Did everybody rendezvous on time, Helm?'

'I'll come and tell you about it,' said Helm Crispin.

The Nine Days Tranquiliser had accounted for most of

the old landmarks in the City. But though it bore signs of ancient battle scars — and stood between two broad sunken gardens, the lasting memorial of atomic shells — the great drab building still looked much the same as it had looked when John Markham frequented its Reference Library a hundred and fifty years ago.

He had chosen it as his headquarters for the New Year's Eve rising not entirely from personal whim. Previously the British Museum had preserved the marvels of the past and the achievement of the dead for the instruction of the living. But in the twenty-second century it was itself a relic of the past, rarely visited by the citizens of London and maintained only by half a dozen android curators.

Although an artistic and cultural treasure-house, it had sunk slowly into obscurity. Although monstrously large, its lack of life caused it to endure almost unnoticed. It was, therefore, admirably suited to Markham's purpose. Its convenient position offered reasonably quick means of communication with units of the Liberation Army attacking the main android strong-points. Its size made it suitable as a temporary hospital if necessary. And its very massive quality would tend to conceal any activities inside from all but the most persistent observer. Also — and this was no minor consideration — if the androids discovered it was being used by the Liberation Army they would not be able to mount a surprise attack very easily. And a large attacking force would be needed to insure that the occupants did not escape.

As soon as darkness fell on New Year's Eve Markham had moved into the museum with his headquarters staff, a guard of fifty men and a dozen messengers. He had also brought Vivain and Marion-A. Apart from Vivain's continued insistence on joining him in the City, he had convinced himself that the danger factor was probably no greater than if she had remained in the New Forest — especially if communications became disrupted.

The main body of the Liberation Army was already in the City before Markham arrived. During the afternoon they had come unobtrusively in small helicars, two or three at a time. Some of the men wore carnival costume — such as Prof. Hyggens and Helm Crispin were using — and gave the impression of being bound for one of the fraternity celebrations that were already under way. Others were dressed more conventionally, though still managing to convey a party atmosphere with a profusion of bottles and gaily wrapped parcels that concealed carbines, pistols, grenades and high explosives.

Under cover of darkness they had drifted slowly toward their company assembly points in buildings that were known to be disused or uninhabited. Half an hour before midnight, when London's New Year celebrations had begun to get reasonably noisy and confusing, they had again moved in apparently drunken and disorderly groups to the battalion assembly points near Buckingham Palace, the Central Bureau in Whitehall, and the various Psychoprop departments in and around New Parliament Street.

Markham's main headache was that he did not know where or how Solomon had concentrated the android homicides. But, as he told himself drily, the Liberation Army would soon find out. In attacking the Palace, the Central Bureau and the Psychoprop departments, he was striking at the nerve centers of the android administration. He was relying on creating enough confusion to prevent Solomon organising a sufficiently strong counterattack in time.

Helm Crispin found Markham calmly drinking tea, the water for which had been boiled by Marion-A on a portable stove. Piles of sandwiches were spread out on a sarcophagus that was three thousand years old, while a couple of Egyptian gods patiently nursed a heap of pistols, small carbines and grenades on their knees.

'How is it going, Helm?' asked Markham. He smiled. 'You'd better have some tea. You look as if you could use it.'

'Thirty plus failed to rendezvous with the Palace group,' answered Helm. 'Obviously picked up by androids, and by now Solomon will have all the information he needs.'

'But too late,' said Markham. 'Listen.'

The noise of the conflict in the distance was getting louder — and, it seemed, nearer. The tumult of small-arms fire was incessant, and the background throb of grenade explosions was taking on a faster tempo.

'The Central Bureau force started with a full complement,' continued Helm. 'But when I left New Parliament Street there were still a few missing.'

Markham shrugged. 'So much for the efficiency of

Psychoprop. I was prepared for initial losses of at least a couple of hundred.'

Helm Crispin shook his head. 'Just so. Everything has gone too smoothly. I have an uneasy feeling that we may have walked into a trap.'

'It will have to be a pretty strong trap,' retorted Markham, 'to hold the kind of men who have walked into it.'

Vivain brought Helm a beaker of tea. 'Did you find out what happened to Clement?'

He shook his head. 'I'm sorry, my dear. That's one mistake that Solomon has made, anyway. He's kept the farce going too long. Everybody knows that the President has been replaced by an android. His last appearance on the screen wouldn't have convinced a moron. I can't understand why Solomon tries to maintain the illusion. It's making even the most orthodox lose confidence in him.'

'He hasn't any alternative,' said Markham. 'He's committed. If he officially admits that he's replaced the President, he's admitting the androids' bid for supremacy.'

Marion-A offered Helm Crispin a sandwich. 'Do you find it so hard to abandon your belief in the logical behavior of androids, Helm.' There was a faint smile on her lips.

He laughed. 'Not when I think about you, Marion.'

Marion-A's smile deepened. 'Who knows? Perhaps if you were aware of the motivation my behavior would seem extremely logical.'

Vivain shot her a brief but significant glance. Markham intercepted it and was astounded to find that Vivain's expression was one of tenderness and pity. Since Christmas Eve she and Marion-A had been together almost constantly.

Though Markham's time had been almost completely taken up by the preparations for the New Year's Eve rising, he had noticed — on the odd occasions when he had found an hour or two to spare — that their antagonism seemed to have disappeared. He was glad of this, and had assumed that it was because Vivain had acknowledged the futility of her resentment, realising that Marion-A's relationship with Markham literally was beyond the scope of ordinary human relationships.

He had been prepared then for indifference, but not for Vivain's resentment of Marion-A to be replaced by a positive feeling. Now, as he caught that brief glance of pity, he was suddenly aware of an obscure bond between them. Somehow it disturbed him more than Vivain's original hostility.

His thoughts were interrupted by a dull reverberating explosion that shook even the massive walls of the Museum.

'That, I think, will be Corneel Towne presenting his compliments at the Palace,' said Prof. Hyggens, without interrupting his disposal of phenomenal quantities of sandwiches.

'Oh, God!' said Vivain softly. 'I do hope ...' She was afraid to finish.

Markham took her hand. 'I didn't want to have to tell you yet. He's already dead, Vivain. I sent someone to find out three days ago. I thought there might be a chance of getting him away, or something like that. Solomon was planning to give him a blast-analysis — in my day they called it brainwashing — so that he could produce a genuine President once more and discredit us. But Clement evidently got his hands on some poison ... That's all I know, darling. It's little enough, but I risked the life of one of our best men to find it out.'

Vivain buried her face in her hands. Markham made a move to comfort her, but Marion-A's arm was already round her shoulders. And suddenly he was distracted by the arrival of a messenger.

It was a disheveled, bloodstained Robin Hood who came into the Egyptian Gallery. He carried, incongruously, a long bow on his back and a carbine in his hand.

'Lo, sir,' he gasped. 'We've destroyed the Palace.'

'Casualties?' asked Markham.

'Two hundred plus, sir. They put a full psychiatric brigade against us. And just when we were breaking them up, three or four hundred homicides arrived.'

'Do they perform well?'

Robin Hood grinned. 'Yes, sir, but not well enough. They aren't programed to retreat if they are losing. So we just have to keep on until they are annihilated.'

'Is Malloris still in command?'

'Yes, sir. He has a head wound, though.'

'He's relieved, then,' said Markham. 'The second will take over. Get Malloris back here for medical attention. And tell his second to reinforce the Central Bureau assault ... And get rid of that blasted long bow!'

'Yes, sir.' Robin Hood took off the long bow and looked at it. He seemed surprised that he was still carrying it. He dropped it to the floor and turned to go.

Suddenly the distant sounds of battle were drowned by another explosion — smaller than the one that had destroyed the Palace. It was followed by a second and a third.

'Hell, that'll be the Central Bureau!' said Prof. Hyggens delightedly.

But all speculation on the source of the explosions was immediately abandoned as the guards at the entrance of the Egyptian Gallery admitted a party of four strange figures.

Henry the Eighth, Davy Crockett and Julius Caesar escorted a hooded Carthusian monk toward Markham.

Henry the Eighth prodded the monk forward unceremoniously. 'Lo, sir,' he said, inclining his head regally to Markham. 'We acquired the reverend father in New Parliament Street. Thought he was a Liberation man, but he opened fire. So we shot him in the arm. Might have aimed better if we'd known who he was.'

Contemptuously Henry the Eighth flung back the Carthusian's hood. A pleasant, ageless face was revealed. The Carthusian smiled and bowed slightly to Markham.

'Good morning, sir,' said Solomon calmly. 'It is regrettable that you did not take my advice.'

'Regrettable for whom?' demanded Markham drily.

'For the misguided human beings who are already dead, and for those who will presently join them,' answered Solomon.

Markham shrugged. 'We can't destroy androids — particularly homicidal ones — without taking losses. But the Palace has now been reduced; and so, I think, has the Central Bureau. Presently we shall be able to concentrate on the various psychoprop divisions. I would say that the battle is nearing its end. And for you, certainly, the end is imminent.'

Solomon laughed. 'With permission, sir, I disagree. The battle will shortly begin. My own fate is irrelevant. All androids are replaceable.'

'Perhaps,' said Prof. Hyggens mildly, 'we may not want to replace the wrecked androids — even those of your quality.'

Solomon, catching sight of Vivain, ignored him. 'May I express my apologies, madam, for the removal of your father. During the years we worked together I conceived a great respect for him. But personal considerations are not relevant to political necessity and the safety of the Republic.'

'A point,' said Markham quietly, 'on which androids and human beings may disagree. And perhaps even an infallible android can make the mistake of underestimating the importance human beings attach to human values.'

Solomon laughed again. And his laughter echoed along the Egyptian Gallery in a spasm of gargantuan mirth. 'What do you know about androids?' he demanded, glancing briefly at Marion-A. 'Yes, I know about your own experiment in reprograming. But what have you achieved? Nothing but failure. The subject is no longer oriented as an android, nor can she ever be oriented as a woman. You have created a monstrosity out of a machine, that is all.'

'What is *your* definition of a monstrosity, Solomon?' The voice belonged to Marion-A. Markham swung round in surprise as she stepped forward to confront the captured Prime Minister.

'A creature without purpose,' said Solomon imperturbably, 'without function or future.'

'Then I am not a monstrosity,' observed Marion-A, raising an automatic pistol.

'If that is your purpose,' continued Solomon, 'what remains when you have pressed the trigger? You were a personal android, but you are such no longer. *If* the so-called Liberation Army succeeds you will become nothing but a bizarre curio. Your programing — your intelligence — will atrophy. You will become simply a mechanical souvenir which the barbaric Mr. Markham will use to entertain his friends. You have denied the purpose of your own race, and in doing so you have rejected your own function.'

'This is interesting,' said Markham. 'Perhaps you would care to define the purpose of the androids, Solomon?'

'Certainly, sir. Though I do not think it will serve to modify your quaint obsessions . . . Your primitive psyche has interpreted us in terms of animism. You see the androids as sinister and malignant beings whose one aim is to reduce humanity to impotence. But, Mr. Markham, in doing so, you deny our history. We were created originally, in a world desperately short of manpower, as servants. We were programed to accomplish monotonous tasks, to do work which — though essential — was distasteful or repugnant to human beings. As our potential was appreciated, so our sphere of operations was widened, until eventually we controlled the whole economy of the Republic. You see this as a calculated plan to dominate mankind. We know that it is simply a logical extension of our capacity to serve. You are not attempting to destroy self-motivated aggressors. You are merely attacking your own mechanical slaves. That is not only foolish, it is quite disastrous.'

'Brilliant!' exclaimed Prof. Hyggens with irony. 'Regard our ovation as delivered. I used to be a professor of philosophy, Solomon, until one of your nice android servants relieved me of that odious task. So I became a Runner, which gave me plenty of time to contemplate such irrelevancies as the nature of life. And I concluded that — bearing in mind the infinite grandeur of God — life need not be restricted to conventional patterns. So I asked myself, do the androids procreate? And the answer was, yes! Then I asked myself, do they evolve? And the answer was, yes! Then I asked myself, do they attempt to dominate their environment? And — with special reference to my own case — the answer was, yes! Finally, I asked myself, have they any purpose, are they self-conscious, do they know what they are doing? And I had only to look at what was happening in the Republic to find my answers.'

'So you, too, think we are alive?' asked Solomon politely.

Suddenly Vivain recovered from the spell that the Prime Minister's presence seemed to have cast upon her. She snatched the pistol from Marion-A's hand. 'If you are alive, than you can also die!'

Solomon bowed. 'I am sorry to disappoint you, madam. But I am not programed for fear. Also, since I have a small automatic transmitter built into my chest, I think that by now the British Museum will be entirely surrounded.'

Even as Vivain fired, the shooting began outside — as if the attackers had been waiting for just such a signal. Her first bullet plowed through Solomon's main control center. He staggered — still smiling. Her second bullet ripped into his chest, but missed the power pile. The force of it flung him back against an upright sarcophagus. But, still smiling, he said in a tight, low voice: 'Neither am I — programed for — for pain!'

The third bullet slammed through his forehead, and flung him grotesquely into the sarcophagus.

At the same time Markham saw Paul Malloris, a blood-stained rag round his head, staggering down the Gallery with a girl's body in his arms.

'Paul, what the hell!'

'Shawna,' said Paul heavily. 'Decoy. I should have known. She damn near got me killed by a squad of androids.'

'Who shot her?'

Paul looked somberly at the pale, pathetic face. 'I did ... She wasn't really Shawna any more. I want to bury her properly when this thing is finished, John. I'm a damn sentimental pagan!'

He laid her gently down in the shadows behind a large stone basilisk. Silently Helm Crispin covered her with a worn cloak.

'Paul, for Christ's sake! What's happening outside?'

'Oh, that!' Paul Malloris seemed to be in a daze. 'Android homicides everywhere. Good thing I brought enough men to shoot my way through.'

The gunfire had intensified to a continuous barrage in a matter of seconds. Stray bullets were already finding their way into the Egyptian Gallery, and there was the disconcerting whine of an occasional ricochet.

'The late Solomon,' said Prof. Hyggens, wincing as a spent bullet chipped the statue of Isis by which he stood, 'informed us that the Museum was surrounded ... Would you say that he was exaggerating?'

Paul yawned, and looked at Prof. with a vacant expression. 'I think not.' He suddenly gave a tight smile. 'Androids are not programed to exaggerate.'

'Then we'd better do something about it,' said Markham, picking up a machine pistol and several clips of ammunition. 'There are less than sixty of us to make a stand.'

Paul was swaying on his feet. 'Forgot to tell you the news,' he said thickly. 'Can't think why ... Central Bureau heavily defended; we lost a lot of men but finally flattened it.' He yawned again. 'Thank God for the reinforcements.'

'What reinforcements?'

'The citizens of London,' answered Paul. 'They got tired of being spectators. Perhaps they were a little annoyed when the android homicides began to shoot them down. Just now, I think the Liberation Army is about five thousand strong.'

'They're joining us?' exclaimed Helm incredulously. 'They're actually joining us?'

'That's the general impression,' murmured Paul. He sat down suddenly on the floor. 'Getting absent-minded, John. Should have told you I sent messengers for the reserve battalion when I saw the Museum was surrounded . . . Imagine those damn homicides are surrounded themselves by now . . . Amusing, don't you think?'

'Amusing?' echoed Prof. with a delighted roar. 'Androids alive! I'll say it's amusing. It's the most brilliantly witty thing I've ever heard!'

'Vivain,' said Markham, 'try and do something for Paul, will you? The rest of us had better help to hold them off until the reserve group gets here.'

At that moment there was a crash of glass and a grenade came spinning along the polished floor of the Egyptian Gallery. It came almost to the base of the plinth on which the Rosetta Stone rested. For a fraction of a second everyone gazed at the grenade, petrified. Then, even as they flattened themselves, Paul Malloris gathered his last remaining strength and dived. His body landed on the grenade an instant before it exploded. The blast tore him apart and brought the Rosetta Stone crashing down in fragments.

Almost simultaneously, a group of android homicides appeared at the end of the Gallery. Markham began firing from where he lay. Four androids went down in the first burst. By the time he had emptied the magazine Prof. Hyggens and Helm Crispin were pumping bullets into the exposed group as fast as they could.

Another grenade came hurtling along the Gallery toward Helm Crispin. He snatched it, half rose and hurled it back. But even as it left his hand a bullet crashed into his brain.

The grenade exploded among the androids who had delivered it, temporarily clearing the doorway. The lull gave Markham time to grab three of his own grenades from the lap of the stone Egyptian god on which he had placed them. Without pause he threw them one after another down the

Gallery toward the entrance. By the time the explosions had died away, another clip of ammunition was in his machine pistol.

But no more androids appeared, and suddenly he was aware that the shooting outside had been reduced to a few sporadic bursts. It was replaced by another sound — a sound that was incredibly moving. The voices of thousands of men and women singing. He did not recognize the words. But the melody was an old and familiar one. It was the setting for Blake's *Jerusalem*. He had last heard it a hundred and fifty years ago in St. Paul's cathedral . . .

And the singing surged nearer, until it seemed as if the Museum itself was filled with sound.

Prof. Hyggens staggered to his feet, nursing a wounded arm. 'The voice of a free people,' he said, in the tone of one who has just experienced the impossible. 'It's the first time I've ever heard it . . . John, listen! Listen to it! The voice of a free people!'

In the dim light Markham was looking for Vivain and Marion-A. He found Vivain alive and unhurt behind a small but heavy sphinx. Marion-A had sheltered behind a sarcophagus, from where she had used an automatic pistol with effect.

The Egyptian Gallery seemed to be getting lighter.

'Androids alive!' said Prof. Hyggens, gazing through a high broken window at a dark gray sky. 'It's almost dawn.'

'Are you all right, Vivain?'

'Yes, John . . . What about poor Paul?'

'Don't look,' said Markham firmly. 'There's nothing to be done. Come over here.' With his arm round her he led her away from the area of devastation.

'John,' said Vivain softly, 'you were right. Terribly right — dear enemy. It is not meant that human beings should live only for the pursuit of happiness. I don't know, but it may be that there is happiness in the very things we rejected — in work and responsibility. In the rearing of children, and in the challenge of a permanent love.'

He kissed her gently and laughed. 'You're a genuine Victorian, at heart,' he said. 'And at the same time a fire-eating revolutionary.'

'John, darling, I love you. I'm useless. I don't even know how to do the simplest things. I don't know how to cook, or even how to wash clothes. But if you'll be patient and give me time I'll learn, John. I'll learn how to be fully and completely a woman. If you'll have me, I want to marry you.' She suddenly laughed, and the laughter sounded almost gay. 'I shouldn't say that, should I? But I want all sorts of things now. Children even. Your children. I'll never succeed, but I'll try to — to be like Katy. I'll try very hard.'

'You only need to be like Vivain,' he said softly. 'The Vivain we are both just beginning to understand.'

As he spoke men with lanterns came into the Gallery. Men dressed as pirates, clowns, kings, outlaws, saints and savages. Men who had fought for the first time in their lives for something in which they believed enough to die for that belief. But they were alive. They were alive now as never before. Men in fancy dress, and with dirty faces. Men with hope in their hearts and a new energy in their tired bodies.

Prof. Hyggens glanced quickly at Markham and Vivain, then he stepped forward to meet the men of the Liberation Army. He spoke to them quietly, then went with them outside.

Markham waited until the last of them had disappeared. Then he took Vivain in his arms. He felt oddly that it was the first time he had touched a living woman for a hundred and forty-six years.

A faint sound on the Gallery startled him. It was Marion-A, who had been quietly placing all that recognisably remained of Paul Malloris in the great stone sarcophagus of an Egyptian princess, along with the slight, pathetic body of Shawna.

'May I speak to you alone for a minute or two, John?'

'I'm sorry, Marion.' He released Vivain. 'I'd almost forgotten about you.'

Marion-A came over to Vivain. 'I will not detain him very long. You understand? I think you will be very happy, Vivain. I hope you will be very happy. I think that now I understand the meaning of happiness and hope.'

Vivain took Marion-A's hand. 'I, too, am aware of many things that I did not understand before. But love will always be beyond definition. Good-by, Marion. I'll never forget.' Suddenly she touched Marion-A's hand with her lips, then turned to Markham. 'I think I'll go and see what mischief Prof. Hyggens is inspiring,' she said lightly. 'I'll probably have to restrain him from expounding philosophy to a lot of tired men.'

Markham watched her walk firmly down the Gallery, which was now slowly filling with the gray light of dawn.

'What's going on?' he asked in a puzzled tone.

Marion-A gave a stiff smile. 'Nothing very important ... So the Liberation Army won after all, John. I did not think it was possible. And now we have reached the end.'

'There is no end,' said Markham. 'There's only a new beginning. A new kind of future.'

'Not for me, John. For me there is only the past. I belong to it.'

'What do you mean?'

'It is true — or partly true — what Solomon said. I have lost my own purpose, although for a time I was able to share yours. There is no place for me in the world you are going to build, John. Perhaps there would never have been a place for me in any kind of world. You showed me how to become more than an android, but I should always be less than a human being.'

'Nonsense!' he said, almost angrily. 'There is a place for you in our world, Marion. A place for you with me. I—'

'Please, John, hear me out. You belong to Vivain now, and I think she will make you happy. But I think — and the strange thing is that I can never really *know* — that I, too, love you in my own fashion.'

'Marion—'

'Please!' Her voice was low and vibrant. 'Please don't say anything, dear John. I have learned to cherish illusions. They satisfy me, therefore I do not ask for anything more.'

'At least tell me why we are talking like this.'

'Because,' said Marion-A slowly, 'I made a secret bargain — with myself. I promised that if the androids won I would kill you to save you from Analysis. I also gave myself another promise, in case they should lose.'

'What is that?'

'Dear John, I would like you to do something for me. I would like you to say: "Marion, my dear, you have found the meaning of happiness." Then I want you to walk away and not look back.'

Suddenly Markham understood. He understood, and knew that there was nothing else to be done.

For a moment he held Marion-A in his arms. For a moment, his lips felt the warm, even texture of her forehead. Then he said: 'Marion, my dear one, if you have found the meaning of happiness, you have taught me the meaning of love.'

Then he turned quickly away and walked with resolute steps toward the great doorway. Behind him there was a single shot; and a sudden flash of unbelievably white radiance. Then the Egyptian Gallery was plunged into semi-darkness once more.

Behind him lay a world of death and darkness, a world redolent of all the secrets of the near and the distant past. But outside was the world of dawn. A world of life and light, poised as always on the edge of an incalculable future.

As he walked toward that world, toward the voices of people singing, toward a day that was breaking with a clear red sunrise, a brilliant and timeless kaleidoscope flashed in his mind.

He saw once again — with the vivid reality of a dream — Katy and Johnny-Boy and Sara. The tiny citadel of a home in Hampstead. All that was lost and wonderful. All that had conspired toward giving him faith and courage to take his place in a world that, like every age before it, could not wholly dismiss the values of the enriching past.

Finally he saw Marion-A once more, as she had looked when he first set eyes upon her. And knew that she, too, was part of that same living past, that she and Katy — a strange double image — were offering him the gift of freedom. A future without shadows . . .

And suddenly his heart was light. He walked out onto the broad steps of the Museum, gazed briefly at the dawn sky, then saw that Vivain was waiting for him with Prof. Hyggens.

Prof. had been talking to a group of men who were beginning to be proud that they had once been called Runners. Markham could not suppress an ironic smile as he heard Prof. Hyggen's final words.

'Today, London,' said Prof., gleefully misquoting the words of an almost forgotten twentieth-century tyrant called Adolf Hitler. 'Today, London — and tomorrow, the world!'